ROAD TO EVIL

A Bridget Bishop FBI Mystery Thriller,
Book Four

Melinda Woodhall

Melinda Woodhall

Melinda Woodhall
Visit my website at www.melindawoodhall.com
Printed in the United States of America
First Printing: September 2022
Creative Magnolia

CHAPTER ONE

Heather Winslow leaned her forehead against the cool pane of glass and trained her emerald-green eyes on the fluffy white clouds just outside the window. As the Boeing 737 settled into a wide holding pattern over the airport ten thousand feet below, her ears began to ache.

Leaning back in her seat, she flipped her long, dark hair over her shoulder and adjusted her earbuds, not wanting to miss the end of the *Chasing Killers* podcast she'd been listening to during the flight.

Her sister had sent her a link to the latest episode, which focused on a gruesome series of murders committed by the serial killer known as the Backroads Butcher.

She'd quickly become transfixed, her interest heightened by the fact that the depraved killer had once been a resident of her own small hometown of Mount Destiny, Virginia.

Of course, that had been years ago.

According to the podcast, the Butcher was now an inmate at Abbeyville State Prison, where he was serving out eight consecutive life sentences in a maximum-security cellblock.

"Ladies and gentlemen, we have begun our descent into

Washington D.C., please turn off all portable electronic devices and stow them until we have arrived at the gate."

Heather looked up as the announcement sounded, then glanced over at her companion, feeling a prickle of irritation.

Ryder Forbes had reclined the back of his seat as far as it would go as soon as the plane's wheels had left the ground.

He'd then proceeded to fall asleep, leaving Heather to occupy herself during the two-hour flight from Chicago O'Hare to Dulles International.

So much for a romantic holiday vacation.

Doubts niggled in her mind as she stared down at her new boyfriend's long, lean figure sprawled out beside her.

She and Ryder Forbes were flying home from Chicago to Virginia for the Thanksgiving break. She hadn't yet told her sister she was bringing a guest, thinking it would be a nice surprise, but she was starting to doubt the decision.

In fact, she was starting to have doubts about Ryder altogether based on his surly, unpleasant attitude so far.

Sure, he was handsome, with brooding eyes, pouty lips, and clear, youthful skin that showed no sign of stubble regardless of the hour.

But he was also arrogant and self-centered. Traits that quickly became apparent on an overcrowded flight.

Sending a sharp elbow into her boyfriend's bony ribs, Heather folded away the tray table in front of her and stuck her phone back into her backpack.

"Sir, I need you to put your seat into an upright position for landing," the flight attendant said as she hurried past.

Ryder opened one eye to stare after the woman but made no move to adjust his seat.

"What a *bitch*," he muttered under his breath. "Like me having my seat down is gonna cause the plane to crash."

He heaved out a dramatic sigh as the plane began to descend, earning a look of reproach from the passenger across the aisle.

"Come on, Ryder," Heather said. "We're landing. Look, I think I can see the Washington Monument."

But Heather's attempt at cheerfulness was met with sullen silence as the plane sunk through the clouds.

By the time the wheels bumped onto the ground, Ryder had managed to raise his seatback, although his tray table was still down.

It banged noisily up and down as the plane barreled over the runway. Unable to stop herself, Heather reached over Ryder's knees and fastened the tray back into place.

A high-pitched screech sounded from the overhead speaker, setting Heather's nerves on edge.

"Ladies and gentlemen, welcome to Washington, D.C. For your safety and the safety of those around you, please remain seated with your seat belt fastened until we're parked at the gate."

Still inwardly fuming as they headed toward the baggage claim, Heather checked her messages but saw nothing from her sister. An uneasy suspicion that she'd forgotten she was coming tried to work its way into Heather's already annoyed brain, but she willed the thought away

I'm not going to get worked up, even if she has forgotten. I'm going to relax and enjoy this break even if it kills me.

Spying her small, silver suitcase making its way toward her on the baggage carousel, Heather hurried forward and pulled it off.

She turned to look for Ryder and saw him dragging a massive white rucksack toward her.

"That's big enough to store a body in," she said, shaking her head. "Don't you have an overnight bag?"

"This *is* my overnight bag," he said with a shrug, moving past her toward the doors, dragging the rucksack behind him.

Heather pasted on a smile and followed after him.

Stepping out of the sprawling concrete and glass building, she dug in her bag for the pair of oversized designer sunglasses she always carried with her, hoping to shield her eyes from the afternoon sun while also hiding the annoyed gleam that filled them.

"My sister should be here any minute," she called.

Ryder stopped and stared around at the chaos outside the ground-level departure area, then pointed to a man in a suit and dark sunglasses holding up a sign with her name on it.

"Looks like she sent a driver," he said, hefting up the rucksack. "So much for the warm welcome."

Wheeling her own small suitcase toward the curb, Heather swallowed back a sharp reply. After all, it wasn't Ryder's fault her sister couldn't be bothered to pick her up.

And of course, she couldn't swallow her pride long enough to ask Dad to pick me up either, could she?

She approached the dark sedan, nodding at the driver.

"I'm Heather Winslow."

"You're also late," the man said, reaching for her case.

As he turned toward the trunk, he nearly tripped over Ryder's rucksack, which had been dropped onto the sidewalk.

The driver stopped and looked up at Ryder in surprise.

"Who are you?" he asked, then turned back to Heather. "I was expecting a single fare."

"And I was expecting my sister," Heather shot back. "But I guess she couldn't be bothered, as usual."

The driver raised his eyebrows, then shrugged.

"That'll be an extra twenty dollars," he said as he moved back to the trunk and deposited Heather's suitcase inside.

"Add it to her sister's tab," Ryder said. "She's paying."

Digging in her purse, Heather pulled out a crumpled twenty-dollar bill and held it out toward the driver.

"You're heading out to Culver County, right?" he said, taking the money and shoving it in his pocket.

Heather nodded and looked to Ryder, who just shrugged.

"We better get going, then," the driver said. "Your flight delay cost me time, and I have another fare to pick up in an hour, so we need to get a move on."

Heather hesitated, glancing down at the ID badge affixed to the lapel of his suit.

The driver followed her eyes.

"I'm Max Bender," he said, gesturing toward the badge as he opened the back door of the sedan.

"And I can assure you, I'll get you home safely."

"Um...Mr. *Bender?*" Ryder called out in an insolent tone that made Heather cringe. "I think you forgot something."

Nodding down at the heavy rucksack on the pavement, Ryder moved toward the back of the sedan.

A faint flush filled Max Bender's face as he watched Ryder slouch toward the car, and for a minute Heather was sure they were going to need to find another ride home.

Then Bender was picking up Ryder's rucksack and hefting it into the trunk alongside her own.

Turning toward the car, Heather saw that Ryder had already climbed into the sedan's backseat and had slammed the door shut behind him.

So much for being a gentleman.

She glared toward the window, but it was so darkly tinted she couldn't see Ryder's face, only her own annoyed reflection.

Heather reached for the door, but Bender was already pulling it open and waving her inside.

Forcing Ryder to slide over, she dropped into the backseat and fastened her seatbelt as the sedan headed west.

The traffic out of the city was always heavy and the upcoming holiday ensured the drive would take over an hour, perhaps closer to two, so she sat back in her seat and stared out at the passing cars.

Stomach grumbling, she imagined the Thanksgiving meal her sister would prepare, focusing on the homemade sweet potato pie topped with cool whipped cream that had been her mother's specialty.

A sudden memory of her mother standing in the warm, fragrant kitchen of her childhood home sent a pang of nostalgia through Heather that bordered on grief.

Closing her eyes, she willed the pain away, determined not to spend the week wallowing in the past.

She couldn't afford to lose focus. She'd come home to Mount Destiny with a mission to fulfill, determined to heal the rift that had formed between her sister and her father.

She needed to get her family back together.

It's what Mom would have wanted.

Her thoughts turned to the upcoming week as the traffic thinned and the car made its way westward.

They'd been on the road for almost an hour, and Ryder had long since dozed off with his head against the window, when Heather reached in her bag for her phone, deciding to listen to the end of the *Chasing Killers* podcast.

Her phone wasn't there.

Sitting forward, Heather held back her fall of long dark hair and looked down at the floor, wondering if the slim black device could have fallen out of her purse when she'd climbed into the car.

"You lose something?" Bender asked, catching her eye in the rearview mirror.

"My phone," she said, sliding her hand along the back of the seat. "I can't find it."

"Your phone? Actually, I think I may have seen it in the trunk," he said, shifting his eyes back to the road. "There's a pull-off ahead for Destiny Peak Overlook. I'll stop there and we can check."

Heather murmured her thanks and leaned back in her seat with a bewildered frown, wondering how her phone could have gotten in the trunk.

Minutes later they were crossing the line into Culver County and were approaching the small town of Mount Destiny just west of Providence Gap.

Bender pointed to a faded sign announcing the turn-off to Destiny Peak Overlook, then pulled the sedan onto a narrow side road lined with thick trees.

After checking the rearview mirror, he took another sharp turn onto a bumpy dirt road that appeared to wind down the mountain between a scattering of oak and maple trees which had started to shed their fading fall leaves.

Heather leaned forward, confused.

"Where are we going?"

She tried to catch the driver's eyes in the rearview mirror, but he continued to stare straight ahead as they bumped further down the mountain.

"I thought you wanted me to look for your phone," Bender said, finally bringing the car to a jerking stop.

An uneasy knot twisted in Heather's stomach as she surveyed the view of the valley below them.

The setting sun cast a violet glow over the army of trees which dominated the sloping terrain.

In the waning light, they appeared to be all alone.

Opening the car door, Bender stepped out onto the narrow strip of dirt and gravel that made up the road and strode to the back of the car.

Heather turned to stare through the back window, but he'd already popped open the trunk, blocking her view.

She waited for a long beat, then reached for the door.

But before she could open it, Bender's face appeared in the window next to Ryder.

As the driver wrenched the door open, Ryder jerked awake with a start and glared up at him.

"What the hell do you think you're doing?"

"Your girlfriend lost her phone," Bender said, unruffled by Ryder's anger. "I checked the trunk and there's something I think you're both going to want to see."

Without waiting for a response, he turned and walked to the back of the car.

"This guy's really beginning to *piss me off,*" Ryder said as he jabbed his thumb down on the buckle to release the seatbelt.

Heather opened her door and climbed out, coming around to the back of the car just in time to see Bender lift a gun in Ryder's direction, aiming it at his smooth, tan forehead.

"What the fuck, man!" Ryder shouted, backing away. "Are you crazy? What the hell are you doing?"

Bender cocked his head.

"Shut up and listen."

His voice was low and hard.

"As long as you do what I say, no one's going to get hurt."

He nodded toward Heather, who stood motionless, frozen in panic and fear.

"Your girlfriend's going to stay with me as collateral, but I'll give you to the count of ten to get out of here."

He waved the muzzle of the gun back toward the

highway.

"Now run before I change my mind...*go!*"

Ryder spun around. Without so much as a farewell glance in Heather's direction, he bolted toward the trees.

"*One...two...*"

He'd traveled less than ten yards when the shot rang out.

"*Three!*"

Blood spurted from the back of Ryder's head and spattered onto the dirt road as he dropped to the ground.

"No!"

Heather's high-pitched shriek pierced the still mountain air. She opened her mouth to scream again, then snapped it shut when she felt the hot metal of the gun under her chin.

Forcing her to walk further down the steep, crumbling embankment, Bender stayed close on her heels.

At one point she stumbled and almost fell, but he ignored her gasp of pain, shoving her forward along the narrowing, overgrown path.

She was unsure how long they'd been walking when he grabbed her shoulder, bringing her to a sudden stop.

"That way," Bender barked.

Turning to her left, Heather's heart stopped as she saw the dark, ragged hole leading into the mountain.

It appeared to be the entrance to the bowels of hell, although Heather knew instantly what it really was.

Her father had taken her out hiking in the mountains plenty of times, back before her mother had died and their lives had fallen apart. He'd always warned her about the dangers of abandoned mines scattered throughout the area.

Backing away, Heather tripped and fell at Bender's feet.

"My sister is expecting me," she shouted up at him, her throat constricting with fear. "She knows I'm with you. She'll call the police. They'll come looking for me."

Bender took off his sunglasses and stared down at her, his eyes bright and hard in the growing darkness.

He reached into his pocket and held up Heather's phone with a cold, unpleasant smile.

The bastard must have had it all along.

The thought sent another wave of panic through her.

"Don't worry. I'll let your sister know you're not going to make it home for the holidays," he said with an ironic twist of his lips. "Now, get inside. I already told you I don't have much time."

Still on her knees, Heather crawled backward, trying to think. She needed to figure out a plan of escape.

Once I go in there, there will be no way out.

But Bender was right behind her, his finger tight on the trigger, his eyes cold and unflinching.

"Go on, get in," he growled. "I don't want to hurt you, but I'll do what I have to do."

She hesitated, then stood on shaking legs and stepped into the mine, sensing Bender directly behind her.

Inching forward, unable to see in the overwhelming darkness, hot tears spilled onto her cheeks.

Suddenly, a beam of light appeared as Bender activated his phone's flashlight, exposing rough stone walls and rusty twin rails leading down into the dark abyss beyond.

"Move!" Bender barked.

She shuffled forward a few feet, then stumbled to her left as she tripped over a splintered piece of wood.

"Watch out for the shaft!" Bender bellowed.

But it was too late.

Heather's arms pinwheeled as she tried to regain her balance. She thrust out both hands to cushion her fall, but only empty air rose up to meet her. With a final scream, she plummeted into the darkness below.

CHAPTER TWO

Dark sunglasses concealed Bridget Bishop's anxious blue eyes as she approached the Culver County Courthouse. Popping up the collar of her suit jacket, the criminal psychologist let her chestnut brown curls fall over one shoulder and ducked her head, not wanting to attract attention from the crowd of reporters and onlookers swarming the steps.

As she entered the old three-story building, she felt a suffocating sense of déjà vu.

I can't believe I'm back here. And that he's back here, too.

Of course, this time was different. This time Bridget was just a spectator. An interested party.

Not an expert witness as she had been at the first trial where she'd given expert testimony in the case against Lyle Grady, the serial killer who had been dubbed the Backroads Butcher after he'd decapitated eight hapless victims on the backroads of Virginia.

Almost four years had passed since the Butcher had been convicted of the gruesome series of homicides and given eight consecutive life sentences at Abbeyville State Prison.

Bridget had been a profiler in the FBI's Behavioral

Analysis Unit when the first victim had been discovered.

The decapitated body of eighteen-year-old Justine Abernathy had been discarded on a dirt road in the foothills of the Appalachian Mountains.

The CSI crew responding to the scene had soon discovered the body of her brother, nineteen-year-old Junior Abernathy, beside his wrecked pickup nearby.

Neither of the young victims' heads had been found at the scene, although a local investigator had quickly identified them as the children of Reverend Virgil Abernathy, a popular pastor at the Mount Destiny Church of Redemption.

More grisly scenes had been left for the FBI to find in the following months, and eventually, after Lyle Grady had been captured, tried, and sentenced for the crimes, Bridget had made the difficult decision to leave the BAU behind.

She'd taken a year off work to help her father recuperate from a debilitating stroke, using the break to heal her traumatized psyche before eventually joining a private forensic psychology group in her hometown of Wisteria Falls.

But the Bureau had been reluctant to let Bridget go.

Her skill as a profiler, and her ability to interpret and predict the motives and actions of psychopaths and serial killers, had proven to be invaluable assets.

In the last year, she'd allowed herself to be persuaded to work on several high-profile cases as a consultant for the BAU, despite the nightmares that continued to plague her.

And now she was back in Mount Destiny, where it had all

started, about to face the man who'd prompted her exit from the Bureau. The man who still roamed free in her most frightening dreams.

Keeping her eyes straight ahead, Bridget pulled off her sunglasses and slipped them into her purse in preparation to pass through the courthouse's security checkpoint.

She grimaced as she spotted a guard talking to a man up ahead in a dark trench coat and a red beanie.

I should have known Chase Grafton would be here.

In no mood to face the abrasive host of the *Chasing Killers* podcast, she quickly averted her eyes, waiting until the man in the beanie had moved out of sight before making her way into the overcrowded courtroom.

Standing in the back of the room, Bridget glanced toward the seats near the front, just behind the bar. The benches reserved for the family and friends of the victims.

Her heart sank as she spotted Reverend Virgil Abernathy's painfully thin shoulders and thatch of thick white hair.

The bereaved father sat stiffly on the uncomfortable wooden bench, his eyes glued to the door from which the man who'd killed both his children would soon emerge.

"I thought you and Santino had gone on vacation," a familiar voice said. "Don't tell me you canceled Aruba?"

Bridget turned to see Special Agent Charlie Day beside her.

The woman's golden blonde hair had been pulled back into a low bun, and her gray eyes were solemn, reflecting Bridget's own unease.

"I couldn't just fly away not knowing what might happen," Bridget said, allowing Charlie to take her elbow and guide her deeper into the courtroom. "When I heard Judge Hawthorne had agreed to hear oral arguments for the appeal, I couldn't believe it."

"What choice did he have?"

Charlie's shoulders lifted in a dejected shrug as she sank onto an empty bench and pulled Bridget down beside her.

"His new lawyer claims material forensic evidence wasn't allowed to be presented at the original trial."

Bridget had already heard the explanation and knew Charlie was right, but it didn't make it any easier to stomach.

New technology had allowed a DNA profile to be extracted from minuscule traces of tissue found under the fingernails of the Butcher's last known victim.

"They claim the DNA collected from Tammy Vicker doesn't match Lyle Grady," Charlie reminded her. "And the FBI lab confirmed their findings. They got the same results."

"But that doesn't prove Grady isn't Tammy's killer," Bridget protested. "That amount of DNA could have been picked up from incidental contact."

Hearing the desperation in her own voice, she sucked in a deep breath, ignoring Charlie's raised eyebrows.

"And the other evidence all pointed to Grady."

"I know, and I hate that he's putting the families through this again," Charlie said. "But we have to follow the science. And right now, that's telling us something isn't right. If the Butcher didn't kill Tammy, we need to know. We need to find out who did."

Her words were followed by a flurry of voices and a sudden rush of activity at the side door. And then Lyle Grady was being hustled into the room.

He wore street clothes instead of a prison uniform, and his short hair had been smoothed neatly into place.

The only indications that he was a convicted murderer were the handcuffs securing his wrists together in front of him and the guard at his side.

Bridget's chest tightened as Grady looked back in her direction as if he could feel her watching him.

Unable to tear her eyes away, she noted that the killer hadn't changed much since the last time she'd seen him.

He wasn't yet thirty, but he'd managed to retain his youthful appearance despite the years spent behind bars.

Eyes darkening, Grady creased his thin, pale face into a familiar sneer that sent a shiver up Bridget's spine. Her fear of coming face to face with the Backroads Butcher again had come true.

Of course, she'd always known something like this was possible since Grady had never actually admitted that he was guilty of any of the brutal murders he'd committed, despite the overwhelming evidence presented at his trial.

He'd remained sullen and quiet, unmoved by the families who had buried only partial remains of their loved ones.

She knew it shouldn't come as a surprise that suddenly, after years of silence, he'd come forward to claim he wasn't the one who had killed Tammy, and that he now had DNA evidence to prove it.

But as Bridget sat beside Charlie waiting for the Butcher to argue his petition for a retrial in front of Judge Hawthorne, she felt a renewed surge of anger.

Hadn't they all been through enough the first time around? Why dredge up the horrors of the past now?

And what good will it do anyway? Trace evidence on one victim won't discount the mountain of evidence linking Grady to the seven other homicides, will it?

She suddenly wondered if Grady's hotshot lawyer would argue that the new DNA evidence justified a complete retrial of all cases.

Would the lawyer throw into question all the evidence they'd so painstakingly collected?

Bridget's stomach gave a sickening lurch as the idea took hold. Turning to Charlie, she gripped her arm.

"What if Grady wins a new trial?" she said in a low voice. "What if he manages to throw doubt on the other cases as well? You never can tell what a jury might decide."

"Even if his petition for a new trial is granted, no jury on earth could look at all the evidence and decide Lyle Grady should be released into society," Charlie assured her.

But her face was grim as she watched Grady take his place between the two lawyers at the defense table.

Bridget noted that Lonnie Millford was seated to Grady's right. Millford was the same public defender who had represented the Butcher at his original trial.

The woman to Grady's left was new to the case.

Her well-tailored suit emphasized her slim, athletic

figure, and her fine features were framed by a sleek brown bob lightened with honey-colored highlights.

Only the first faint lines around the woman's eyes and a subtle softness around her jawline hinted that she was approaching her fortieth birthday.

Bridget recognized the woman as Reagan Rivera, a defense attorney known for her pro bono legal and investigative work with prisoners claiming wrongful conviction.

Bridget wasn't sure how many of Reagan's clients had been exonerated and were now out of prison and back with their families, but she'd recently seen an interview on the local news that had gotten her attention.

The attorney had filed an appeal for a convicted child killer named Elliot Fisher. The man had ultimately won his release from Abbeyville following a decade of confinement.

But that man was likely innocent. Lyle Grady definitely is not.

Loud footsteps drew her eyes away from Grady as the bailiff stepped forward.

"All rise for the Honorable Judge Frederick Hawthorne."

Standing abruptly, Bridget felt a wave of dizziness wash over her. She swayed as the judge entered and took his place behind the bench.

"You may be seated."

As the bailiff's order echoed through the courtroom, a solid figure slipped up beside Bridget and put a steadying hand on her elbow. She looked up to see Special Agent Terrance Gage.

The man she'd previously worked for in the BAU was

dressed in a dark suit and blood-red tie. His face was clean-shaven and the smooth skin on his hairless head was the coppery color of a newly minted penny.

Bridget sank onto the bench beside him.

"We can't let this happen," she said in a pained whisper. "We can't let the Butcher go free."

CHAPTER THREE

Terrance Gage glanced over at Lyle Grady as Bridget's soft warning echoed in his ear. He couldn't blame the criminal psychologist for being scared. Few men he'd encountered were as scary as Lyle Grady.

But before Gage could offer up a reassuring response, Judge Hawthorne brought his gavel down on the wooden bench with a resounding *bang*.

"Silence in the courtroom!"

The judge studied the occupants at the table for the defense with hard, assessing eyes, before moving his gaze to the table for the prosecution. The chronic frown he usually wore had long ago formed deep furrows on his forehead.

"I will not allow this hearing to be turned into a circus," he barked as he slid on his glasses and peered around the room. "I've allowed cameras in the courtroom for now, but I can just as easily bar them if anyone gets out of hand."

He waited as if expecting someone to object. When no one did, he looked down at an open file in front of him.

"Okay, Ms. Rivera," Hawthorne finally said, not looking up. "You've petitioned this court for a hearing and your petition has been granted. Now, am I to understand that your client is seeking to have the conviction against him for the first-degree murder of Ms. Tammy Vicker overturned?"

Gage watched the judge's face as he spoke.

Based on his past experience with Hawthorne, who had presided over Grady's original trial, he knew the old jurist was no pushover. Reagan Rivera would have little hope of manipulating or bulldozing over him.

Studying the lawyer as she confidently faced the bench, Gage saw right away that the woman wasn't intimidated by Hawthorne's testy, combative demeanor.

He hadn't expected anything less. Well known as an activist against wrongful convictions, Reagan's reputation as a tenacious litigator preceded her.

Like most people in the area, Gage had read plenty of stories about Reagan in the news and had seen innumerable interviews and special reports highlighting her work with convicted criminals over the years.

Based on the interviews he'd seen, Gage judged Reagan's activism to be well-intended, if not a touch naïve.

Which was why he'd attempted to contact her after rumors had started circulating that she was considering taking on Lyle Grady as a pro bono client.

Hoping to set her straight, he'd left several messages asking why she would want to waste her time helping a psychopathic killer like the Backroads Butcher.

He couldn't say he was surprised when she'd simply ignored his calls and emails. The snub was to be expected, based on the role he had played in Grady's capture and conviction.

Gage's team of analysts at the BAU had created the original profile for the unsub known as the Backroads Butcher, and Reagan likely considered him to be an adversary.

She probably thought he was motivated by a desire to save his team's reputation above all else. In that, she was wrong.

His motivation had nothing to do with his ego or his reputation. It was all about the victims' families. All about his determination to spare them the excruciating pain of another high-profile trial.

After all, the Backroads Butcher had earned his nickname by using a meat cleaver to decapitate Justine and Junior Abernathy alongside a narrow dirt road only a few miles from the courthouse they were sitting in now.

The details of Grady's crimes and the accompanying photographic evidence were traumatizing, not just for the victims' loved ones, but for the witnesses and jurors as well.

Pushing back the unwanted images that flashed through his mind, Gage returned his eyes to the prosecution's table, where Reagan was still sitting, making no move to rise.

"Your Honor, handcuffing my client in the courtroom is unnecessary and potentially prejudicial, considering that media has been allowed inside," she said in a crisp, cool voice. "Photos in the press showing Mr. Grady in handcuffs will suggest to future jurors that he was deemed too dangerous to sit in the courtroom unrestrained."

"Objection, Your Honor!"

The cry came from the prosecution's table.

Alistair Kennedy was on his feet, and the anxious expression and five o'clock shadow on the Commonwealth attorney's normally smooth, boyish face made it clear he was finding it hard to believe he was facing Lyle Grady in court once again.

Culver County's lead prosecutor had earned hero status in Mount Destiny for his role in convicting the infamous Backroads Butcher. Now the entire case, and his impressive conviction rate, was in jeopardy of being overturned.

The prosecutor tugged at the navy-blue tie knotted at his throat as Judge Hawthorne glared down at him.

"The defendant is a dangerous man already convicted of eight counts of first-degree murder," Alistair protested. "We can't allow him to-"

"Overruled!" Hawthorne barked.

Clearly annoyed at the prosecutor's objection, he turned to the uniformed guard who had escorted Grady into the room.

"Officer Pickering, you may remove the defendant's restraints," he said, earning a gasp from the crowd.

The guard momentarily froze as all eyes turned in his direction. Then, hitching up his pants, which had settled low on his substantial hips, he moved forward.

Fumbling with the key, Pickering managed to unlock the cuffs around Grady's wrists before returning to his position against the wall.

"Now, Ms. Rivera, please enlighten the court as to your petition for a retrial," the judge ordered with a heavy sigh.

Reagan stood and circled around the table to stand at a podium facing the judge.

"Thank you, Your Honor," she said, not bothering to look down at the folder she'd placed in front of her. "New DNA evidence has come to light which calls my client's previous conviction into serious question."

The lawyer spoke quickly, glossing over the gruesome details of the original case that had been presented against Grady, never referring to his first seven victims by name as she laid out her argument.

Fighting back a wave of outrage at the woman's callous tone, Gage forced himself to maintain a calm façade, knowing that the media would be thrilled to capture any sign of distress from him or his team at the possibility of Grady's possible exoneration.

He glanced over to see how Bridget was holding up as Reagan paused to exhale and was relieved to see that she was staring straight ahead, a fixed, stoic expression masking the turmoil he knew must be churning inside.

"I'd like to call an expert witness to the stand," Reagan said, glancing down at the folder on the podium. "I call the Commonwealth's medical examiner, Opal Fitzgerald."

Gage turned as a familiar figure entered the courtroom. He watched as Opal made her way up the aisle, her short, sturdy legs moving quickly as if she wanted to get the whole thing over with as soon as possible.

As she took a seat on the witness stand, the medical examiner's gray curls seemed to quiver with indignation.

"Dr. Fitzgerald, you examined Tammy Vicker's body at

the crime scene before she was taken to the medical examiner's office for autopsy, did you not?" Reagan asked once Opal had been sworn in by the bailiff.

"Yes, I was the M.E. on duty that day," Opal agreed with a stiff nod. "I went to the scene and examined the poor girl. At least, what was left of her."

A soft murmur rolled through the crowd, prompting Judge Hawthorne to reach for his gavel.

"Was that when you discovered the tissue under her fingernails?" Reagan asked.

"Good lord, no," Opal said, rolling her eyes. "After a visual inspection, I always bag the hands as per protocol."

Reagan hesitated, waiting for Opal to continue. When she didn't, Reagan raised her eyebrows.

It was the first sign of frustration Gage had seen from the lawyer, and he allowed his shoulders to relax slightly at the proof that she was human after all.

"And why do you bag the hands, Dr. Fitzgerald?"

"To avoid losing any trace evidence during transport, of course," Opal said, folding her arms over her ample chest. "It's all pretty obvious if you ask me."

Opal paused and then spoke again under her breath.

"Just like Lyle Grady's guilty verdict."

Another ripple rolled through the courtroom. Someone to Gage's left let out a soft laugh.

Face hardening at the remark, Reagan waited without comment as Judge Hawthorne banged his gavel on the bench.

"Quiet in the court!"

Opal caught Gage's eye and winked, obviously enjoying the commotion, unfazed by Hawthorne's anger.

"Dr. Fitzgerald, did you or did you not collect tissue from under the fingernails of Tammy Vicker during autopsy?"

Reagan's voice was flat.

"I did," Opal said.

"And what did you do with that tissue?" the lawyer asked. "Please describe your procedures to the court."

Opal walked through the painstaking process of collecting, packaging, and shipping biological samples to the FBI lab for testing, emphasizing the need to maintain chain of custody records.

"So, you're confident the tissue collected from Ms. Vicker was received by the FBI lab?" Reagan asked in follow up. "Is it true that the tissue sample you sent was too small to allow for them to construct a DNA profile?"

Shrugging her round shoulders, Opal frowned.

"I'm sure we sent it to the right address, but you'd have to ask the lab if they received it and what they did with it," she said, preparing to stand. "Now, is that all?"

With a curt nod, Reagan turned to Hawthorne.

"That's all I have for this witness, Your Honor," she said.

"Do you have any questions for the witness, Mr. Kennedy?" the Judge asked, looking toward the prosecution's table.

"Not at this time, Your Honor," Alistair said.

The judge nodded.

"Then you may step down, Dr. Fitzgerald."

Lips pressed into a thin line, Reagan watched Opal exit

the witness box and retrace her steps down the aisle.

"Well then, go ahead and call your next witness," the judge said impatiently as the M.E. disappeared into the hall.

Reagan leaned past Grady to confer with Lonnie Millford, then straightened again with a faint sigh.

"Your Honor, we were planning on calling a forensic examiner from the FBI lab as our next witness, but it seems she hasn't arrived yet," Reagan admitted. "I'd like to request a short recess so we can check and see where she is. I'd also like a chance to confer with my client in private."

Glancing up at the clock, Judge Hawthorne exhaled and once again banged his gavel, causing Gage and most people around him to jump.

"Court will adjourn for a ten-minute recess," Hawthorne called out. "Officer Pickering, can you escort the defendant and his counsel into the conference room?"

The guard stepped forward to lead Grady away as the judge retired to his chambers, freeing the spectators in the courtroom to talk or move around.

Gage looked over at Bridget, but her eyes were trained on the door leading to the back, where the attorney-client conference room and holding cells were located.

"I wonder who they were sending over from the lab to give testimony," he said, trying to get Bridget's attention, not liking the anxiety he saw in her eyes.

He attempted to keep up a stream of conversation, but the voices around them rose in intensity as the minutes passed, until it was impossible to hear his own voice without yelling.

The noise died suddenly as the gavel reverberated through the room, announcing the judge's return to the bench.

"Bailiff, please bring in the defendant and his counsel."

The bailiff turned and pushed through the door.

Judge Hawthorne had just settled back into his big leather chair behind the bench when the door slammed open and the bailiff lunged through, his eyes wide with fear.

"He's gone. The Butcher's gone!"

Someone in the courtroom screamed, and then the room erupted into chaos as the bailiff yelled out again.

"Officer down!" he yelled. "Call an ambulance."

Charlie Day was out of her seat first, drawing her Glock as she charged toward the open door to the back.

Jumping to his feet, Gage raced after her, his heart hammering against his ribs as he approached the door.

Before he could slip through the doorway, the bailiff stuck out both hands to block him from charging past.

"Everyone, step back and calm down," he yelled as several uniformed security guards ran into the courtroom.

Gage strained to see past the bailiff.

"I'm FBI," he said, digging in his pocket for his credentials. "My colleague is in there, let me through."

The bailiff dropped his arm and let Gage slip past.

He stepped forward into the hall and looked toward the conference room. The door was open, revealing blood spatter on the inner wall. His stomach lurched at the sight of the slim leg sprawled just inside the doorway.

Reagan Rivera had been assaulted by her client, that

much was clear. But Gage couldn't see if she was moving. He couldn't tell how many more victims the Butcher had added to his list.

Suddenly Charlie was standing beside him, her breath coming in deep gasps.

"Grady stabbed...Pickering and went out...the window," she said, trying to catch her breath. "The Butcher is gone."

CHAPTER FOUR

C harlie Day pushed through the heavy doors of the Culver County Courthouse and inhaled a deep lungful of cool, crisp air. Standing at the top of the wide, concrete steps, she looked up and down Buchanan Street, trying to figure out how Grady had made such a quick escape, wondering where he could be now that he was a free man.

Uniformed officers guarded the perimeter of the courthouse, which had been cordoned-off in yellow crime scene tape. They'd been instructed not to let anyone in or out of the building until further notice, and from what Charlie could tell, they were going to have their hands full.

The road beyond the perimeter had quickly filled with local news vans. Reporters and their crews spilled onto the sidewalk, each desperate for an update on Lyle Grady's rumored escape, each hoping to be first to break the story.

News that the depraved monster known as the Backroads Butcher had somehow managed to knock his lawyer unconscious, slash a guard's throat, and disappear down the old building's fire escape, hadn't been made public yet.

When it did, she knew that press from all over the

country would rush to the little town of Mount Destiny, just as they had during the first trial, when the Backroads Butcher's true identity had finally been revealed.

Turning to study the gray three-story building, Charlie noted the crumbling, cracked stone facade, and the narrow, dust-coated windows.

Apparently, the city council lacked either the will or the resources to renovate and maintain the old building. Their failure to dismantle the disused fire escape on the west side of the building had given Grady the chance he needed.

But how did he know it was still there? And how did he get hold of a knife? It doesn't make sense. Someone must have helped him...

A headache started up behind Charlie's temple as unanswered questions filled her head.

"Agent Day!"

She looked around and spotted the owner of the high-pitched voice coming around the far end of the building.

Detective Shannon Larkin from the Mount Destiny PD strode toward her. The town's first-ever female detective wore a shapeless black jacket and pants that were a size too big for her generous curves.

As she approached, Larkin pushed back a strand of dirty blonde hair that had escaped her loose ponytail. It immediately fell back over one eye.

"I've been around the block twice," the detective huffed, her face strained and flushed. "There's no sign of Grady anywhere. Looks like he's well and truly gone."

"Then we better put out an APB," Charlie said, gritting

her teeth. "He can't have gotten far. At least, not yet."

A siren wailed in the distance, quickly growing louder and closer. Charlie and Larkin watched the ambulance appear at the corner of Buchanan and Central, red lights flashing frantically, forced to slow to a crawl along the packed street.

Jogging down the steps, Charlie greeted the two paramedics who emerged.

"We've got an officer down and a civilian injured."

She followed behind as they pushed the gurney up the ramp to the entrance, then pointed them toward the blood-spattered conference room on the second floor.

Bridget Bishop knelt next to Reagan Rivera holding a cloth to her head. The lawyer blinked up at the newcomers with a dazed expression.

"She's just coming around," Bridget said, moving aside for the paramedics. "There's a cut on her head. I think that's where the blood's been coming from."

One of the paramedics crossed to Officer Pickering, who lay motionless, his head resting in a thick pool of blood. He studied the wide gash that had been carved across his throat.

"There's nothing we can do for him," he said, meeting Charlie's eyes briefly, before turning back to Reagan.

Once they'd loaded the lawyer onto the gurney and wheeled her into the hall, Bridget walked to the door and called to someone outside.

"He's in here."

Charlie looked up to see Opal Fitzgerald standing in the

doorway. The M.E. was already dressed in protective gear.

"You came back," Charlie said, her voice reflecting her surprise. "You couldn't have gotten very far."

"I actually didn't get anywhere at all," Opal admitted. "I couldn't just leave without finding out if that monster was going to get a retrial, could I? I was loitering out in the hall when the alarm was raised."

Her eyes dropped to Officer Pickering.

"He's a lot fresher than I'm used to," the M.E. said with a heavy sigh. "I don't usually get to meet my patients before I examine them."

Before stepping closer, she pulled her phone from her pocket and began to take photos from every angle, making sure to get a shot of all visible wounds, as well as the blood spatter and open window.

"The evidence response team is on the way," Charlie assured Opal as she knelt next to Pickering.

"That's good," Opal said, then sat back on her heels. "You do know his gun is gone, right?"

She pointed to the empty holster strapped around the dead man's waist with a gloved hand.

"That's right," Charlie confirmed with a grim nod. "Grady's armed and he's on the run."

Leaving the M.E. to her work, Charlie went back into the courtroom, where a handful of nervous-looking officers from the Mount Destiny PD were interviewing anyone who'd been in the courthouse when Grady had escaped.

As she looked around at the shell-shocked crowd, her eyes landed on Lonnie Millford. Grady's lawyer stood by himself in the back of the room, shifting nervously from one foot to the other as he scrolled through his phone.

Anger percolated in her chest as she made her way toward him, although she wasn't sure why.

After all, it's his job as a public defender to represent his assigned defendants to the best of his ability. Even those defendants who are murderous psychopaths. Isn't that right?

The only problem was, he and Reagan Rivera had used a legal loophole to put their murderous psychopathic client in a position where he could be released, or, even worse, escape.

Perhaps it wasn't logical, or even fair, but she was suddenly and uncontrollably furious as she came to a stop in front of the lawyer.

"This is all your fault," she hissed, eliciting a startled gasp from Lonnie. "Why would you try to get a known *serial killer* a retrial anyway?"

"My fault?" he blustered. "You've got to be kidding. This was all Reagan Rivera's doing. I told that woman she was asking for trouble, but what woman ever listens to reason?"

Charlie couldn't hide her disgust. The man's obnoxious attitude was nothing new.

"Why didn't you mention the blood and tissue found under Tammy's fingernails during the original case?" she asked. "Was it a legal strategy, or just pure incompetence?"

Lonnie shrugged his meaty shoulders.

"The attempt to extract DNA failed," he said. "So, Judge Hawthorne refused to let the sample be entered into evidence. What did you want me to do about it?"

Her eyes narrowed into two gray slits.

"So, you're saying you were just a helpless bystander?" she demanded. "Just like you were helpless to prevent your client from killing a guard and going on the run?"

"Don't try to blame *me* for this," he protested. "If you want someone to blame, how about the lax security at the courthouse? This place is like a hundred years old. They don't even have proper metal detectors at the doors."

Charlie had to agree that the courthouse security measures were woefully inadequate. She'd noticed earlier that the guards were using simple handheld wands and a manual search of bags rather than the walk-through metal detectors used at newer courthouses.

And who knows what they used to check the prisoners.

But then, the lax security wouldn't have mattered if Lonnie and Reagan had left well enough alone.

About to give Lonnie another piece of her mind, Charlie's attention was drawn to a tall figure in the doorway.

Her pulse quickened as Special Agent Tristan Hale stepped inside, his eyes searching the courtroom until he found her and began to move in her direction.

Meeting him in the middle of the room, Charlie offered a casual greeting. Her heart jumped when he leaned forward to speak in her ear as if sharing an important update.

"I was worried about you," he said softly. "Are you okay?"

Charlie nodded, wishing they were alone so she could hold his hand and rest her head on his shoulder.

"I was worried about you, too," she admitted.

After years of working together on a series of intense investigations, Charlie's stony resistance to their mutual attraction had suddenly crumbled the previous winter after she'd seen Hale at Bea Allen's bedside.

The elderly woman had lost her only son during an undercover FBI operation, and Hale had stepped in, offering himself up as a surrogate, caring for Bea after she'd received a terminal cancer diagnosis.

His kindness and compassion had proven irresistible, overcoming Charlie's doubts about dating a colleague after his good looks and charm alone had failed to convince her.

And so far, things between them had gone smoothly, although she knew it was inevitable that there would be bumps in the road ahead.

"I thought you were going to the hospital," she said, wanting to ask him for an update on Bea, but knowing it wasn't the right time or place. "How did you find out about Grady escaping anyway?"

"I overheard the news when I was leaving your house," he said quietly. "Why didn't you wake me up before you left?"

Her answer caught in her throat as she saw Judge Hawthorne exiting his chambers. As he walked toward them, Charlie stepped to the side, blocking his path.

"Sorry, Judge Hawthorne, but we need to ask you some questions before you leave."

The judge jerked to a stop.

"What questions?" he demanded.

As the annoyed frown she'd seen him wearing on the

bench earlier reappeared, Charlie decided it was definitely more intimidating up close.

"We're interviewing everyone who was in the courtroom when Lyle Grady escaped," she explained. "Just a simple series of questions. Can I start by asking where you were during the recess?"

Pulling himself up to his full height, which was only a few inches taller than Charlie, the judge shook his head.

"You most certainly may not," he said with an indignant scowl. "This is my courtroom and I'll be the one setting the rules and asking the questions."

Before she could stop him, Hawthorne had stepped past her and was once again heading for the door.

Charlie considered going after him, then sighed and turned back to Hale. Picking a battle with the judge would do little to bring Grady back now.

Instead, she followed Hale to the prosecution's table, where Alistair Kennedy and Detective Larkin stood.

The prosecutor had taken off his jacket, and his dark, close-cropped hair stood up at odd angles.

"How could he have just...*vanished*?"

He lifted a hand to scratch at his head, revealing nervous patches of sweat under his arms.

"We should have had more officers assigned to the courthouse," Larkin admitted. "But we're short-handed as it is, and Mayor Sibley said we need to watch the overtime."

"This is Reagan Rivera's fault, not ours," Alistair protested. "But either way, we're going to be crucified on the news tonight."

The prosecutor's phone buzzed in his pocket.

He turned away to answer as Charlie updated Hale on the steps they'd taken so far to bring Grady in. By the time she'd finished her update, Alistair had ended his call.

"This is going to be a PR nightmare," he said morosely. "Now I've got to go update Mayor Sibley in person."

"I'm glad to see the mayor has his priorities straight," Charlie said dryly as Alistair hurried away. "I bet he's more concerned about protecting his reputation than about losing an officer."

"Any word on how Reagan's doing?"

Charlie looked up to see Bridget.

"No, I haven't heard," Charlie admitted, trying to keep her eyes off the blood stains on Bridget's sleeve.

"We need to talk to her soon," Bridget said. "We need to find out exactly what happened in that conference room."

Turning on her heel, she moved away, leaving Charlie and Hale staring after her.

"This is her worst nightmare come true," Charlie said, keeping her voice low. "She won't be able to rest until Grady is back in custody."

Hale nodded.

"You've put out an APB and every cop in Virginia is looking for the guy. Someone's bound to see him soon," he assured her. "In the meantime, I agree with Bridget. We need to talk to Reagan Rivera and find out what she knows."

* * *

Charlie parked her black Expedition in the Culver County Hospital garage, then followed Hale into the old building. The worn, dated exterior was a sharp contrast to the sleek, modern reception desk and polished tiles inside the lobby.

"Can I help you with anything?"

A young woman behind the desk flashed a smile.

"Yes," Charlie said, pulling out her FBI credentials. "I'm looking for a woman brought in earlier by ambulance."

The smile on the receptionist's face faded.

"I can't give you a patient's information, even with that badge," she said. "You'd have to-"

"We don't want information," Hale assured her. "We just want to talk to her. Her name is Reagan Rivera. Can you let her know she has visitors? *Please?*"

He softened his tone on the last word, and the receptionist's face relaxed back into a shy smile.

"The only patient who came in by ambulance today is still in the E.R.," she said. "Just through those doors."

Heading toward the *Emergency Room* sign on the far wall, Charlie glanced over at Hale and raised a smooth eyebrow.

"I didn't know you were such a sweet talker," she said. "Does that usually work for you?"

Hale shrugged.

"It works with the nurses on Bea's floor," he said. "She always gets her pain meds on time when I'm there."

"I bet she does," Charlie said dryly, imagining the nurses swooning behind Hale's broad back.

The doors to the E.R. slid open as they approached, and Charlie made a beeline toward the nurse's station, then stopped as Hale called out to her.

"Over there," he said, pointing to a row of vinyl chairs by the window. "Isn't that her?"

Reagan Rivera sat with her back to the room, staring out at the patient drop-off lane just outside.

"What is she doing?" Charlie gasped.

Striding across the room, she almost collided with a man on crutches, before coming to a stop beside Reagan.

"Reagan Rivera?"

She flashed the credentials still held in her hand.

"I'm Agent Day with the FBI. Are you okay?"

Reagan studied her photo for a long beat, then nodded.

"I've got a hell of a headache," she mumbled. "But the doctors say I'm going to be alright as long as I get some rest."

Based on the pallor of Reagan's skin, and the shakiness of her voice, Charlie wasn't so sure.

Why would the doctors send her home so soon? Don't they know she's a lawyer? Aren't all doctors afraid of malpractice lawsuits?

"I can't believe they would discharge you already," she heard herself say. "I mean, you were unconscious, and-"

"They wanted to keep me overnight for observation," Reagan admitted in a dull voice. "But I refused."

She held up a packet of paperwork.

"Once I signed the waiver, they couldn't keep me, so I called an Uber."

"We can give you a ride home," Hale said, sinking into the chair beside Reagan. "You shouldn't be on your own."

"And you shouldn't be telling *me* what to do," the lawyer replied. "I'm perfectly fine. Unlike Officer Pickering."

Charlie was surprised to see a tear slip from Reagan's eye and slide down her cheek.

"That man is dead and I...well, I'm just *fine*."

She ground out the words, her eyes on her hands.

"I'm sorry, but we need to ask you some questions," Charlie said, the mention of Pickering suddenly reminding her why they were there in the first place. "We need to know what you can remember. How did Grady manage to escape?"

Shaking her head, Reagan pointed out the window.

"My ride is here," she said, slowly rising to her feet. "And I can't remember anything. It's all just a blank."

As the lawyer moved toward the door, Charlie turned to Hale, who remained motionless in the chair.

"Now would be a good time to use your powers of persuasion," she said between gritted teeth. "We've got to get her to talk."

"She says she doesn't remember," Hale replied. "Besides, she's in no shape for an interview."

Waving away his objections, Charlie hurried after Reagan, catching up to her just before she could climb into the backseat of a sleek, black sedan.

"We need you to give a statement, Reagan," Charlie said, reaching out a hand to steady the lawyer as she swayed beside the car. "Lyle Grady is out there right now. Do you know where he might be?"

"I can't help you," Reagan said. "I have no idea where

that man is. Now, I want to go home. I need to rest."

She looked down at Charlie's hand, which still rested on the sleeve of her coat.

"I'm sorry," she choked out. "Hopefully tomorrow I'll feel better. Maybe then I can answer your questions."

Charlie pulled her hand back as Reagan slumped into the backseat, then watched as the sedan pulled away from the curb. Once the car had disappeared from view, Charlie dug in her pocket for her phone.

Tapping in the number Shannon Larkin had given her earlier, she waited as the phone began to ring.

"Agent Day?"

The detective's voice boomed through the phone, a siren wailing in the background.

"I need you to do me a favor," Charlie said, raising her own voice, wanting to make sure Larkin could hear her. "I need you to assign a patrol car to watch Reagan Rivera's house tonight. If anyone goes in or out, I want to know."

CHAPTER FIVE

Bridget stood at the courtroom window, staring down at the growing crowd on the street below. She wondered how much time they had before the news broke. How long before the public was told that the Backroads Butcher had killed a guard, assaulted a lawyer, and been allowed to escape into the quiet community?

The citizens of Mount Destiny were sure to be angry, and Bridget couldn't blame them. Lyle Grady had terrorized the community for months before he'd been caught the first time. They had no reason to suspect he'd be any easier to catch this time around.

Sensing movement out of the corner of her eye, Bridget turned just as a woman in baggy pants and a messy blonde ponytail hurried through the near-empty room.

Most of the people who'd been in the courtroom during Grady's escape had now spoken to the police. Those who had provided their name and contact details, along with any connection they had to Grady, had been free to go.

Only a handful of law enforcement resources remained as the Bureau's evidence response team worked to collect evidence in the conference room.

"Detective Larkin?"

Bridget's voice came out louder than she'd intended, but it did the trick. Larkin stopped and spun around to face her.

"I was just wondering if you'd gotten an update on Reagan Rivera," Bridget said. "I know the hospital won't give out information, so-"

"Actually, I spoke to Ms. Rivera a while ago," Larkin said. "She'd already been examined by the E.R. doctor and was waiting for a ride home."

The detective held up her phone.

"Then Agent Day called and asked me to set up a patrol outside Ms. Rivera's house tonight."

She started to move toward the door.

"I assume that means she got home safely. I'm just heading over to make the arrangements now."

"Does Reagan Rivera live nearby?"

Larkin lifted her hand, giving Bridget a thumbs up.

"Yeah, she lives just off Cumberland Road," she called over her shoulder. "She's one of Mount Destiny's hometown success stories. Or at least she was before this happened."

Watching as the detective strode out of sight, Bridget noticed that Gage was also heading toward the exit.

She'd almost forgotten he was still there.

"I think I'm going to head back to Quantico," he said, shrugging on his coat as she trailed after him.

"Oh, no, you're not."

Bridget laid a hand on his arm.

"I need to talk to Reagan, and you're coming with me."

Following Gage out to his dark gray Navigator, Bridget typed *Cumberland Road* into his sat nav, then shifted impatiently in her seat as he inched the big SUV through the traffic jam outside the courthouse.

Twenty minutes later they were cruising down a quiet street lined with colonial-style houses.

"That's it," Bridget said, pointing to a white house with faded blue shutters. "It says *Rivera* on the mailbox."

Gage stopped the Navigator, and they both stared up at the silent house, which seemed a bit rundown considering it belonged to a local hero.

"I'd say Reagan spends too much time at the office," Bridget said, noting the withered plants outside.

"I know the feeling," Gage muttered under his breath as he pulled into the driveway.

Opening the door before the SUV had come to a stop, Bridget jumped out and walked up the front path.

"Hold on," Gage called, coming up behind her. "You do remember that Grady's on the loose, don't you?"

She glanced back to see Gage reaching for his Glock.

"You think he'll stay in Mount Destiny?" she asked, scanning the street behind him.

"I don't know what that man might do," Gage snapped. "But we've got to be ready for anything."

The anxiety in his voice was contagious, causing Bridget's heart to beat faster as she knocked on Reagan's door.

"She's not here," Bridget said, hearing only silence from inside. "Maybe we should wait in the car."

"Maybe we should just leave and come back later," Gage said, checking his watch. "I've got to get back and–"

His words stuck in his throat as a sleek, black sedan pulled onto the driveway. Reagan climbed out of the backseat.

The lawyer stared at the Navigator, then turned unfriendly eyes to Bridget and Gage as she walked slowly up the driveway toward the porch.

"Sorry to just stop by," Bridget said, noting the woman's unsteady gait. "We're with the FBI's Behavioral Analysis Unit. We need to ask you a few questions. It won't take long."

When Reagan didn't respond, Bridget held out her hand.

"This is Agent Terrance Gage, and I'm–"

"I know who you are," the lawyer said, brushing past her to unlock the door. "But I'm too tired to talk to anyone right now. I need to rest. Doctor's orders."

Struggling with the lock, Reagan fumbled the key. It dropped to the ground with a metallic *clink*.

Gage stepped forward and scooped it up.

"Let us help you inside," he said, smoothly unlocking the door. "We can check the house while we're here and make sure everything's okay. Better safe than sorry."

After a long pause, Reagan nodded stiffly.

"Okay, but then you need to go."

She didn't wait for a reply, just pushed her way inside, leaving the door open for Gage and Bridget to follow her.

As Gage checked the doors and looked into every room, Bridget trailed Reagan into the kitchen.

"I'll make some tea," Bridget said, picking up the kettle on the stove and crossing to the sink. "It'll help you sleep."

"Nothing will help me sleep until Lyle Grady is back behind bars," the lawyer said. "I wish I'd never met him."

Taking the opening she'd been given, Bridget cleared her throat as she searched for a tea bag.

"How did you get involved with Grady, anyway?" she asked. "Why take on his particular case?"

Reagan sighed and sank into a chair at the table.

"Grady was cellmates with a man I represented," she said. "I'm sure you've heard of him. His name is Elliott Fisher."

Bridget nodded.

"He was exonerated of a little girl's murder," Reagan explained. "He's the one who told me about Grady."

"What exactly did he tell you?"

Setting the kettle on the burner, Bridget held her breath, hoping she wasn't pushing too hard.

"Elliot told me that Grady hadn't killed Tammy Vicker and that he'd been poorly represented at trial by his lawyer," Reagan said, "After talking to Lonnie Millford and looking through the old case files, I had to agree."

Footsteps sounded in the hall and both women jumped, then relaxed as Gage stepped into the room.

"Was it the blood and tissue under Tammy Vicker's fingernails that convinced you?" Bridget prodded.

Reagan rubbed her head and sighed.

"Originally, there wasn't enough blood and tissue to extract DNA," Reagan said. "So, there was no way to conclusively link the evidence to Grady or anyone else. When Lonnie Millford tried to introduce it into evidence anyway, Judge Hawthorne refused to allow it. That was a mistake in my opinion, but it actually works in Grady's favor now."

"So, you think the DNA profile proves Grady is innocent?" Bridget asked. "Was that the only thing that convinced you to take on the case?"

Reagan hesitated, then shook her head.

"Several sources confirmed Tammy had started dating a new man a few weeks before her death. That fact hadn't come up at the trial," Reagan said. "It made me wonder."

"You suspect that this other man killed Tammy?" Gage asked. "You think it was his DNA under her nails?"

The lawyer stared up at him with foggy eyes.

"I'm pretty sure Grady didn't kill Tammy Vicker."

Her voice was slurred.

"That doesn't mean I know who did," she said. "But whoever he is, his DNA is now in CODIS waiting for a match."

Summoned by the shriek of the kettle, Bridget crossed to the counter and poured the boiling water into a mug.

As she finished preparing the tea, Gage lowered himself into the chair across from Reagan.

"So, you believe the real killer is still out there?" he asked.

Reagan lifted a trembling hand to her bruised forehead.

"Of course, I do," she sighed. "Why else would I be trying to get Grady's conviction overturned?"

She closed her eyes, and for a minute Bridget thought she'd fallen asleep.

"I never wanted to get Lyle Grady out of jail," she finally said in a small, weary voice. "It was quite obvious he'd killed seven other people. I had no doubt he would have continued killing if he hadn't been taken off the street."

Setting the steaming mug in front of Reagan, Bridget waited for her to continue.

"What I do isn't just about exonerating innocent men," Reagan said. "It's also about holding the guilty accountable."

She lifted her eyes to Bridget.

"If a murder case is closed through a false conviction, the real killer remains free. Possibly to kill again," she insisted. "All I wanted was to make sure Tammy's real killer didn't get away with murder. I never wanted Grady back out there."

Reagan's voice cracked on the words, and she bent her head to sip at the hot tea.

Looking over the lawyer's head, Bridget met Gage's eyes. He gave her an almost imperceptible nod. It was time to move on to the hard questions.

"I understand your motivation," Bridget said. "But what I don't understand is what happened at the courthouse today. How did Grady get the knife? How did he manage to overpower Officer Pickering? We need you to tell us anything you can remember. Lives could depend on it."

Reagan's eyes darkened and her jaws clenched.

"That's just it, I can't remember *anything*," she gritted

out. "I already told you that."

Pushing the tea away, she stood.

"Now, I need you both to leave so I can get some rest."

Bridget hesitated, sensing that the lawyer's anger hid some other emotion. Was it fear?

"Look, if you're scared of Grady...if that's why you don't want to talk, we can get you protection."

But Reagan wasn't listening, she was already walking toward the door, her mouth set in a hard line.

Changing tactics, Bridget followed behind her.

"You're right, you probably need some rest," she said, spotting the *Happy Thanksgiving* rug in front of the door. "I imagine you're probably having family over for the holiday, but maybe we can come back when-"

"I'm not in a holiday mood," Reagan said curtly, swinging open the door and ushering Bridget and Gage outside. "But I'll be sure to let you know if I remember anything else."

Before Bridget could protest, Reagan closed the door behind them.

* * *

Bridget checked the lock on her front door again, then crossed to the front window and pulled back the curtain.

As she looked out onto Fern Creek Road, she couldn't shake the thought that Lyle Grady could be somewhere out there in the dark.

Now that he's free, will the Butcher come for me?

After all, Bridget had been the one to figure out that the young delivery driver was in reality a serial killer.

No one who had known Grady back then had guessed his secret. But the profile Bridget had come up with had described him perfectly.

And by the time she'd finally met Grady in person for the first time, she'd had no doubt he was the Backroads Butcher.

Pushing away thoughts of the frightening encounter, Bridget checked the lock on the window, then looked over to where she'd left her purse, wanting to make sure her Glock was within easy reach.

If he comes, you've got to be ready. Your life depends on it.

The little voice in her head repeated what Gage had already told her. What she already knew in her heart.

A soft nuzzle at her hand drew her eyes down to Hank, who stared up at her with dark, worried eyes.

The Irish setter could sense her anxiety.

"Don't worry, boy," she said, ruffling the soft reddish fur on his head. "Everything's going to be okay."

Suddenly headlights illuminated the window as a vehicle pulled into the driveway. Bridget squinted against the harsh light as Hank let out a rare bark.

Surprised to see two figures climbing out of a red pickup truck, Bridget let the curtain fall back into place and crossed to the front door.

Deputy Marshal Vic Santino was already halfway up the front steps by the time Bridget swung open the door.

His worried eyes searched her face as he stopped in front

of her and took both her hands in his.

"Are you okay?"

His voice was low and urgent as he looked over her shoulder into the house.

"Are you here alone?" he asked. "Why didn't you go to your father's house?"

"I'm fine," she said, shrugging off his concern. "Hank and I are perfectly capable of taking care of ourselves."

Santino looked down at the Irish setter beside Bridget and raised an eyebrow.

"No offense, but Hank isn't exactly a guard dog."

Before Bridget could object, a tall shadow fell over her.

A muscular figure appeared behind Santino, stepping into the soft glow cast by the porch light.

Her eyes widened as she recognized the man's shaggy blonde hair and clean-shaven, boyish face.

U.S. Deputy Marshal Howie Decker had played a key role in bringing in Lyle Grady the first time the serial killer had been captured. If he was here with Santino, he must be ready for round two.

"Decker?" she said, forcing a smile. "It's been a while."

"It sure has," the big man agreed, his eyes lighting up with an appreciative gleam. "But you're still looking mighty good, Doc. Private practice suits you."

Santino spoke up before Bridget could respond.

"Mind your manners, Decker," he said, aiming a sharp look at his companion. "Or you'll be waiting outside."

Shrugging his thick shoulders, Decker laughed.

"Since when is it bad manners to appreciate a beautiful

woman?" he asked, then held up both hands in supplication when Santino turned on him. "Okay, okay, message received loud and clear, bro. You've made your claim. I'll back off."

An annoyed flush spread over Bridget's face at the crass comment, but she swallowed back a protest, reminding herself that she owed Decker.

If it wasn't for Howie Decker, I might not be here now.

Bridget waved the men inside and followed their broad backs down the hall and into the kitchen. She watched as Hank first circled around Santino's feet, then sniffed at Decker's hand in a friendly way, excited to have visitors.

So much for being a guard dog.

Suppressing a sigh, she turned to Santino, who was checking the lock on the back door.

"I couldn't believe it when I heard the news," he said, bending to rub Hank behind one floppy ear. "I wanted to make sure you're okay. But then, of course, you're not..."

He reached for her hand, pulling her toward him, knowing without asking that she wasn't okay.

Not when headless bodies still filled her dreams. Not when the man who had haunted her nightmares for years had been set free in the real world and she had no idea where he could be or what he might do.

Shooting an embarrassed glance at Decker, Bridget gently extracted herself from Santino's embrace.

"I'll be fine," she said, looking toward the dark sky outside the kitchen window. "Grady's likely hundreds of miles away by now. He's probably running for the Canadian border."

"Then it looks like we'll be heading north!" Decker bellowed, banging a big hand on the counter.

Bridget winced as her eyes found Santino.

"You're going after him?" she asked, her voice hoarse.

Nodding solemnly, Santino checked his watch.

"Decker and I are on the team responsible for bringing Grady in," he confirmed. "We'll be heading over to Abbeyville State prison once we leave here to interview the warden."

"You think Grady may have told someone there where he was heading?" she asked. "Or that he had help?"

Santino shrugged.

"Warden Crawford's men were supposed to be guarding Grady. Officer Pickering shouldn't have been in that room."

"And we don't know how Grady managed to get hold of a knife," Decker added. "We need to find out who Grady had been talking to lately. He had help with this, that's for sure."

Bridget nodded in agreement.

Grady couldn't have managed the escape without help from someone who knew what they were doing. Maybe even someone on the inside.

"I hate to leave you alone," Santino said, his eyes searching her face. "Do you want protection? I could ask Cecil to send a patrol car–"

"No," Bridget said, refusing his offer to call the Wisteria Falls chief of police. "I've got Hank and my Glock. The three of us will be just fine."

"Maybe you should go stay with your father," Santino suggested, still looking anxious.

Sensing his reluctance to leave, Bridget took Santino's arm and guided him back toward the front door.

As much as she wanted him to stay, she knew he had a job to do. It was a job he'd done before.

They'd both worked on the initial Backroads Butcher Task Force. Only back then, they had barely known each other as they'd raced to find the man who had been butchering and beheading innocent people along the backroads of Virginia.

And now that same psychopath was free again.

As Bridget watched the men get back into Santino's pick-up truck, her phone buzzed in her pocket.

Ignoring the phone until the red Chevy had turned onto Landsend Road, Bridget looked down at the phone's display.

She grimaced as she saw the text was from Chase Grafton.

Over the years the *Chasing Killers* podcaster had relentlessly hounded her for an exclusive interview, wanting confidential details from the high-profile cases she'd worked.

He'd even gone as far as dating Daphne Finch, her best friend, in an attempt to get closer to Bridget.

Luckily, Daphne had discovered that the podcaster was already in a relationship before things had gotten too serious. She'd broken things off with Chase over the summer.

But he wasn't the type to give up so easily, and his

obsession with Bridget had only grown since Daphne had cut off his one connection to the profiler.

Tapping on Chase's text, Bridget read the message, her stomach tightening with dread.

"I hear the Butcher's out. Better lock your doors."

CHAPTER SIX

S antino and Decker arrived at Abbeyville State Prison well after dark. A waxing crescent moon hung in the sky overhead as the Chevy pulled up to the security gate. Santino flashed his badge at the stone-faced guard, then steered the pickup into the administrative parking lot.

Following the guard's instructions, the two deputies approached the *Official Prison Staff Only* entrance.

Decker jabbed at a button beside the metal door.

A long buzz sounded, and then the door clicked open.

"Come on through," a deep voice called out as they stepped inside. "Leave your weapons in one of the lockers. Take the key with you."

Two uniformed guards waited, their arms crossed over their chests, as Santino and Decker complied, removing guns from shoulder and ankle holsters.

Feeling strangely vulnerable without his weapons, Santino followed a short, stocky guard through a depressing maze of dank, empty corridors.

The guard finally stopped outside a locked gate and waved his badge over an electronic keypad.

Pushing the door open, he waved them into a carpeted

reception area. The room was tastefully decorated and comfortably furnished, looking to Santino more like a hotel lobby than a prison warden's office.

"Warden Crawford is in there," the guard said, nodding toward an open door at the end of the hall. "He'll walk you out when you're ready to leave."

The door clanked shut behind them as Santino followed Decker down the hall.

A man with a thick headful of sandy brown hair sat behind an enormous desk, a stack of paperwork in front of him.

"Warden Crawford?"

The man looked up with a faint frown.

"We spoke earlier on the phone," Santino said from the doorway. "I'm Deputy Santino and this is Deputy Decker."

Crawford's face cleared.

"Ah, Deputy Santino," he said, getting to his feet and circling the desk to offer a hand. "You're here about Lyle Grady, right?"

The warden was tall and broad-shouldered with a square jaw, thick eyebrows, and a prominent nose.

He would have been a handsome man if not for his eyes, which were too small and close-set for his long face.

"Yes, thanks for staying late to speak to us," Santino said as he shook the warden's hand. "I appreciate your help. We're looking for any information that could assist us in finding Grady and bringing him back in."

Crawford crossed his arms over his wide chest and leaned back on his heels.

"I'm not sure how much help I can give you, seeing that someone down in Culver County let the little bastard get away," he said. "But I did pull up the visitors' log you asked about. Got it right over here."

Moving toward a small conference table against the wall, he gestured to an open laptop.

"Looks as if Grady had been getting more visitors than usual lately," he said, tapping on the keypad to wake up the computer. "We keep a record of all visitors coming through."

Santino bent over the desk as Crawford tapped a long finger on the screen.

"Reagan Rivera is his new lawyer," the warden said. "She's visited a couple of times a week from what I can tell."

He scrolled down.

"And Lonnie Millford comes with her sometimes, although not as often. He's the old lawyer."

"You said Grady had more visitors than usual," Decker interjected over Santino's shoulder. "We already know about his lawyers. Tell us something we don't know."

Wincing at Decker's impatient tone, Santino motioned for Crawford to continue.

"No, this is good," he said. "I'm going to want printouts of every visit, even the ones from his lawyers. Now, who else has been here to see him?"

Crawford scrolled back to the previous month.

"Does the name Max Bender ring a bell?" he asked. 'The guy was here twice last month."

Santino shook his head.

"Well, he gave us a driver's license when he checked into the visitor's desk," the warden said. "Does that help?"

"You guys keep a copy of the ID?" Santino asked.

The warden shook his head, then pointed to a series of numbers on the screen.

"We don't take copies, but we record the ID number."

"I'll ask Ivy to run a full check on the name," Decker said, pulling his phone out of his pocket and tapping in a text.

Minutes later, his phone dinged with a response.

"Well, I'll be damned," he said. "Sounds like Max Bender's a very naughty boy."

Santino's pulse picked up a notch as Decker's phone rang.

After listening intently to the caller, he put the phone on speaker and held it up.

"Do me a favor, Ivy, and repeat that for Santino."

A brisk female voice filled the room.

"Looks like a clear case of identity theft. The real Maxwell Bender died as a child. The dead kid's social security number and other data were used to obtain a license and several credit cards. Happens more than you'd like to think."

"Thanks, Ivy," Santino said. "Keep digging and let us know if you find out anything else."

Decker ended the call and stuck his phone in his pocket.

"Is there a camera in the visitor's area?" Santino asked. "Would there be pictures or a video of this guy?"

"There's a video camera in the visitor's hall alright," Crawford said. "But it won't do you much good. The footage gets overwritten every seven days."

He tapped on the computer screen.

"And the last time this guy Bender visited was several weeks ago, so you're out of luck."

"But...why overwrite the video?" Decker demanded.

Crawford flashed an apologetic smile.

"Budget constraints I imagine," he replied. "But that policy was implemented before my time, so..."

Shrugging his shoulders, he was about to close the laptop when Santino saw a familiar name on the visitor's list.

"Chase Grafton was one of Grady's visitors?" Santino asked, not sure he could be seeing correctly.

Crawford frowned and followed his gaze.

"Oh, yes, of course," he said with a nod. "Chase Grafton has also visited Lyle Grady on several occasions."

"Who's Chase Grafton?" Decker asked.

He looked back and forth from Santino to Crawford.

"He's the host of a true crime podcast called *Chasing Killers*," Santino explained. "He's a real piece of work. Always hounding Bridget for information or pressuring her for an interview. He must have persuaded Grady to add him to his approved visitor's list."

Crawford cleared his throat.

"Mr. Grafton *is* a persuasive man," he said, looking uncomfortable. "He even talked me into giving a brief interview for one of his recent episodes."

Santino raised an eyebrow, momentarily too surprised to

respond.

"You see, my wife is a big fan of his show," he admitted, red-faced. "The interview didn't take long, but it sure earned me a few brownie points at home."

"Did he interview Lyle Grady as well?" Santino asked.

He sucked in a deep breath as he awaited Crawford's response, trying hard not to show his disapproval.

"He sure did," the warden said. "Apparently, the Butcher case was what got Chase interested in true crime."

"Is that what he told you?" Santino asked.

The warden shrugged.

"Well, that's what he said in his podcast," Crawford said. "It was in the episode about Grady's capture, I think. The one about that profiler who figured out who he was."

"The *profiler*?" Santino asked.

A simmer of anger started up in his chest.

"Yeah, you know. The woman who's always on the news," he said. "The brunette with the-"

"You mean Bridget Bishop?" Decker asked.

Stepping between Santino and Crawford, he quickly guided the conversation back to the visitors' log.

"We're going to need that printout," he said. "We need to know everyone who visited Grady in the last ninety days."

Crawford looked at his watch.

"I'll get my IT guy to send you the files," he said. "But he won't be back in until tomorrow. Now...my wife's waiting-"

"We also need to see Grady's cell before we go," Santino

said with a tight smile. "We'll try to keep it brief."

Crawford led the men back to the metal door. Following his imposing figure through another warren of corridors, Santino and Decker eventually arrived at the maximum-security block.

A guard escorted the three men into Grady's ward, which was filled with stale air and loud, angry voices. A row of closed metal doors ran down the corridor.

"The inmates are required to stay in their cells after chow," the warden explained. "This one is Grady's."

As the guard opened the door, Santino noted that the cell had two bunks, a toilet, and a narrow window protected by iron bars.

"We're keeping it free for Grady," Crawford said. "It'll be here waiting when you guys bring him back."

"Have your men searched it, yet?" Santino asked.

Crawford shook his head.

"I got a call from an Agent Day with the FBI asking me to leave the cell untouched until they could send over an evidence response team. Haven't seen anyone yet."

Santino looked at Decker, then shrugged.

"I don't think we can afford to wait," he said.

Stepping inside, he began to inspect the meager contents of the cell, not sure what he was expecting to find.

Adrenaline surged through him as he lifted the mattress and a small piece of paper fluttered onto the floor.

Grady had left them a note.

Time to get on the road again. But don't worry, I'll be in touch.

CHAPTER SEVEN

Reagan Rivera bolted upright in the dim room, jarred awake by a high-pitched ring that filled her with instant dread. Swinging her legs over the edge of the sofa, she held a hand to her aching head and stared down at the coffee table where she'd dropped her cell phone.

Tired of the incessant calls and questions, she'd shut off the ringer hours before. The little screen was filled with alerts and notifications of missed calls and messages, but the phone was quiet, just as expected.

Ring...ring...ring.

Turning toward the shrill sound, Reagan's eyes fell on the credenza under the front window where a sliver of moonlight shone through a gap in the curtains, illuminating a white landline phone.

She hadn't used the phone in months, intending to have it disconnected. But patience wasn't one of her virtues and each time she'd called the telephone company, they'd kept her on hold so long she'd eventually hung up in frustration.

Reagan stood and walked slowly across the living room on trembling legs, still groggy from the pain medication they'd given her at the hospital.

Who managed to get my unlisted number?

Over the years, Reagan's legal work with several high-profile convicted murderers had earned her plenty of overzealous fans, obsessed stalkers, and angry vigilantes determined to make her life hell.

And then there were the reporters, both professional and amateur, who felt it was their duty to follow and harass her, hoping for a comment or soundbite that could boost their ratings.

Reagan wasn't interested in speaking to any of them. But as she looked down at the phone, she hesitated.

What if it's Heather? What if he's let her go? What if she needs me? If she couldn't get through on my cell...

Realizing that her younger sister was one of the few people who might call the unlisted number, Reagan snatched up the receiver and held it to her ear.

Lyle Grady's voice sent a chill up her spine.

"Are you alone?"

She nodded, then remembered he couldn't see her.

"Yes," she croaked between dry lips. "The feds have been here, but I didn't tell them anything. How did you get this number?"

"I have my sources," he said. "The feds will already be tracing your cell, but I doubt they're tapping your landline yet. It'll take them time to get their shit together."

"Where are you?" she asked, automatically switching into lawyer mode, trying to assess the risk. "What phone are you using?"

"I'm calling from Officer Pickering's phone," Grady said,

sounding amused. "I didn't think he'd be needing it anymore, so I took it."

Reagan closed her eyes and held the phone to her ear.

"That *poor man*. I have his blood on my hands now."

"Stop with the guilt trip already," Grady muttered. "It wasn't your fault. It wasn't mine either, for that matter."

The killer's callous tone suggested he didn't much care whose fault it was one way or the other.

"The cop wasn't supposed to be there," he complained. "I didn't set out to kill him, but I did what I had to do. Lucky for me, the knife was taped under the conference table just as I'd instructed."

Picturing the sudden slash of metal, and the blood spurting up from the guard's throat, Reagan suppressed an urge to gag.

"So, how'd he talk you into keeping quiet?" Grady continued. "Why'd you help me get away?"

"You expect me to believe you don't know?" Reagan asked in disbelief. "That you weren't in on the whole thing? He has *my sister...*"

She swallowed back a sob and steadied her voice, not wanting to give him the satisfaction of hearing her cry.

"He has Heather. He said he'd kill her if I didn't help you."

There was a long pause on the other end of the connection.

"*Who* has your sister?"

"Max Bender," she said. "At least, that's the name he's using, although I can't find evidence he actually exists."

A soft chuckle sounded in her ear.

"Is that what he's calling himself?" Grady asked.

She detected glee in his voice and pictured the half-grin she'd become familiar with during the last few months. The one that revealed a mouthful of small, crooked teeth.

"The guy has balls, I'll give him that," Grady said, oblivious to Reagan's distress. "But don't blame me. I didn't tell him to mix you up in all this. I just told the guy to get me out of prison. It was his job to figure out the fastest way."

She gripped the phone harder, letting his words sink in.

"He did it for *you*."

Her voice broke as she struggled to rein in her anger.

"He took Heather so that I'd help *you* escape."

Closing her eyes, she pictured the text the man named Bender had sent to her the day before. A photo of her sister exiting the airport, along with a message.

I have Heather. If you ever want to see your sister again, you'll do exactly what I tell you. If you call the police, she's dead.

Reagan had immediately tried to call Heather's number, hoping it was just some type of stupid prank, but the call had rolled to voicemail. Moments later, she'd received a text from Heather's phone.

I told you I have your sister. Which means I have her phone. Try anything like that again, and I'll slit her throat.

Heart thumping erratically in her chest, it had taken Reagan all her strength to tap in another text.

Who are you and what do you want?

The response had come back quickly.

I'm Max Bender, and what I want is for you to do exactly as I say.

He'd instructed her to arrange for Grady to be alone in the conference room at the Culver County courthouse during the hearing.

She'd agonized over what to do, reading the instructions he had texted to her again and again.

Grady will know what to do. Stay quiet and stay out of the way. Stall for time. If it goes wrong, you'll never see Heather again.

In the end, what choice had she had? She knew too well what an evil man might do to an innocent girl like Heather.

"What are you planning?" she asked Grady, knowing he might be her only chance to get Heather back alive. "Where will you go now?"

"I have scores to settle. A whole list, actually."

He was starting to sound impatient.

"But don't worry, you're not on it. You tried to help me. You're about the only person who ever did."

He chuckled again.

"Well, you and another do-gooder. A man of God as they say. He tried to help me, but it didn't end well. Not for him."

"You could still redeem yourself," Reagan cried. "There's still a chance to make amends. You could tell Bender to bring back my sister. You could-"

"This guy *Bender* is nothing but a two-faced *crook*."

Anger had seeped in under the amusement.

"A crook who will do anything not to get caught."

"But he has my *sister*," Reagan said, swallowing hard.

"You've got to tell him to let Heather go."

She clutched the phone to her ear.

"Please, I'm begging you. She's not-"

Her words were cut short by a loud knock on the door.

"Sounds like you've got company," Grady said, ignoring her plea. "Just remember to keep your mouth shut."

She started to protest, but the line was already dead.

Reagan stared at the phone with welling eyes.

Grady was gone.

Crossing the room, Reagan looked out the window, half expecting to see Grady's soulless eyes staring back at her.

She felt an initial surge of relief at the sight of the man under the porchlight, then her heart sank.

Resisting the urge to turn away, she reached down and slid back the deadbolt, forcing herself to meet the man's gaze as she pulled the door open.

Reverend Virgil Abernathy stood stiffly on the porch, his tall, thin body draped in a black cassock, white surplice, and stiff collar. A wild shock of white hair surrounded his head like a bristly halo.

"You look dressed for the pulpit, Reverend," Reagan said, not quite meeting his eyes. "But you'll have to excuse me. I'm not really up for a sermon today."

She'd already had several run-ins with the reverend over the last few months. Ever since he'd heard she had taken on Grady's appeal he'd been a constant presence in her life.

If he hadn't been the bereaved father of two murdered teens, she would have accused him of being a stalker.

But can I really blame him for grieving his children? For trying to keep the man who killed them locked away?

The reverend's grief and rage had manifested as righteous anger. She could understand that. She didn't take it personally.

But now, with everything going on, she felt as if she might crack under his reproachful gaze.

"Your ambition and pride have led you astray," the old man said, sounding sorrowful. "You listened to the Butcher's whispers and fell for his evil lies. And now we all must pay."

His words echoed in the cool, dark air, sending a ripple of unease through her.

"This isn't my fault," she said, shaking her head. "I never meant for him to escape. I just wanted to find the truth..."

She faltered as she met the old man's unflinching gaze.

"The *truth*? The truth is your client butchered both my children," he said, visibly shaking with emotion. "The truth is their heads were never found."

Reagan recoiled as she tried to block the disturbing images his words conjured.

"I don't know about you," he said in a strangled voice, "but I won't be able to rest until I find out what he did with them. What he did with all of them."

Abernathy gave a weary shake of his head as Reagan dropped her own head into her hands, unable to bear the pain she saw in the reverend's red-rimmed eyes.

"Be careful," he said softly. "He'll come for you and yours next. One day soon the Butcher will find you."

Reagan lifted her eyes. Were the tortured words a warning, or a premonition?

But she didn't get the chance to ask.

Abernathy had turned and was already walking away.

Stepping back into the house, she slid the deadbolt into place before hurrying to the kitchen to make sure the back door was locked.

Once the doors were secured, she moved into the bedroom and opened the top drawer of her bedside table.

The Glock was wrapped in a silk scarf and nestled into the back corner. It wasn't the safest way to store a firearm, she knew, but she liked to have the gun easily accessible.

Men such as Lyle Grady have taught me that much, at least.

As she turned to go back into the living room, Reagan's eyes were drawn to a photo on the mantle.

In the picture, she and Heather stood side by side, arms slung over each other's shoulders.

Tears filled her eyes as she studied their happy faces.

What I did, I did for Heather's sake. Just like everything else I've done over the last ten years.

Reagan wondered if the words were still true.

For so long she had tried to be a stand-in for her own mother, who had died while Heather was still in high school.

And she'd done her best to shield the younger girl from their father's alcoholism.

But to be honest, Reagan had never been the maternal type. And over the years, she'd let Heather down too many times to count while convincing herself that she was doing her best.

Once Heather had gone off to college, Reagan had hoped to be free to focus on her own burgeoning career.

Unfortunately, she now realized she had lost all sense of perspective, allowing her work to take over her life, causing her marriage to flounder and her father to all but disown her.

Her little sister had been the only one who had accepted her invitation to Thanksgiving Dinner. The only family she had left. The only person she could count on.

And now Heather was missing.

And it's all my fault.

Picking up her cell phone with trembling hands, Reagan tapped in a text to the number she had saved under the name Max Bender, unable to wait any longer.

I've done what you wanted. Now, give me back my sister!

CHAPTER EIGHT

The mild morning sun was still low in the blue Virginia sky as Bridget steered her old Ford Explorer onto Maplewood Drive. Pulling onto the driveway of her childhood home, she looked over her shoulder to where Hank waited patiently in the backseat.

"You be a good boy, today," she said, trying to stifle a yawn. "Don't give Paloma any reason to complain."

The Irish setter regarded her with an innocent expression, then moved to the open window and stuck his nose into the cool fall air, waiting for Bridget to open his door.

The dog would spend the day with her father and stepmother while she drove over to the Mount Destiny police station for an emergency task force meeting.

Lyle Grady was now officially a wanted fugitive by the U.S. Marshal Service, the FBI, and the Mount Destiny PD, and the agencies had agreed to work together to try to bring him in before anyone else got killed.

As Hank jumped down from the backseat, Bridget saw Bob Bishop open the front door and step out onto the porch.

Walking up the front path, she noted that his salt and

pepper hair had been neatly combed, and his shirt and slacks appeared to have been freshly pressed.

If Bridget hadn't known better, she'd have said he was dressed and ready for work. But her father had retired from his role as a detective at the Wisteria Falls Police Department several years earlier after he'd suffered a sudden stroke.

He'd been rushed to the hospital only days after Lyle Grady had been found guilty at his original trial.

Her father's stroke, along with the stress of the recent investigation and trial, had prompted Bridget to quit her job at the BAU so she could help with his recovery.

She'd always suspected his health crisis had been brought on by the stress she'd put him through as he'd watched his only daughter work the high-profile Backroads Butcher case.

And now, as Bridget stood in front of her father, outside her childhood home, she felt the usual twinge of guilt.

It was one of several unwelcome, recurring emotions she was working to dispel with her therapist Faye Thackery. And while she'd managed to identify the source of her guilt, she hadn't yet managed to overcome it.

"You were supposed to be here twenty minutes ago," her father scolded as Hank ran past his legs into the house. "I was beginning to worry. Grady could be anywhere."

"There's no need to worry," Bridget said, trying to keep her voice light. "Every law enforcement agency in the country is looking for him. If he has any sense, he's already left the area by now."

Bob shook his head, unconvinced.

"That's just it, honey," he said. "Grady isn't driven by logic or good sense. He's driven by evil. You of all people should know that by now."

Footsteps sounded in the hall, and then her stepmother appeared in the doorway wearing a fluffy, white bathrobe, her wispy hair twisted into a buttery-blonde chignon.

"Your father's been worried sick about that man."

Paloma's accusing tone suggested that Grady's escape was somehow Bridget's fault.

"Stress isn't good for him, remember?" she said as if speaking to a particularly foolish child. "The doctor said so just last week."

"I'm sorry, Dad," Bridget said, not quite sure what she was apologizing for. "I didn't want this to happen."

She studied her father's lined but still handsome face. Did he look thinner than he had the last time she'd seen him?

Why was he at the doctor's last week, anyway?

Tucking the question away for later, when she and her father were alone, she made her way back to the Explorer.

"I'll be back before dinner time to pick up Hank," she called, giving one last wave to her father.

With a sigh of both regret and relief, Bridget pulled the SUV onto the road and headed toward Mount Destiny.

* * *

Bridget parked the Explorer along the curb on Central

Avenue and walked into the Mount Destiny police station just as the task force began filing into the little department's only conference room.

She took an empty seat next to Charlie Day, who sat at the head of the table. As their eyes met, Bridget was again overcome by a sense of déjà vu.

Hasn't this all happened before?

They'd already found the Backroads Butcher once, and they'd ensured that justice had been done. Hadn't they? So why were they here again, searching for a man who had caused unimaginable fear and misery?

Catching a glimpse of her own stunned disbelief mirrored in Charlie's somber gray eyes, Bridget forced herself to suck in a deep, fortifying breath.

If she and Charlie and the rest of the team had stopped the Butcher once before, they could do it again.

She surveyed the attendees gathered around the long, oval table. Her eyes stopped on Terrance Gage, and she nodded a grim greeting.

"You holding up?" her former boss asked.

"If tossing and turning half the night is *holding up*, then I'm fine," Bridget said, producing a wry smile. "But you know, for just a minute, when I woke up this morning, I thought Grady's escape must have been a bad dream. It just seems so surreal to be sitting around this table again."

Gage had already opened his mouth to reply when Argus Murphy leaned past him. The BAU's new behavioral analyst's amber eyes were anxious behind his glasses and his carrot-hued hair was uncharacteristically disheveled.

"I know, I can't believe this is happening," he said, shaking his head. "I have to admit I was gutted not to be invited to the original Butcher task force meetings."

His cheeks flushed pink behind his freckles.

"I thought I was missing out on the excitement," he said. "But now that this is happening again, and I'm here trying to stop a man like Lyle Grady, I realize how naïve I was."

Bridget tried and failed to muster a reassuring smile.

Argus had been a profiler coordinator during the original investigation. Although he hadn't been officially assigned to the task force, his persistent efforts to provide analytical and statistical support from behind the front line had paid off, eventually earning him a coveted analyst position at the BAU.

Feeling someone sink into the chair beside her, Bridget looked over to see Opal Fitzgerald. The M.E. looked as tired as Bridget felt but still managed a smile as she began to arrange a stack of folders on the table in front of her.

Just as Charlie stood to call the meeting to order, Detective Larkin hurried in looking flustered, her hair loose around her shoulders as if it had finally burst free from the ponytail she'd worn the day before.

"Okay, everybody, let's get started," Charlie said from her place at the front of the room. "As you all know, Lyle Grady escaped from the Culver County Courthouse yesterday and we've been tasked with finding him."

Before she could continue, the door opened again and Vivian Burke slipped into the room, her tall thin, figure immaculate in slim black pants and a white jacket, her flame-red hair smoothed into a high ponytail.

"Sorry I'm late," she murmured, finding a seat at the end of the table. "I was wrapping up a few things at the lab."

"You actually got here just in time today," Charlie said. "We're reviewing the events leading up to Grady's escape. Turns out your tardiness yesterday played a pivotal role."

Vivian blinked.

"Excuse me?"

"I'm not sure if you're aware, but Judge Hawthorne called a recess while we waited for a forensic expert to arrive. An expert who was scheduled to give testimony on a DNA test related to a murder," Charlie said. "I learned this morning we were waiting for *you*."

She didn't wait for Vivian to respond.

"During that recess, Grady used a knife to slit a guard's throat, knock his lawyer unconscious, and slip out the window onto the fire escape."

"And you think that's *my* fault?" Vivian asked, raising an already arched eyebrow.

Charlie shrugged.

"I think it created a window of opportunity," she said. "It makes me wonder what Grady would have done if you'd showed up on time."

"I did show up on time," Vivian insisted. "The request I received asked me to give testimony at the Mount Destiny Courthouse at noon. I arrived well before that, but the roads were closed, so I turned around and went back to Quantico."

"You're lucky that Grady had already made his escape by then," Opal said in Vivian's direction. "Otherwise, Judge Hawthorne would have surely held you in contempt for being a no-show. He's a real stickler for protocol."

Shrugging her narrow shoulders dismissively, Vivian leaned back in her chair with a peeved expression.

Bridget made a note to herself to find out who had sent the request to Vivian as Charlie turned toward Opal.

"Now Opal, you *were* there on time to give testimony yesterday, which meant you were also able to examine Officer Pickering's body immediately after he was attacked. What can you tell us about that?"

"I can tell you that Officer Pickering's neck was sliced open with a switchblade," the M.E. said bluntly. "And that the murder weapon was recovered from the scene. Turns out it got trapped under Pickering's body when he fell."

Looking up at Charlie, Opal cocked her head.

"What I can't figure out is how Grady got hold of a switchblade in the first place."

"Well, if you figure that one out, be sure to tell me," Charlie said. "In the meantime, our colleagues in the FBI lab can let us know if they find any DNA on the blade other than the victim's. If someone gave the knife to Grady, their DNA could be on there, too."

She glanced in Vivian's direction, but the forensic examiner appeared to be scrolling through her phone.

Charlie's jaw tightened in irritation. Shaking her head, she turned to Shannon Larkin.

"Now, I thought we'd review Grady's history of offenses

for the benefit of the new members of the task force. It's important they understand exactly what we're dealing with."

Larkin froze, then gave an awkward nod as everyone looked in her direction.

"The Butcher's first victims were Justine and Junior Abernathy," Charlie said. "Both siblings were found on the side of the road out near Hickory Pass. They'd both been decapitated."

"Is it true that their heads have never been found?"

The room fell silent at Larkin's question.

"That's right," Bridget said. "We never were able to recover the heads of any of Grady's victims. We think he kept them as trophies."

She hesitated, giving Larkin a minute for the information to sink in. She knew only too well that the horror of it all could be overwhelming.

"Michelle Ewing was the third victim," Charlie said, picking up the thread. "She was a high-school senior from West Virginia. She missed the bus home from school and was seen hitchhiking. Her body was found near Providence Gap three days later."

Charlie continued to recap the atrocities Grady had committed, describing the next four victims who'd been found, and the growing hysteria in the community.

Two more lone women and another young couple had been killed in brutal attacks, their decapitated bodies discarded by the side of the road. All seemed to be random victims of chance encounters.

Then Tammy Vicker's body had been discovered.

Charlie held up a head shot of the young reporter as she described the gruesome crime scene.

The photo showed a vivacious blonde with a wide smile.

Bridget knew the reporter had gotten a reputation as a wild child and had been known to go to extreme lengths to get a story. She'd certainly been relentless in her coverage of the Backroads Butcher before her death.

No one on the task force had believed she'd been a random victim, but they'd never figured out why she'd been chosen.

Most investigators assumed Tammy had crossed paths with Lyle Grady during her coverage of the high-profile investigation, and that the serial killer had impulsively decided to make her his next victim.

Bridget had wondered if the reporter had found out too much. Maybe Grady had wanted to shut her up. Or maybe he'd seen her on the news and decided to hunt her down.

But all those scenarios went against his previous M.O. of random victim selection based on opportunity.

As she'd struggled to work it out, Bridget had begun to suspect the Butcher had known his first victims. That he may have even lived close to them.

The idea that Justine and Junior Abernathy were just random victims of opportunity, as the next four victims appeared to be, had suddenly felt wrong after she'd studied the data Argus had been sending her.

She had begun to think that if the Butcher had targeted Tammy Vicker, maybe he had targeted Justine, too. Perhaps

Junior had just been in the wrong place at the wrong time.

"Thanks to Bridget's profiling work, Grady was captured only a few weeks after Tammy's murder," Charlie said, still holding up the reporter's photo.

"Actually, it was Argus' geographic profiling that made me keep coming back to Mount Destiny, and to Justine and Junior," Bridget admitted. "It had all started with them."

Larkin shook her head, confused.

"Geographic profiling?"

"It's not as confusing as it sounds," Argus said. "It's actually pretty basic."

He flipped through the folder in front of him and pulled out a map sprinkled with red dots and intersecting lines.

"This is the geographic profile I sent to the task force right before Tammy Vicker's body was found."

"If we assumed some of these were random attacks, we could also assume the killer and his victims must have both been at the same place at the same time during the course of their normal routines."

Turning the map in Larkin's direction, he used a finger to trace the perimeter of a large red circle.

"I mapped out the victim's travel patterns to work, school, home, or wherever, and then determined a probable area where the killer lived or worked."

Bridget didn't bother looking at the map. She already knew it by heart. Already knew that downtown Mount Destiny sat in the middle of the circle.

"The reports and data Argus sent got me thinking," Bridget said, explaining how she had watched the recorded interviews of dozens of subjects and persons of interest without finding a viable suspect.

"I kept turning back to the map that indicated the killer was likely living in downtown Mount Destiny."

Her stomach tightened at the memory.

"On impulse, I decided to attend and observe the church where Justine and Junior's father had preached. Reverend Abernathy was still out on leave, but I soon became aware of a young man who fit my profile perfectly."

"Do you still have your original profile of the Butcher?" Larkin asked, her eyes on the folder in front of Bridget.

Flipping through the documents inside, Bridget stopped and stared down at a printout.

She scanned the text, then handed the page to the detective, reciting the profile from memory.

"The unsub is a single white male in his mid-to-late twenties. He lives with his mother or another domineering maternal figure. He is socially awkward, has trouble relating to women, and is not currently in a relationship. He has a job or other responsibilities that require him to travel extensively in the area.

"He is a psychopath with a history of petty crimes who is motivated by a desire to exert total power over his victims. He most likely keeps the heads to extend the feeling of having control over his victims and their families."

Larkin's face grew pale, and the room fell silent. After a long beat, the detective cocked her head.

"But how did you know Lyle Grady matched your profile?"

The image of a young girl's earnest face flashed through Bridget's mind as she thought back to her first visit to the Mount Destiny Church of Redemption.

"I talked to most of the teenage parishioners at the church," Bridget explained. "I asked about Justine and Junior, trying to find out if there had been anything unusual going on prior to their deaths."

She shook her head at the memory of how close she'd been to giving up on her theory before Zadie Monroe had called.

"Eventually, one of the girls called the number I'd left. She said she'd been a close friend of Justine's. She suspected the son of a parishioner had been involved in Justine's murder."

Bridget could still hear the sound of Zadie's soft, frightened voice on the phone that day.

There's this guy...his name is Lyle Grady. He gives me the creeps.

A shiver ran through Bridget at the thought of how quickly everything had happened after that.

"Turns out this girl was right. Lyle Grady had attended church with his mother occasionally. He stopped going after the Reverend caught him stealing money out of the collection plate one Sunday, but not before he'd made several unwanted advances at Justine. I thought it was likely he held a grudge against the whole family."

Bridget took the profile from Larkin and placed it back in the folder.

"With a little digging, I soon discovered Grady worked

for a local delivery service. Needless to say, he moved to the top of my list. It wasn't long before he was arrested."

Gage cleared his throat.

"Bridget actually managed to find Grady and his van before he was caught and–"

Holding up a hand, Bridget stopped him before he could continue. She wasn't ready to talk about the events of that day. Not with everyone in the room listening in.

She'd had a hard enough time discussing it with Faye Thackery during their therapy sessions. She wasn't prepared to share it with the rest of the world.

Suddenly eager to shift the focus away from herself and back to the investigation, Bridget looked past Gage.

"Argus, if I remember correctly, you had expressed doubts that Tammy Vicker was one of Grady's victims."

The analyst's pale, freckled face was solemn, his eyes thoughtful behind his glasses as he nodded.

"That's right," he said. "I never could find a satisfying pattern in the data once Tammy was added into the victimology. She didn't fit the other victim types. And she skewed the geographic profile."

"What do you mean?" Larkin asked.

Digging into the bag beside him, he rummaged around, eventually pulling out another folder.

"When I added Tammy into the mix, the geographic profile included a much wider zone. It moved away from Mount Destiny."

He opened the folder and pulled out another map. This one had a much larger area in the red circle.

"Are you saying that, even back then, your data suggested another killer had been involved?" Charlie asked. "But what about the scene? It fit Grady's M.O. perfectly."

"What if whoever killed Tammy wanted it to look as if she was a Butcher victim?" Bridget said slowly, her mind flashing back to the grisly crime scene. "What if that had been the intention all along?"

Gage cleared his throat.

"Hold on, now," he said. "Grady's claim that he didn't kill Tammy could still be a ploy. Maybe he used the new DNA evidence as justification to get to the courthouse. It could have been part of his plan to escape."

His theory was reasonable, even logical, but Bridget wasn't convinced.

"There are too many signs that someone else was involved to ignore," she said. "Both with Tammy's homicide and Grady's escape. I'd say for now we have to assume we've got another killer."

"Were there ever any other suspects in Tammy's case?" Larkin asked, looking around at the somber faces. "I mean, if the Butcher didn't kill her, do you have any idea who did?"

Bridget thought of the rumors Reagan had mentioned. The mystery man Tammy had been seeing before her death.

"First things first," Charlie said, interrupting her train of thought. "We need to find Lyle Grady and get him back where he belongs before anyone else is hurt. And we need to talk to the families of all of Grady's victims."

"I'm sure they've already heard," Opal said. "Cecil was

listening to a report on the news when I left the house."

Charlie nodded.

"I'm sure you're right, Opal. But we need to ask them to let us know if Grady tries to make contact. We need to warn them to be careful."

Bridget met and held Charlie's gaze, wondering if they were having the same thought.

She's worried about Reverend Abernathy, too. She's thinking Grady might try to finish off the old man once and for all.

CHAPTER NINE

G age climbed out of his Navigator and stood on the cracked sidewalk, looking up at the white spire of the Mount Destiny Church of Redemption. Gray clouds had rolled in to dot the sky overhead, and a new chill hung in the air as he waited for Bridget and Argus to join him.

"What do you say to someone who lost both their kids to a serial killer?" he asked Bridget as they headed up the steps.

Just the thought of anything happening to Russell, his foster son, was enough to start up one of his panic attacks. How did anyone manage to survive such a tragedy intact?

"You say you're sorry for their loss," Bridget said. "And then you listen to whatever it is they want to tell you."

She pulled one of the big double doors open just as Argus reached for the other one. With the path opened wide before him, Gage stepped into the church.

The sanctuary seemed deserted. But as he looked down the aisle and past the empty pews, he saw they weren't alone.

A thin man with spiky white hair knelt at the altar. His

head was down, and his hands were clasped in front of him.

Not wanting to disturb the man's prayers, Gage turned and motioned for Argus and Bridget to be quiet. He hadn't counted on the doors banging shut behind them.

The old man's head jerked up at the sudden noise.

He stood slowly and turned toward them expectantly, his face a mask of wrinkled sorrow as he moved down the aisle.

As he came closer, Gage thought he detected a hint of disappointment in the old man's eyes. Then it was gone.

"Welcome to the house of the lord," Abernathy called in a thin, cracked voice. "All souls are welcome here."

Bridget stepped forward to meet him.

"Reverend Abernathy, it's good to see you looking so well," she said. "We're sorry to come unannounced, but we were hoping to talk to you. I'm Bridget Bishop, and-"

"I know you. You're that psychologist," he said. "You came and saw me in the hospital. I wasn't in very good shape back then, but I remember you looking in on me."

A pained expression settled over his face as he looked past Bridget to where Gage and Argus stood.

"I had a breakdown you see," he said. "Once the Butcher took my children, the grief took my mind. I got it back eventually, at least that's what they tell me."

He forced a strained smile and nodded toward Bridget.

"Bridget came to visit me. Just like an angel lighting up the darkness," he said. "I wasn't sure I'd make it out..."

His voice trailed off as if he was miles away, and then suddenly he was back, his eyes pinned on Gage.

"I considered leaving Mount Destiny, you know. Thought

I could start over in a new city at a new church," he said, shaking his head. "But I found the kindness of strangers sustained me. And I couldn't bear to leave Mount Destiny. Not when my wife and children are interred here in the family mausoleum."

A glimmer of anger lit up his eyes.

"I only wish I had *all* their remains with me," he said, as a flush filled his face. "You see, my faith is still strong, but I struggle to forgive, even after all this time."

Sucking in a deep, painful breath, he projected his voice as if standing at the pulpit, prompting Gage to take a step back.

"The poison of the serpent, whose head you crush, enters you through the wound in your heel; and thus the serpent becomes more dangerous than it was before."

Gage looked to Argus, who stood transfixed, then to Bridget. Was the old man having another breakdown? Should they prepare to run?

But Bridget looked more curious than scared.

"That's not from the Bible, is it?" she asked with a faint frown. "It's a quote by Carl Jung, right? Are you a student of psychology as well as theology, Reverend?"

"I'm a student of evil," he said simply. "Whatever form it comes in, and whatever it may be called. The more I know about it, the better equipped I'll be when it shows its face."

His answer seemed to satisfy Bridget.

"Well, let's hope Lyle Grady doesn't show his face around here," she said, giving no indication she thought the man's behavior was peculiar. "You were there in the courthouse yesterday when he escaped custody, weren't you?"

"Yes, it's dreadful that he's out, isn't it?"

The reverend gave a woeful shake of his head.

"I've been praying for his capture all morning," he said. "Praying that no other innocent souls are taken."

He turned to Gage.

"Are you with the U.S. Marshals?" he asked hopefully. "They're the ones who track down fugitives."

"We're behavioral analysts with the FBI," Gage admitted. "But we're on the task force looking for Grady."

He felt Bridget watching him, knew she was waiting for him to say something more, but Gage's throat had suddenly constricted. He wasn't sure he could force out another word.

Feeling the familiar tightening of his chest, he worried he may be having another panic attack.

"We mainly came by to ask you to be careful," Bridget said after an awkward pause. "We aren't sure where Grady is right now. It's possible he could show up here."

She cocked her head.

"We could provide you with protection if you wanted."

Abernathy shook his head and reached into the pocket of his robes, pulling out a small gun.

Both Gage and Argus jumped back as he held it up, their hands reaching toward their holsters.

"God will protect me," the reverend said calmly. "But just in case he's busy, I keep this as a back-up."

Motioning for Gage and Argus to put their guns away, Bridget turned back to the old man.

"Please, be careful with that, Reverend," she said. "And be sure to let us know if you see or hear anything that makes you think Grady might be nearby."

Her mood was more somber as she followed Gage back to the Navigator. She waved to Abernathy, who stood on the front steps as they drove away.

Once they'd turned the corner, Bridget pulled out her phone and tapped in a number.

"Detective Larkin? This is Bridget Bishop."

The calm demeanor she'd kept in the church had been replaced with an anxious frown.

"Can you assign a few uniforms to watch Abernathy's church? I think he needs protection."

Gage gaped at her in surprise.

The idea that the reverend needed protection seemed unlikely. The old man was a ticking timebomb who could lose his shaky grip on reality at any time.

And I don't want to be there when he does.

* * *

Gage steered the Navigator off the highway and turned toward home, exhausted and on edge after fighting rush hour traffic the whole way back to Stafford County.

His mind kept replaying the events of the last few days, even as he tried to unwind and clear his head, wanting to decompress before he got home.

It wasn't fair for him to bring his stress home to Russell. He didn't want to ruin the little time he and his foster son got to spend together during the week.

The thought of Russell waiting for him at home brought thoughts of dinner, and the near-empty refrigerator and pantry shelves.

Russell was a teenage boy, which meant that he was always hungry, and that Gage was constantly trying to figure out what to feed him and how to keep the kitchen stocked.

Checking the clock on the dashboard, Gage pushed his foot down harder on the accelerator. It was getting late, and he didn't like leaving Russell alone in the house for too long.

After all, the teenager had lost his father to a tragic accident the year before, and his mother was locked up in a women's detention center for the foreseeable future.

He needed stability and guidance, not an empty house and dinnertime spent watching TV on his own.

As Gage sped around the corner onto Mansfield Way and pulled onto his driveway, he had to stomp on the brakes to avoid hitting the unfamiliar car blocking the garage.

Wondering who was in the house with Russell, he jumped out of the SUV and hurried up the walk.

A delicious aroma greeted him as he pushed his way through the front door. It was coming from the kitchen.

"We're in here, Uncle Gage!"

Russell stuck his head into the hall.

"You'll never guess who showed up."

The pure happiness in Russell's voice made Gage's irritation and worry evaporate.

Moving into the kitchen, he stopped in surprise to see Kyla Malone standing in front of the stove wearing the red apron his sister Anne had given him the Christmas before.

"Aunt Kyla came to visit," Russell said, as Gage continued to stare. "And she's making dinner. Isn't that great?"

Gage nodded mutely, then stepped forward, almost tripping over Sarge in the process.

The tiger-striped tomcat meowed plaintively and walked over to the empty bowl in the corner. He didn't seem happy to have a stranger in the house.

Of course, Kyla Malone was no stranger. At least not to Gage. She was Kenny's little sister and Russell's aunt.

His real family.

"How are you, Gage?" Kyla asked, setting down the spoon she'd been holding and wiping her hands on the apron.

"I'm good," he said, his voice catching in his throat.

Seeing her there reminded him all at once how much he missed Kenny. His sister had his same kind, brown eyes. The same dimples when she smiled. And her heart-shaped face was the same rich shade of mahogany.

"Wow, how long has it been since we saw each other? Was it back at Kenny's funeral?" he asked. "I didn't even know you were back in the States."

"And I didn't know Russell was living with you, now," she said. "I had to hear it from a neighbor when I stopped by to see my nephew."

The smile slipped from her face, revealing an expression

of hurt underneath.

"Russell, why don't you go to your room so I can speak to your Aunt Kyla alone?" Gage suggested. "We'll call you when it's time to eat."

The teenager started to protest, then thought better of it. He scooped up Sarge, carting the big cat with him as he headed toward the stairs.

"Listen, Kyla, I didn't mean to shut you out," Gage said, keeping his voice low. "Not on purpose. I just didn't think..."

The last year had been harder than he'd expected. He'd suddenly been totally responsible for another human being after a whole life of being single and pretty much only worrying about himself.

"Besides, I didn't know how to reach you," he added. "Estelle never mentioned you should be called, and-"

"My sister-law and I never have gotten along," Kyla admitted. "Estelle would like nothing better than for me to stay away. But that's not what Kenny would want. And it's not the right thing to do. Russell should be with family."

A knot twisted in Gage's stomach at her words.

"What are you saying?"

"I'm saying that Kenny's son should be with me," she said. "After all, I'm his family."

Suddenly Russell was standing in the doorway, holding Sarge tight to his chest, his face stricken.

"That's not fair," he said. "Uncle Gage is family, too."

Kyla looked up in surprise.

"Of course, he is, sweetheart," she agreed. "And I

appreciate everything he's done for you. But you're my responsibility now. I owe your father that much."

A look of panic flashed into Russell's eyes, tightening the knot in Gage's stomach, but he forced his voice to stay calm.

"Let's not rush into any decisions," he said, turning to Kyla. "We'll figure this out I'm sure, but for now, the court has assigned me as Russell's guardian, so he stays here."

Kyla opened her mouth, as if ready to argue, then sighed.

"I've got to go back to my post at the end of the month," she said. "But I plan to ask for a permanent transfer to the States. When I get back, we'll need to discuss this again."

"That's a deal," Gage said, noting Russell's relieved expression. "Now, let's eat dinner. It smells delicious."

As he set the table and dished out the casserole, Gage kept a smile on his face, refusing to give in to the fear that was simmering just under the surface.

But once Kyla was gone, and Russell had gone up to his room to work on his homework, Gage crossed into the living room and immediately sank onto the sofa, dropping his head into his hands.

For the last year, he'd been dealing with his own sister's disapproval for bringing Russell into his home, and now he was going to have to deal with Kenny's sister's sudden appearance and the possibility of losing Russell for good.

Taking in a series of deep, cleansing breaths, he began counting backward from one hundred. It was a technique his therapist Faye Thackery had shown him to cope with the panic attacks he'd started having after Russell had moved in.

As his anxiety faded, Gage stood and walked to the window, looking out into the dark street beyond, wondering where Grady could be.

The killer had been on the run for over twenty-four hours now. There had been no sightings of him, and no hint at what he planned to do next. None of it made sense.

Not unless he'd had help.

CHAPTER TEN

The sleek black sedan slipped past the Mount Destiny city limit without being seen, although the man behind the wheel couldn't resist another look in the rearview mirror just to make sure he wasn't being followed.

Now that a serial killer had escaped custody and was once again loose in the community, he knew he could be stopped and questioned at any time.

Local and federal agents were patrolling the whole area. They'd be sure to question any man who was out on the mountain skulking around in the dark.

And if they decided to search me, well, that could be a problem.

After all, he had two driver's licenses in his wallet. The one bearing his legal name was easily accessible, ready to be pulled out and presented at a moment's notice in the event a passing cop got nosy.

The other license, the one naming him as Maxwell Bender, had been stashed under the wallet's expensive leather lining in preparation for a potential need to cut and run.

He whispered the name aloud, enjoying the sound.

"*Max Bender.*"

It was the perfect alias for someone who had a penchant for bending the rules. Someone who made the maximum effort in every task he took on, no matter how unsavory.

He'd liked the name as soon as he'd heard it, which was lucky. He might have to get used to it.

It could be his name permanently if he didn't figure out what to do about the situation he'd gotten himself into.

Spotting the turnoff for Destiny Peak Overlook ahead, Bender forced himself to focus on the road and the task at hand. He couldn't afford to worry about Lyle Grady now.

The fact that the serial killer had used him to escape custody and had then vanished into thin air certainly threw his grand plan into jeopardy.

How can I kill the bastard if I can't find him?

The thought circled Bender's mind as he nosed the sedan onto the narrow road leading to the overlook.

Bringing the car to a stop, he shut off the lights and sat in the dark, listening to the sounds of the mountain.

He leaned over and took a small flashlight from the glove compartment, then resolutely opened the car door.

As he stepped out onto the uneven, sloping road, a dead branch cracked under his boot, and he heard something rustle in the bushes behind him.

Switching on the flashlight, he shone the light into the darkness ahead, then jumped back as a black snake slithered past his feet. He resisted the temptation to pull out his Glock as he watched it disappear into a tall patch of wild grass growing beside the road.

Now that the search was on for Grady, it wouldn't be

wise to draw unwanted attention to himself, and any random gunshots on the mountain would surely be investigated.

His goal was to get down to the mine unnoticed and confirm that Heather Winslow wouldn't be a problem.

He had started to worry that the college coed could still be alive at the bottom of the shaft. That she might even be capable of calling out for help.

If a search party did spread out over the mountain, it could present a major problem.

He hurried down the path, his boots skidding on loose gravel and fallen leaves.

Fall was quickly moving toward winter, and the light from the flashlight revealed a profusion of red, orange, and yellow leaves on the ground.

When he got to the mine he hesitated. The mine hadn't been active for over fifty years. Maybe even longer.

Bender remembered his grandfather telling him that the miners had worked twelve-hour days but still couldn't manage to make the mine profitable.

Many workers had died young, some down in the hellish innards of the mine, thus earning the nickname, the Iron Graveyard.

But that had been decades ago, and most people in Mount Destiny had long ago forgotten the mine had ever existed. Even the path down to the mine was now overgrown although a pair of iron rails could still be seen, marking the way to the dark opening.

Ducking his head, Bender slowly stepped inside. He

listened but heard nothing.

That's a good thing, right?

He had planned to take Heather Winslow deep into the mine and tether her to the splintered timbers that seemed to stand guard along the tunnels.

But she'd had to go and fall into the vertical shaft.

Looking down into the shaft, he could see only shadows and vague shapes on the pitted walls.

He called down, trying to sound properly concerned.

"Hello? Anybody down there?"

There was no response. Nothing moved.

He tried again.

"Heather? Are you okay? Do you need some help?"

Still nothing.

He relaxed his shoulders and exhaled.

She was already dead.

He'd known all along that she would have to die, although it wasn't a task he'd looked forward to.

I'm not an animal. Not like Grady.

He'd originally planned to keep her alive, at least for a while. He'd wanted to use her as leverage.

Of course, there was nothing to be done about it now.

And when the time came, he would make it look as if Grady was responsible. He would set it up to look as if the serial killer had kidnapped Heather.

Looking down into the dark shaft, Bender wondered if the black garbage bag was still down there. The one he'd thrown into the shaft years before.

Allowing his mind to drift back, he replayed the events of

that hot summer night. The night he'd become a killer.

He knocked on the door and waited in the moonlight.

When Tammy Vicker appeared in the window, her blonde hair gleamed, as did her angry eyes.

The crime reporter had caught his attention from the first time he'd seen her on the local news. But he hadn't known then that within weeks they would begin a torrid affair...if you could call a few late-night trysts an affair.

Of course, it had been stupid and impulsive of him to get involved with another woman when he already had Erica.

He quickly realized he'd make a terrible mistake. That it never should have happened. Once he'd ended it, Tammy had become hell-bent on exposing their relationship to the world.

But he couldn't allow that to happen.

Erica would leave him for sure.

The life he'd so carefully constructed would be over if he didn't clean up the mess he'd made.

Pulling back the deadbolt, Tammy opened the door.

He knew the only reason she was opening her door to him was the promise of a scoop on the Backroads Butcher.

Foolishly, she still trusted him, even now. She never even noticed that his car wasn't in the driveway as he followed her inside.

Once he was in the house, his rage took over, making his hands strong as he began to strangle her, allowing him to squeeze, and squeeze, and squeeze.

When she finally stopped fighting, he dragged her to the bathroom, steeling himself for what was to come.

He refused to think or allow himself to feel as he used the cleaver he'd brought with him. One that was very similar to the cleaver the Butcher had used on Justine and Junior Abernathy.

By the time he'd completed the job and began maneuvering her head into a black garbage bag, there was blood everywhere.

After washing most of the sticky mess down the drain, he carried the body and the black bag out to Tammy's car in the garage.

He dumped her body into the underbrush beside a backroad just as the Butcher would have done, all the while fearful that a SWAT team would descend on him at any moment and the truth would be revealed for all to see.

After driving out to Destiny Peak Overlook, he carried the black bag down to the opening to the Iron Graveyard, which he'd scouted out the previous day.

With a shudder of distaste, he dropped the bag into the shaft, listening to it land far below with a resounding thud.

As he stared down into the same dark shaft, Bender realized his actions that night had sealed his fate to the Butcher's.

At first, he'd thought that his plan had worked perfectly.

Everyone had immediately assumed that Tammy was the Butcher's latest victim.

It had been only a matter of weeks before Lyle Grady had been captured, and although he'd insisted he was innocent of all the murders, within the year he'd been tried and convicted of eight homicides.

Years had passed without any sign of the trouble to come.

Then Reagan Rivera held a press conference announcing that she was taking on Lyle Grady's appeal for a retrial based on new evidence coming to light.

He'd felt like he'd taken a blow to his lower belly when she'd given an interview on the news, claiming that DNA evidence found during Tammy Vicker's autopsy had been re-examined by a private lab and that they were requesting the FBI lab to confirm their findings.

But the real shock came with the phone call from Abbeyville State Prison.

Lyle Grady said he knew who Tammy's real killer was and that Reagan Rivera was going to help him win a retrial.

The serial killer had vowed to tell the world what he knew if he didn't get exactly what he wanted.

The threat had worked.

Using his new stolen identity for the first time, Bender had gone to see Grady at the prison.

The Butcher had crowed about the new technology that allowed the FBI lab to extract a DNA profile to match against possible suspects.

He'd boasted about Reagan Rivera, the hotshot attorney who had taken on his case, and said she was going to finally be able to prove that he wasn't the one who'd killed Tammy.

Then Grady had proposed what he'd called a mutually beneficial arrangement.

"Getting you locked up for Tammy Vicker's death won't get me out of prison," he'd said. "They know I did the other ones. So, I'm willing to make a deal."

He'd flashed his small, crooked teeth in an ugly grin.

"You're a smart guy with connections and resources. A guy who's willing to kill to get what you what."

The words had sent a rush of anger through Bender's blood stream, but he'd had no choice but to sit and listen.

"If you can figure out a way to get me out of here in the next ninety days, I'll keep my mouth shut about you killing that reporter. I'll even forget about you pinning it on me. If not, I start talking to anyone who will listen. Once they test your DNA..."

So, Bender had concocted a plan to help Grady escape.

The plan to kidnap the lawyer's sister had ensured Reagan Rivera's cooperation and guaranteed she'd keep her mouth shut about anything she might suspect in the meantime, although Grady had known better than to tell her the truth.

The Butcher hadn't given his lawyer the name of Tammy Vicker's real killer. He hadn't told anyone. At least, not yet.

What Grady didn't realize, was that helping him escape would work to Bender's advantage in the end.

After all, if he remained locked up in Abbeyville, Grady would remain a threat to Bender's freedom.

But if the Butcher was on the outside, then Bender would have the chance to silence him for good.

All he had to do was make it appear as if Grady had killed Heather, her whiny boyfriend, and anyone else who ended up getting in his way.

CHAPTER ELEVEN

B ridget lowered the temperature on the stove, leaving the creamy alfredo sauce to simmer as she hurried toward the front door with Hank at her heels. Wiping her hands on a dishtowel, she was already reaching for the knob when she hesitated, remembering that Lyle Grady was on the loose and could be anywhere by now, including on her front doorstep.

Leaning forward, she held her breath and peered through the peephole. The porchlight shone down on Santino and Decker, prompting a sigh of relief as Bridget flung open the door and waved the deputy marshals inside.

Hank wove himself between the men's boots, his tail wagging in welcome as they made their way back to the kitchen, led by the smell of warm bread crisping in the oven.

"Dinner's just about ready," Bridget said, scooping mounds of fettucine onto plates. "I figured you guys would be pretty hungry by now. Any luck with the search?"

Santino grimaced and shook his head.

"No sign of that bastard," Decker said, watching hungrily as Bridget spooned Alfredo sauce onto a plate of pasta. "He must be holed up somewhere close by. No way he could have gotten past the roadblocks without being seen."

Bridget met Santino's eyes and lifted an eyebrow but refrained from voicing her doubts. A man as desperate and ruthless as Lyle Grady was capable of almost anything.

If he wants to get out of the area, he'll find a way.

She handed the heaping plate to Decker, who immediately crossed to the kitchen table and began stuffing messy forkfuls of pasta into his mouth.

"No need to wait for us, Decker," she said with a wry grin toward Santino. "You go ahead and get started."

Nodding toward an open bottle of wine on the counter, Bridget picked up another plate while Santino pulled three glasses out of the cabinet.

"What about your visit to Abbeyville last night?" she asked. "Did you learn anything helpful?"

"We learned that Chase Grafton had been visiting Grady in Abbeyville," Santino said, earning a look of surprise from Bridget. "Warden Crawford even gave the guy an interview."

Decker laughed out loud despite his mouthful of food.

"Apparently, Warden Crawford's old lady is a *Chasing Killers* fan," he said as he chewed. "She never misses an episode. That was Crawford's justification for talking to Chase. Can you believe it?"

Actually, Bridget could believe it. *Chasing Killers* was the number one true-crime podcast on all the charts, and its persistent host was relentless when he had a target in sight.

"Are you going to talk to Chase?" Bridget asked, setting two plates of pasta on the table as Santino carried over the wine. "Don't you want to know what he and Grady talked about during his visits?"

Decker dropped his fork on his now empty plate and leaned back in his chair.

"Waste of time," he stated, shaking his head. "There's no way Grady would have told the guy what he was planning. Grady was probably just playing with him. Maybe even manipulating him to get some sympathy in the press in case he did win a retrial."

The theory had some merit, Bridget thought.

But then again, maybe there's more to it. Maybe Chase was somehow involved with Grady's escape.

Before she could voice the question, Santino spoke.

"We'll talk to Chase and find out what he knows," he said, his voice firm. "In fact, we'll need to talk to everyone on Grady's visitor list in the last few months. But the man I really want to talk to is Max Bender."

Bridget frowned. The name wasn't familiar to her.

"Is that a friend of Grady's?" she asked.

"We don't know who he is. The name is an alias based on a stolen identity," Santino admitted. "But whoever he is, he visited Grady several times in the last few months."

Wondering who Grady's mystery visitor could be, Bridget finished her pasta and carried her plate to the sink.

She picked up her wine glass and took a sip as they moved out to the living room, where she began to recount her visit to Reverend Abernathy's church.

"The man is eccentric, I'll give you that," she said. "But he's suffered a great loss. What I don't understand is why Gage thinks he's dangerous."

"Well, the DNA evidence does point to another killer," Decker said. "So, maybe Gage thinks Abernathy's the one."

Bridget rolled her eyes at the idea unable to imagine the frail older man could be capable of violence.

"I don't buy that, no matter what Gage thinks," she protested. "Even if Abernathy had wanted to kill Tammy, he wouldn't have the means."

"Okay, then maybe the guy who killed Tammy is Grady's partner," Decker suggested. "Maybe it's even this Bender guy, whoever he really is. He could have visited Grady in prison to help plan his escape."

"Do you think Grady could have had a partner all along?" Santino asked Bridget.

Bridget considered the question, then shook her head. She wasn't convinced.

"I doubt it. Grady is a loner and a psychopath. He wouldn't accept a partner. Not unless it was the only way to get what he wanted. And only as long as it served his purpose."

"What exactly was his purpose?" Decker asked. "Why did he kill all those people?"

Bridget crossed to the window and looked out into the dark. She had asked herself that question a million times.

"With Lyle Grady, it's all about power," she said, keeping her eyes on the street beyond. "At least that's my theory, although Grady never did open up after he was arrested.

Perhaps that was his way of trying to retain his power over us. To keep us guessing...to keep us from finding the answers we'd been looking for."

A car turned onto Fern Creek Road, its headlights moving closer. Her chest tightened and then relaxed as it passed by.

"And now Grady has the power to make us afraid again," she said softly. "Only he knows what he's going to do next."

*   *   *

The next morning Bridget woke up to the sound of her phone buzzing on her bedside table. Opening one sleepy eye, she saw that it was Chase Grafton calling again.

Ignoring the call, she squeezed her eyes shut, willing herself to go back to sleep.

When a high-pitched ding sounded a minute later, alerting her that Chase had left a voicemail, she grabbed the phone and hit *delete* without listening to the message.

Chase Grafton is a problem for Santino and Decker now.

But she was already wide awake, so she climbed out of bed with a sigh and pulled on jeans and a t-shirt.

"You ready for a walk, Hank?" she called out, earning a happy tail wag from the Irish setter.

Pulling on a warm jacket to combat the fall chill, she set off toward Landsend Road, her nerves still on-edge, half-expecting Lyle Grady to jump out at her at any minute even though it was broad daylight and plenty of people were passing by on their way to work or school.

Relax, Bridget. This was supposed to be your vacation after all.
The thought depressed her.

She'd scheduled two weeks of vacation from her job at the Wisteria Falls Forensic Psychology group so that she and Santino could go on their first vacation together to Aruba.

They'd imagined spending the Thanksgiving holiday in the sun and sand, and the timing allowed them to avoid a decision between Bridget's father's house or Santino's mother's house for Thanksgiving dinner.

Her island vacation would have to wait for another time.

And since Bridget wasn't expected back at the office until early December, the time she and Santino had planned to spend together at the exclusive resort would now be spent on a task force tracking down a serial killer.

"Looks like Aruba is definitely off, Hank. At least for now," Bridget said as she waited for the Irish setter to inspect a fallen tree branch. "I guess we'll be going over to Dad's for Thanksgiving dinner after all."

When she and Hank got back to the house, she turned on the news. As expected, every channel seemed to be running a report on Grady's escape.

She had just poured herself a cup of coffee when her phone buzzed in her jacket pocket.

Digging it out, she saw Charlie's number on the display.

"Detective Larkin just called. She said a man came into the station this morning and reported his daughter missing."

Charlie sounded wired.

"He claimed the girl got off a plane from Chicago a few days ago and just...vanished. She's young, attractive, and traveling to Mount Destiny."

Bridget's heart sank.

"So, she matches Grady's victim profile perfectly."

"Exactly," Charlie agreed. "I thought maybe you could come with me to the station and talk to the father. Just in case. If Grady is already back to his old tricks, we'll need to alert the public asap."

* * *

Thirty minutes later Bridget was walking through the crowd of reporters and camera crews camped in front of the Mount Destiny Police station.

The news about the infamous Backroads Butcher's escape had hit the local and national press like a bomb, exploding over every front page and morning news show in the country.

Noticing Chase Grafton's signature red beanie sticking out in the small pack of press and reporters, Bridget tried to hurry pass without being noticed.

"Hey Bridget, did you get my message," he called out, trying to sidestep a burly man wielding a hefty broadcast camera in front of him.

Ignoring the *Chasing Killers* host, Bridget slipped through the front door, nearly bumping into Charlie, who stood next to Hale just inside the lobby.

"They've put him in an interview room back here,"

Charlie said, leading Bridget and Hale down a narrow hall.

As they rounded the corner, Bridget saw Shannon Larkin standing outside a closed door marked *Interview Room 2*.

The detective looked tired. Her eyes were puffy and red-rimmed, and she yawned as she motioned toward the door.

"He's been waiting a while," she said. "But I think there's something you should know before we go in."

Bridget raised her eyebrows.

"Sure, what is it?"

"The man in there is Dale Winslow," she said. "He filed a missing person report. Claims his daughter Heather is missing."

Larkin lowered her voice and leaned forward as if worried the man might be listening through the door.

"Everyone in town knows Dale. He runs the local food bank," she said. "And he has *two* daughters. Heather is his youngest, and Reagan the oldest."

Bridget's eyes widened.

"Reagan?"

The detective nodded.

"Yes, Reagan Rivera's maiden name was Winslow. Heather is her younger sister."

CHAPTER TWELVE

harlie rapped twice on the interview room door, then opened it and stepped into the little room. The man inside was pacing back and forth. When he saw Charlie, he stopped short and looked at her expectantly, as if she might produce his daughter from behind her back.

"Mr. Winslow, I'm Agent Charlie Day with the FBI and this is Bridget Bishop, a consultant with the BAU," she said, motioning for him to have a seat at the table. "I understand you've filed a missing person report for your daughter Heather."

Dale sank into the chair and exhaled.

He appeared to be in his sixties, with puffy, weary eyes that looked as if they'd seen a lot of pain in the last six decades. His hair was a silvery gray that matched his full mustache, and he lifted a big hand to push it back from his sunburned forehead.

"My daughter was supposed to come back to Mount Destiny for Thanksgiving," he said. "She's in grad school up in Chicago. She's very independent."

Charlie placed the folder with the missing person report on the table in front of her and began to take notes.

She glanced at Bridget, wondering if she, too, thought it was odd that the man didn't say his daughter was coming home, only that she was coming back to town.

"I see from your report that Heather was scheduled to arrive on Sunday," she said. "That was three days ago. Why are you only reporting this now?"

Twisting his hands on the table, Dale dropped his eyes.

"She wasn't staying with me, you see. She planned to stay with her sister. She was going to have Thanksgiving Dinner over there, but she'd agreed to help me out at the food bank."

As he leaned forward, Charlie got a whiff of alcohol and mouth wash. She stared at his red face and slightly misshapen nose, making a few quick deductions.

The man was obviously struggling to keep it together long enough to file the report. It was all he could do to stay seated in the chair.

"And you've tried to contact Heather's sister?" Charlie asked. "What is your other daughter's name?"

She poised her pen over the report.

"Reagan Rivera," Dale said, clenching his jaw. "She lives over on Cumberland Road not far from here."

A disapproving frown wrinkled his forehead.

"You've probably heard of her, like everyone else in the country," he said. "She's a big-time lawyer. Only, we've had a falling out over her choice of clients."

He dropped his eyes.

"As well as some other things."

Leaning back in his chair, he ran a hand through his hair

again, clearly restless.

"When Heather never called me, and wouldn't answer my call, I tried to contact Reagan, but she didn't pick up either."

Holding up his phone, he thrust it toward Charlie.

"But I know Heather arrived as planned on Sunday," he said. "She even posted a photo. I saw it on my feed. It was taken at the gate when she landed."

Charlie studied the picture of the young woman, then passed the phone to Bridget.

A caption had been added to the post.

There's no place like home.

"Do you know who took this photo?" Charlie asked. "Was she traveling alone?"

Dale shook his head.

"I thought she was until I saw this."

He took the phone from Bridget and scrolled to the next post, which included a selfie of Heather and a handsome young man with an annoyed expression.

Bringing new BF to meet the family. Kind of a surprise....

Studying the photo, Charlie felt the stirring of worry.

Had the young couple simply decided to spend a week on their own without family hassles or had they really disappeared?

"When I still couldn't get in touch with Heather yesterday, I started to get worried," he said. "She hasn't posted anything online since Sunday, and now when I call, her phone immediately goes to voicemail, like it's turned off."

He used a big finger to tap on his phone several times.

"Heather tagged the guy she's with in her post," he said. "His name is Ryder Forbes, and he goes to grad school with her. He hasn't posted anything since Sunday, either."

Scrolling through a number of photos, he stopped on an image of a glamorous-looking couple in their fifties relaxing on the beach, cocktails in hand.

"Looks like Ryder's parents went to Fiji for the Thanksgiving holidays," he said, holding up the phone for Bridget and Charlie to see. "They probably don't even realize their kid is missing."

Charlie raised an eyebrow at Dale's investigative work.

He could have made a good detective...if he'd kicked the booze.

She jotted down the information Dale had found on Ryder and added it to the missing person report.

"Okay, so have you tried going to Reagan's house?" Charlie asked. "To see if Heather is there?"

Dale shook his head.

"Not yet. Reagan has got a mess of her own going on, as you may have heard," he snorted. "She's gotten herself involved with all kinds of criminals. They're mostly killers."

A gleam of anger, or maybe fear, crossed his face.

"But this morning, I heard this latest one had escaped, so it made me start thinking."

Charlie nodded as an unsettling suspicion began to form.

Could Heather's disappearance somehow be related to Reagan's work with Lyle Grady?

Deciding it was best not to jump to conclusions, or to mention anything to Dale Winslow that would exacerbate his already shot nerves, she slipped the report back into the folder.

"I'll ask Detective Larkin with the MDPD to assign someone to go to Reagan's house and see if Heather is there," she said. "If she's not, they'll open an investigation."

She started to rise, then hesitated.

"Do you happen to have a recent photo of Heather we can add to the file?" she asked. "It could help in the search."

A look of pained guilt fell over Dale's face.

"We haven't taken any photos together for quite a while."

Sticking a hand in his back pocket, he pulled out an ancient wallet and opened it. He fished out a wrinkled school photo.

"This was her in high school," he said, swallowing hard.

Charlie reached out and took the small photo from his hand, sensing how hard it was for him to release it.

"I'll go scan a copy of this," Bridget said, taking the photo. "That way you can get it back before you leave."

As Bridget slipped out of the room, Charlie turned back to Dale, who was staring down at the empty space in his wallet with a forlorn expression.

She wanted to reassure him that all would be well and that his daughter would surely be found safe and sound. But she knew from past experience that she was unable to offer that kind of false comfort.

Once Dale had left the station with the photo of Heather back in his wallet, Charlie turned to Bridget.

"I think it's time to pay Reagan Rivera another visit."

CHAPTER THIRTEEN

R eagan Rivera was still in her nightgown even though it was almost noon. She paced back and forth in front of the television, holding the remote in one hand and her phone in the other. She'd been unable to sleep, tortured by worry and doubt, not sure what to do next.

Letting herself be blackmailed in the first place had been a terrible mistake, she knew that now.

But there could be no going back. Not after she'd helped a convicted killer escape, thus becoming an accomplice to Officer Pickering's murder.

And the murder of anyone else he kills going forward.

How had she let herself get caught up with the likes of Lyle Grady in the first place? How had her life become focused on killers and criminals instead of her sister and family?

Shame coursed through her as her eyes fell on the high school photo of Heather that sat on the mantel. They'd once been so close, but she'd let her ambition come between them.

She'd been so determined to play the hero. To ride in and

give innocent people convicted of crimes their lives back, that she'd lost sight of what had mattered most.

Obsessed with her own crusade, she'd ended up sacrificing her relationship with her father and her sister.

And now it was Heather paying the price for her mistakes.

How could I have been so stupid...so selfish?

The phone that she'd kept clutched in her hand all night suddenly buzzed, causing her to jump.

Looking down at the message on the screen, Reagan's heart started to race.

Your sister is safe. Keep your mouth shut and she'll be home soon. Start talking and you'll never see her again.

Her fingers shook as she tapped back a reply.

Don't hurt her. She is innocent in all this.

Reagan tapped *Send*, then hesitated, wanting to beg for her sister's safety, but knowing that showing weakness only excited monsters like Lyle Grady and Max Bender.

She stood and crossed to the kitchen, wanting another cup of coffee to help her stay alert. She would need all her senses to be sharp for whatever might happen.

A rap at the front door made her spill the coffee as she started to pour. She jumped up, knocking her phone unto the floor, cursing as it disappeared under the counter.

Creeping into the front room, she peered out the window.

Agent Charlie Day, the attractive blonde FBI agent who'd been at the courtroom the day before stood on her front porch. Bridget Bishop stood beside her.

Looking down at the text, Reagan hesitated, tempted to

turn and run. She could hide away in her room.

But that would only draw more attention and make her actions seem more suspicious.

With slow, heavy steps, she crossed to the door and opened it, forcing a strained smile onto her face.

"Listen, I'm still not feeling up to an interview and-"

Charlie's eyes rested fixedly on Reagan's face.

"Your father filed a report with the Mount Destiny PD this morning. He claims your sister Heather has gone missing. We need to know if she's here."

Reagan's look of horror and surprise was genuine. It had never occurred to her that her father might involve the FBI.

"My father filed a...*missing person report?*" she gasped, stalling for time. "That's ridiculous. Heather's not here...but she's not *missing.* She's probably just avoiding him."

"Can we come in, Reagan?" Bridget asked.

The profiler looked back at the street as if expecting someone to come up behind her at any minute.

"We won't stay long."

Reluctantly stepping back, Reagan allowed Charlie and Bridget into the foyer but didn't lead them further into the house. She needed to get rid of them as soon as possible.

No telling what Bender might do if he sees the FBI here.

Tying her robe tighter around her waist, Reagan crossed both arms over her chest defiantly.

"I really am supposed to be resting," she said. "And I'm sure my sister is just taking time off from my father. I hate to share our family's dirty secrets, but he's an alcoholic.

He's alienated both his daughters with his addiction."

The words tasted bitter in her mouth.

As angry as she was with her father, she hated the feeling of betrayal that washed over her as she uttered the words.

"Where is your sister now?" Charlie asked. "She was supposed to be heading here, wasn't she?"

"I...don't know where she is," Reagan stuttered. "When she didn't show up, I assumed she'd stayed in Chicago."

Pulling out her phone, Charlie showed Reagan a post.

It was a picture of Heather at the airport.

"Your sister arrived at Dulles as planned," Charlie said. "She was with a man named Ryder Forbes. You know him?"

Relieved to be able to answer at least one question honestly, Reagan shook her head.

"No, I don't know who he is," she said. "Heather never mentioned that she was bringing anyone with her."

"This is the last post on Heather's feed, and there have been no more posts from Ryder Forbe's accounts since he left Chicago Sunday afternoon."

Reagan shrugged, trying to ignore the sick feeling in her stomach. Worried she might throw up right there in the foyer if she didn't get rid of the women soon.

"I'm sure they just decided to hole up somewhere for a romantic break," Reagan said. "Heather's very...impulsive."

The skeptical frown on Charlie's face told her the agent wasn't buying her nonchalant act.

"We're wondering if Heather's disappearance could have something to do with Lyle Grady's escape."

Reagan's throat went dry.

She shook her head.

"That's...ridiculous," she repeated.

"Have you ever heard of a man named Max Bender?" Bridget suddenly asked.

Reagan's blood turned to ice water at the softly spoken words, but her years of practice hiding her emotions in court kicked in, and she managed to keep the dismay out of her voice and off her face.

"No, that name doesn't ring a bell," Reagan replied as she turned toward the door. "Is he related to the case?"

"A man named Max Bender had been visiting Lyle Grady in Abbeyville. Turns out he was using a fake identity. I just wondered if you knew anything about that."

Reagan's throat was almost too dry to allow her to answer.

"That's news to me," she managed to say, but her words sounded weak and unconvincing even to her own ears.

Both women were frowning at her now.

"If you're in some kind of trouble, you'd better tell us now before someone else gets hurt or killed."

Suddenly picturing the photo of Heather on the mantel, Reagan shook her head.

"I've told you everything I know," she said stiffly. "Now, I think you should be out there looking for Lyle Grady, not here wasting time interrogating me."

After she'd closed the door behind the women, Reagan went back to the living room, where the television was still tuned to the news.

As a photo of Lyle Grady flashed onto the screen, Reagan sank onto the sofa and began to cry.

* * *

A sound from somewhere in the back of the house jerked Reagan out of her much-needed sleep.

She stretched and sat upright, her back and shoulders aching from the slumped positioned she'd been in for the last few hours.

The sun had already started to make its slow descent to the west of the house, casting a shadow over the doorway leading into the hall.

The sick ache in her stomach had become a sharp hunger pang, and she was debating getting up to fix herself a bowl of soup when a floorboard creaked behind her.

A bolt of adrenaline shot through her as a deep voice sounded in her ear.

"I told you not to talk to the feds."

Before she could move, an arm shot out and wrapped around her neck. The man behind her began to squeeze.

"What did you tell them?" he demanded.

"Nothing," she choked out. "I...promise."

The arm loosened slightly, allowing Reagan to suck in a shallow gulp of air.

"So, no one knows about me?" he asked in a low growl. "No one knows that Heather's been taken?"

"No one knows," she gasped.

His arm tightened again.

"Good," he said. "That's very good."

Instinctively lifting her hands, she tried to pry away his arm. Her fingers caught hold of something around his wrist. Pulling with all her strength, she felt the leather bracelet give way and come off in her hand, then fall to the floor.

Panicking as a wave of dizziness descended, she flailed back, reaching for his face, her fingernails catching on soft, warm skin, before her hand was jerked away.

"Stop fighting," the voice commanded. "It'll just make this harder for both of us."

Reagan's eyes widened as he lifted the cleaver in front of her face, displaying the razor-sharp blade.

She gasped as she saw his reflection in the shiny steel.

"I'm going to have to make it look like the Butcher was here," he muttered beside her ear. "Just like I did with Tammy. And from what I recall, it's going to get very messy."

CHAPTER FOURTEEN

Bridget sat in the passenger's seat of Charlie's black Expedition, oblivious to the fading fall colors outside her window as they made their way toward Wisteria Falls. Lost in thought, she replayed the earlier conversation they'd had with Reagan Rivera, curious about the lawyer's refusal to acknowledge her sister might be missing.

As the Expedition began to cross Landsend Bridge, Bridget turned to Charlie, ignoring the dark water churning below.

"I get the feeling Reagan's hiding something," she said. "She seemed determined to get us out of the house as quickly as possible. It was almost as if she was scared of us."

"She's scared of something, alright," Charlie agreed. "I'm just not sure what that is."

Charlie's phone buzzed on the dashboard.

"It's Hale," Bridget said, checking the display.

She frowned as Charlie let the call roll to voicemail.

"Don't you want to take it?" she asked.

"I'll talk to him later."

Charlie's cheeks flushed pink as Bridget stared at her.

"You aren't avoiding him, are you?" Bridget asked in dismay. "I thought you two were an item now."

Steering the Expedition safely off the old truss bridge, Charlie shot a startled look in Bridget's direction.

"What, you think I didn't notice?" Bridget asked. "Was it supposed to be a secret?"

"Not a secret exactly," Charlie said testily. "But we weren't exactly hoping to broadcast it."

She winced at the ding of a voicemail alert.

"So, why isn't Hale here now?" Bridget prodded. "I'd have thought he'd want to be in on the interview with Reagan."

"It's complicated," Charlie said, her voice suddenly strained and small. "You see, there's a woman...someone Hale cares about very much."

She paused as if considering her words, leaving Bridget to shift uncomfortably in her seat while the little voice in her head gave a disapproving tut.

You really should learn to mind your own business, you know. This isn't one of your therapy sessions.

As Charlie's eyes grew bright with what appeared to be unshed tears, Bridget wished the little voice in her head had spoken up a bit sooner.

"I'm sorry," Charlie said, blinking hard, keeping her eyes on the road. "It's just that Bea...that's the woman...she has cancer. Hale thought she'd beaten it, but it's back. There's nothing else they can do. She's moving to the hospice today."

Bridget swallowed hard. She wasn't sure what to say.

She'd never seen the FBI agent cry before, at least not that she could remember, and something told her Charlie wouldn't like this to be the first time.

"I'm sorry for Hale...for both of them," she finally managed. "But I'm glad he's taking time to spend with her while he can. A lot of agents choose work over family and loved ones, and I'm pretty sure they end up regretting it."

Looking up, Bridget could see that they were getting close to her father's house. She gathered her purse and laptop bag as Charlie turned onto Maplewood Drive and pulled the Expedition onto the driveway.

Still feeling awkward, Bridget reached for the handle.

"Don't say anything to Hale," Charlie said before Bridget could climb out. "I don't think he wants anyone to know."

"Don't worry, I'm a psychologist," Bridget said, flashing a reassuring smile. "I have a degree in keeping secrets."

She opened the door and climbed out.

"You sure your father can give you a ride home?" Charlie called to her, looking up at the house.

Bridget nodded.

"He's been watching Hank all day," she said. "He'll probably welcome an excuse to get out of the house."

Waving as Charlie pulled away, Bridget walked toward the front door, seeing her father and Hank waiting just inside.

"No run-ins with the Butcher today?" Bob asked, only half-joking. "I've been keeping an eye on the news."

As he stepped back to let Bridget inside, she bent down to give Hank a hug, glancing around warily for Paloma, bracing herself against her stepmother's wrath.

"You can relax, Paloma's at the store," her father said. "And don't worry, I set her straight about Grady. It's not your fault he escaped, and it's certainly not your fault I worry about you too much. That's on me."

His attempt to make her feel better only added to her guilt.

"Lyle Grady must be up in Canada by now," she said, as he plucked his keys off the rack. "There's been no sign of him. So, there's no need for you to worry."

She followed him out to his car, a sedate Buick that she suspected Paloma had picked out and helped Hank climb into the backseat.

The clouds dotting the sky earlier had expanded and thickened over the afternoon. They now formed a gray blanket that blocked the waning sun.

As they pulled out of the driveway, fat raindrops began to plop onto the car and roll down the windshield in front of Bridget with increasing frequency.

"Are you coming for Thanksgiving dinner?"

Her father's question took Bridget by surprise. With everything going on, she hadn't really thought about the holiday, or where she would be eating.

"I'm not really sure," she admitted, not wanting to make a promise she couldn't keep.

Seeing the disappointed look on his face, she sighed.

"I'll try to make it," she said. "What time?"

"I'll check with Paloma and let you know," he said. "And bring that boyfriend of yours. I like him."

The rain was bucketing down by the time the Buick pulled up to Bridget's house.

"Wait for it to slow down," her father said, shutting off the car. "You don't want to get wet and catch a cold."

"You do know that's just an old wives' tale, don't you?" Bridget asked with a smile. "Rain doesn't give you a cold."

He shrugged.

"I know, but it's a good excuse to have you sit here with me a little while longer."

Looking at her father's face, half hidden by shadows in the cozy car, Bridget was suddenly filled with an irrational fear that she might never see him again.

She grabbed his hand and squeezed, trying to read the emotion in his eyes, never quite sure what he was thinking.

"You remind me so much of your mother," he said, suddenly sounding tired. "I still miss her, you know? A lot. Especially when I catch a glimpse of her in you."

Bridget's throat closed and for a long moment she couldn't speak.

"I miss her, too," she finally managed to say. "But most of the time I feel as if she's with me. It's like she's in my head. And she..."

Hesitating, Bridget tried to find the right words. She didn't want to scare her father. She wasn't delusional.

"I know...it's like she's talking to you, right? Giving you advice? She does that to me, too."

As the rain began to slow, Bridget impulsively leaned over and gave her father a kiss on the cheek.

"I love you, Dad," she said, wondering when she'd last

spoken the words out loud.

"I know you do, baby," he said, his eyes locked on hers. "That's about the only thing in this world I never doubt."

He cleared his throat and looked back at Hank, who was watching the raindrops drizzle down his window.

"Now, you better get in there. Hank's ready for dinner."

* * *

Once Hank had been fed, Bridget stood by the sink staring out through the kitchen window.

She couldn't stop worrying about her father. Couldn't stop thinking of the last stressful weeks of the original Backroads Butcher investigation.

She'd been fixated on finding the serial killer, and her father had been convinced she was putting herself in danger.

In the end, he'd been right. But he'd also been sick.

Only Bridget had been too busy to notice or to do anything about it. Was history repeating itself all over again?

Picturing her father's worried face, she felt her pulse jump, and an uneasy ache started in her stomach.

She sucked in a deep breath as she poured herself a glass of water. As she sipped it, she considered scheduling an appointment with Faye Thackery.

She'd canceled her two upcoming appointments with the therapist after planning her trip to Aruba.

Now that the trip wasn't happening, she should probably

reschedule. Especially now that Grady had escaped and was on the run. Faye was one of the only people she could talk to openly about the trauma she'd been through.

And the only person she'd ever talked to about her run-in with Lyle Grady during the hunt for the Backroads Butcher.

It had taken months of therapy to become comfortable enough to share the traumatic experience. Even thinking about it now, as she stood in the kitchen, caused Bridget's breath to grow shallow and her pulse to quicken.

Deciding a cup of chamomile tea might help calm her nerves, she put the kettle on to boil and returned to the window, allowing her mind to return to the day she had finally come face to face with the Butcher.

Bridget stepped through the backdoor of the old church and looked out at the deserted parking lot. Her eyes scanned the thick forest of trees that lined the hardpacked dirt, disappointed that the delivery van Zadie Monroe had mentioned wasn't in the lot.

Justine Abernathy's friend had described Lyle Grady's van, saying he often parked it out behind the church because his mother wouldn't let him park it in her driveway.

"She says it makes the neighborhood look tacky," the girl had explained. "But I think she just likes to be difficult."

Bridget was about to turn away when she saw a flash of white behind the row of trees.

She hesitated, checking her watch, wondering where Gage could be. He'd promised to meet her at the church, but he was late.

Tapping out a message with impatient fingers, she pressed Send, then began to walk over the rutted ground.

As she approached a gap in the trees, she saw the van.

The Mount Destiny Delivery Express logo was painted in red on the side, just as Zadie had described.

Moving closer, she strained to look through the front window.

From what she could see, the van appeared to be empty.

Lyle Grady, the man she believed to be the Backroads Butcher, could come back at any minute and find her there.

This might be her only chance to look inside his van. Her only chance to find out if she was right about him being a serial killer, or if she'd tracked down an innocent man.

She didn't need a warrant, she told herself because all she wanted to do was look. She wouldn't touch anything or take anything. She just wanted to know the truth. Had to know.

There was no way she could walk away now without knowing.

Checking that her Glock was still safe in her holster, Bridget reached out with a trembling hand and pulled back on the handle.

The side door slid open smoothly.

She hesitated, then looked around at the trees again, expecting to see Lyle Grady looming up behind her, but no one was there.

As she climbed inside the van, she saw that all the back windows had been blacked out with a thin layer of paint.

Taking out her phone, she activated her flashlight, shining it down in front of her, lighting up a bloody shoeprint on the floor.

Her heart seemed to jump into her throat as she lifted the light, moving it around the interior of the van, which was nearly empty, other than a few boxes and an old-fashioned steamer trunk.

As she inched further into the van, she saw a cardboard box

positioned in front of the back doors.

The flaps of the box were open.

An image of Michelle Ewing's headless body flashed through her mind and for one terrifying moment she was convinced the girl's head would be inside.

It could be Michelle's, or one of the Butcher's other victims.

After all, none of his victims had been found intact.

Bridget slowly stepped forward, her heart hammering, her mouth dry, and looked into the box.

It was empty.

She stepped back with a sigh of relief.

"That one I saved for you," a deep voice said from behind her. "I was hoping you'd be the one to find me."

With a scream, she turned to see Lyle Grady standing only inches behind her.

He grabbed her and spun her around before she could react, pressing his chest against her back as he held a knife to her throat.

"The feds know you're the Butcher," she grasped out, reaching for the gun in her holster.

"I wouldn't do that if I were you," he said, pressing the knife into the soft flesh under her chin.

Her hand froze as he wrapped his free arm around her throat and began to squeeze.

"Are you ready to die today, Dr. Bishop?"

She cringed at the killer's hot breath in her ear.

"Cause this is the time to say your prayers."

Bridget squeezed her eyes shut, calling silently for the little voice in her head, her mother's voice, to tell her what to do.

But all she could hear was Grady's nasty laugh.

Opening her eyes, she saw him lift the sharp blade in his hand, noting the leather bracelet tied around his wrist.

He was the Butcher alright, and the blood knot was ready for her. She'd be wearing it when they found her body.

"You thought I always used a meat cleaver, didn't you?" he said gleefully. "But I'll use whatever does the job. And this little beauty slices right through without-"

Suddenly the back doors of the van were wrenched open to reveal a tall figure.

Deputy Marshal Howie Decker stood looking into the cargo area with his gun already drawn, his face as hard as stone.

"Let her go," he ordered, keeping his voice calm. "I'm armed and there's no place to go. Just put down the-"

"Move back or I'll slit her throat," Grady shouted, tightening his arm until Bridget could barely breathe.

Decker hesitated, giving Grady just enough time to reach down and pull the Glock from Bridget's holster.

She screamed a warning as he lifted the gun toward Decker.

The deputy marshal dove to the left as the gunshot exploded beside Bridget's ear, the bullet missing Decker by mere inches.

Throwing back her head as hard as she could, Bridget felt her skull connect with something soft and flexible as she dropped to the ground, then rolled toward the van doors.

Grady howled in pain behind her, holding his gushing nose as she scrambled out onto the rocky ground, falling to her knees.

"Watch out!" Decker yelled as a bullet whizzed past her head, kicking up dirt and grass behind her.

Grabbing her hand, he yanked her behind him toward the cover of the trees as Grady got off another shot.

As the van's engine roared to life, Decker jumped back on his feet. But it was too late. The van was already speeding away.

"What were you doing here?" Bridget asked, looking toward the deserted lot behind the church.

"Saving your ass," Decker replied, using one hand to help her to her feet and the other to pull his phone from his pocket. "Now, I need to call for back-up. It looks like you just found the Butcher."

The scream of the kettle drew Bridget's mind back into the kitchen with a start.

Pouring boiling water over the tea bag, she watched as the steam rose to fill the air, thinking back to the days that had followed her close encounter with the Butcher.

While she had finally figured out the killer's true identity, their encounter had left her shaken, and she'd been terrified he would come back to find her and finish her off.

When she'd heard that Decker and Santino had tracked Grady down in West Virginia, sans his delivery van, her relief had been overwhelming.

But it wasn't until Grady had been safely convicted that she'd allowed herself to think about anything other than making sure he was locked away for good.

Then, once he'd been sent away to Abbeyville, Bridget had begun to assess the emotional fallout from Grady's assault, which had left her suffering with nightmares and anxiety.

She'd finally allowed herself to acknowledge the trauma she'd suffered during her brush with death and her violent confrontation with her own mortality

Taking a sip of the scalding tea, Bridget assured herself that, thanks to her work with Faye Thackery, she'd managed to get back to something akin to normal.

The thought was interrupted by the sound of soft footsteps outside the back door. Her eyes scanned the room for her purse. Her Glock was in it. But she'd left it in the living room.

She looked around the kitchen, then pulled a knife out of the block before walking silently toward the door.

Has Grady finally come to take his revenge? Or maybe it's the mysterious Max Bender coming to do Grady's dirty work.

A soft knock stopped her heart.

"Bridget? Are you in there? It's me, Santino."

CHAPTER FIFTEEN

Vic Santino looked down at Bridget and saw that she had fallen asleep on the sofa, her face relaxed and peaceful in the soft glow of the television. After ordering pizza and finishing off a bottle of merlot, they'd retired to the living room to unwind, and had ended up watching the news, even though they knew there had been no major breakthroughs in the search for Grady to report.

Thinking of the ninety-minute commute between Wisteria Falls and Arlington, Santino brushed a strand of silky hair back from Bridget's forehead and sighed.

Their relationship had flourished over the last few months despite the distance, although he doubted he'd ever be completely free from the guilt and pain he felt whenever he thought of his late wife, Maribel.

While he'd come to believe that Maribel would want him to be happy and that perhaps her spirit or her memory, or whatever part of her that remained with him, had played a part in guiding him to Bridget in the first place, he couldn't yet move on. Not until justice for her death had been served.

The depressing thought was interrupted by dramatic intro music announcing a special television report.

The anchor spoke with somber urgency as she described the shocking details of Lyle Grady's escape, and then began to recount his original crimes and his eventual capture.

Santino couldn't tear his eyes away from the footage taken on the day Grady had been captured.

He watched a younger version of himself lead the serial killer into the Mount Destiny Police Department, with Decker at his side.

Leaning forward, he inhaled sharply as video taken from within the courthouse showed a visibly shaken Bridget giving testimony at Grady's trial.

The report moved on to cover the years Grady had spent in Abbeyville, his recent petition for a retrial due to new DNA evidence, and his puzzling escape at the Culver County Courthouse.

"After speculation that the serial killer has an accomplice helping him, the U.S. Marshals Service asks for any information on the fugitive to be called into their tip line."

Drained from the impromptu tour down memory lane, Santino switched off the television and checked his watch.

Holiday traffic would be heavy, with everyone heading home for the big meal the following day.

The thought made him long for the safe confines of his mother's place on the Chesapeake Bay, although he would have little time for a Thanksgiving meal at home this year even now that Aruba had been canceled.

Despite the holiday, he and the task force would have to continue their hunt for the escaped serial killer. They may even be forced to search for a missing couple if Heather

Winslow and her boyfriend weren't found soon.

Even as he told himself to get up and start the drive back to Arlington so he would be ready for the long day that lay ahead, he remained seated.

He was worried about leaving Bridget on her own.

She had played a pivotal role in Grady's capture, and Santino couldn't help thinking that the killer would want to pay her back if he had the chance.

Hank moved at his feet, arranging his soft body into a more comfortable position as Santino looked down.

"You don't act much like a guard dog, do you?" he asked in a low voice. "I guess I'll just have to stay and protect both of you."

"We'll be fine," Bridget said, her voice groggy as she sat up and stretched her neck. "I've got my Glock, and I'll set my alarm. No one will get in here without a fight."

"Now, why doesn't the thought of you having another gunfight with a deranged serial killer make me feel any better?" he asked, cocking his head.

Bridget produced a weary sigh and hefted herself up and off the sofa.

"Well, nothing's going to make *me* feel better until Lyle Grady is back behind bars where he belongs."

Santino caught her eyes.

"Grady isn't the only one we need to worry about," he reminded her. "Whoever helped him plot his getaway could also pose a danger. Someone who went to the extent of slipping him a weapon-"

He stopped short when he saw the thoughtful look on

Bridget's face.

"What are you thinking about?" he asked.

"I've been thinking about what Decker said."

Bridget suddenly seemed wide awake.

"He suggested Max Bender could be Grady's partner and that he could be the one who killed Tammy Vicker," she said. "Which would mean the DNA under Tammy's fingernails belongs to his partner."

Santino shrugged.

"I guess so," he agreed. "But whoever's DNA it is, there wasn't a match in CODIS, so it doesn't tell us much. At least not until we have a suspect."

She nodded, looking more than a little dejected.

Sensing her anxiety, Santino reached for her hand.

"If you're worried Bender or Grady will come for you, I can still request a patrol car to keep an eye on the house."

"I'm more worried about Heather Winslow and Ryder Forbes," Bridget said, nudging him toward the door. "And anyone else who doesn't know how dangerous Grady really is."

CHAPTER SIXTEEN

Dale Winslow woke on Thanksgiving morning with a pounding head and a cotton-dry mouth. The hangover was made worse by the heavy blanket of depression that had settled over him during the last few days. Looking in the mirror, he ran a finger over the stiff, silver hair of his mustache. He could use a trim but decided he didn't have time.

He needed to see Reagan before he started his shift at the food bank. Thanksgiving was their biggest day of the year, and he couldn't let the community down.

But I can't let down Heather, either. She's missing, and I need to let Reagan know. Maybe Reagan will know how to find her.

The thought stayed with him as he washed and shaved, then pulled on his Sunday best and opened the door.

He stopped with a groan when he saw that his beat-up Volvo wasn't in the driveway.

Flashes from the night before came back to him. He remembered struggling with someone for his car keys.

Looking out at the empty driveway, he exhaled loudly.

I guess I lost the fight.

Figuring his car was outside one of the three bars in

town, he decided it could wait.

After changing his shoes, he walked the two miles to Cumberland Road, reaching his eldest daughter's house just after nine, determined to ask for her help.

Too bad if she was still mad at him.

It was time for them both to let go of their grievances.

Reagan had been after him to stop drinking ever since her mother had died, and he'd been furious when he found out she was working to free convicted murders.

"There's enough evil in this world already, why work to let it loose on society?"

Although his opinion about her work hadn't changed, for Heather's sake, he was ready to move on and put their differences behind them.

As he stood on Reagan's porch, he spotted a police car cruise past the house. He prepared to explain his presence, but the car didn't stop, and the two uniformed officers inside didn't appear to notice him.

With a shrug, he turned and knocked on the door, steeling himself for his daughter's reaction, whatever it may be.

He waited, but there was no sound from inside.

Pulling out his phone, he tapped on Reagan's number.

Seconds later he heard a faint ringing coming from inside.

He leaned forward and put his mouth close to the door, calling out in a loud but amiable voice.

"Reagan! You in there?"

Still hearing no response, Dale hesitated, then pulled his

key ring from his pocket, his eyes falling on the spare key Reagan had given him before they'd fallen out.

The key slipped into the lock with ease, but as he turned the handle and tried to push the door open, something heavy seemed to be blocking the way.

Shoving against the door with his shoulder, he managed to open the door wide enough to stick his head inside and look down at the obstruction on the floor.

His eyes struggled to adjust to the dim light in the foyer.

Dale blinked, sure his eyes must be playing tricks on him.

Then, as he stared down at the headless, blood-soaked figure sprawled on the floor, he began to scream.

* * *

"Mr. Winslow?"

The woman's voice sounded as if she was far away.

"Mr. Winslow, are you okay?"

Dale resisted the urge to open his eyes, not wanting to wake up. Not ready to continue the nightmare that had started that morning when he'd discovered Reagan's mutilated body.

"He was pretty upset when he ran out to flag us down," a man's voice said. "He was shouting and banging on the hood. I thought he must be having some kind of episode."

An image of the cop in the patrol car flashed into Dale's mind, but he pushed it away, not wanting to remember the way he'd screamed for help.

Not wanting to remember anything at all.

"I think he even called 911, but I'm not sure they could understand what he was trying to say."

"I've called an ambulance," the woman said. "And there will be an FBI evidence response team here within the hour. In the meantime, I need you to cordon off the whole house."

Moving his hand, Dale felt the scratch of concrete under his fingers. He turned his head and eased open his eyes.

He was lying on the driveway outside Reagan's house.

So, it wasn't a bad dream. It had all really happened.

He'd made a mess of his life. Allowing the booze to take over, allowing himself to wallow in his own grief and self-pity after his wife had died.

Of course, he'd always planned to get sober. To make up with his daughters eventually. He'd assumed that someday they'd all be together.

Now, by some cruel, unfair twist of fate, his beautiful wife and daughters were all gone, and he had been left alone to be tormented by the memories of his failures.

Footsteps sounded beside his head.

"Mr. Winslow, I need you to sit up now."

Charlie Day crouched down beside him and leaned over, studying him with worried gray eyes.

"I'm sorry, Mr. Winslow, I know this is difficult, but I need to understand what happened," she said. "Do you know who did this to your daughter?"

Shaking his head, he lifted a hand to cover his eyes.

"No," he said. "I don't know who did this. But if I find out who it is, I swear, I'll tear him limb from limb."

"I understand," Charlie said, sticking out a hand. "Let's go sit on the porch. You can tell me what happened."

Dale allowed himself to be helped up off the pavement. He walked slowly and stiffly after Charlie before sinking down onto the top step with a soft moan.

"Okay, now tell me what happened," Charlie asked, sitting beside him. "Tell me everything you can remember."

"I came here to make up with my daughter," he said, wiping at his eyes. "I wanted her to help me find Heather."

Reaching into her jacket pocket, Charlie pulled out a crumpled tissue and handed it to Dale.

"I knocked but Reagan didn't come to the door," he said, dabbing at his eyes. "I heard her phone ringing inside, and so I knew she must be there. I tried to open the door, but something was...blocking it."

He dropped his head into his hands, unable to go on.

"Detective Larkin is here," Charlie said, as a woman in baggy pants and a stretched-out sweater hurried up the driveway. "She'll sit here with you while I go inside and see if I can find the phone. I didn't see it earlier, but I'll call the number now and see if I can find it."

Voices whispered next to him, and then Charlie was gone, and Larkin was sitting stiffly next to him, her feet drumming nervously on the pavement.

Soon a faint ringing sounded somewhere inside the house, then Charlie was back holding a phone in her gloved hand.

"It had fallen under the kitchen counter," she said. "Mr. Winslow, do you know the password?"

149

Dale's head felt too heavy to look up.

"I know it's hard," Charlie said. "But whatever's on this phone could help us find the person who did this."

"Let's try her birthday," Larkin said.

Shaking his head, Dale spoke without looking up.

"Try Heather's birthday. Reagan always used her little sister's birthday as her password."

Charlie tapped in the numbers as he recited them.

"That was it," she said.

He glanced up to see her scrolling through the recent messages, her face growing increasingly alarmed.

"What is it?" he asked.

"Mr. Winslow, do you know a man named Max Bender?"

The name wasn't familiar.

"No, I've never heard of the guy. Why, who is he?"

"I'm not really sure," she admitted. "But he's sent Reagan some texts that indicate he might know where Heather is."

Dale's chest tightened at the mention of his youngest daughter. He'd almost forgotten that she was missing. That it had been her disappearance that had brought him to Reagan's house that morning.

"I'm sorry to have to tell you this now, after what's happened," Charlie said, looking torn. "But you have a right to know, and-"

Reaching out, Dale grabbed the phone from Charlie's hand, taking her by surprise.

She made no move to stop him as he scrolled through the messages from the man named Bender. A mix of despair and hope flooded through him as he stopped on the last one.

Your sister is safe. Keep your mouth shut and she'll be home soon. Start talking and you'll never see her again.

His hand dropped to his lap, and Charlie caught the phone just before it could fall to the ground.

"She's safe," he said numbly, closing his eyes. "That's what the messages are saying. Heather is still alive."

"Mr. Winslow, I'm going to need you to go down to the station with Detective Larkin," Charlie said, placing a soft hand on his arm. "We need to take a full statement from you."

Dale shook off her hand.

"You can't afford to waste time with me. You need to go find out if Heather is alive. And you need to find the man who killed my daughter."

CHAPTER SEVENTEEN

Bridget poured freshly brewed coffee into a Christmas mug and added a generous splash of milk. Carrying the mug into the living room, she turned on the television and sank onto the sofa, hoping to catch a few minutes of the Macy's Thanksgiving Day Parade.

She had loved watching the parade each year with her mother as a little girl, and the giant floats and marching bands never failed to get her in a holiday mood.

Her phone buzzed on the table before she could take a sip of the strong, sweet coffee. Seeing Charlie's number, she set the mug down and picked up her phone.

"Reagan Rivera is dead," Charlie said as soon as she picked up. "She was attacked in her home this morning."

"Was it him?" Bridget asked, reaching for the remote, and shutting off the television. "Was it Grady?"

Charlie hesitated before answering.

"It does look like the Butcher's work," she said. "She was decapitated with a meat cleaver for one thing."

A wave of nausea rolled through Bridget at the words.

"But we found evidence on her phone suggesting someone else could be responsible," Charlie said. "It also confirms what we feared. Heather Winslow has been abducted. We're not sure about Ryder Forbes."

"Evidence?" Bridget asked, trying to absorb everything Charlie was saying. "What kind of evidence?"

She was already moving toward the bedroom.

"Text messages and a photo," Charlie said. "From a man named Max Bender. Why does that name sound familiar?"

Bridget stopped and stared down at the phone.

"That's the name of the man who had been visiting Grady in Abbeyville," she said. "Santino and Decker found his name on the visitors' log, but apparently he was using a stolen identity. Max Bender is just an alias."

After assuring Charlie she was on her way, Bridget threw a warm jacket over her sweater, tucked her black pants into knee-high boots, and headed toward the door, stopping only to assure Hank she'd be home in time to take him to her father's house for Thanksgiving dinner.

When she arrived in Mount Destiny, the downtown area appeared to be deserted. All businesses had closed for the holiday, and most people were at home with their families.

But as she tried to pull onto Cumberland Road, she couldn't find room for her Explorer to squeeze past all the cars and people who had gathered outside Reagan's house.

Finally parking along the curb a block away, Bridget threaded her way through the crowd.

She'd just reached the driveway when a hand fell on her shoulder. Spinning around, she saw Chase Grafton holding out his trusty recorder.

"I'm here outside the scene of the latest murder in

Mount Destiny with Dr. Bridget Bishop, the well-known criminal psychologist and FBI profiler who helped nab Lyle Grady, the man known as the Backroads Butcher."

Chase thrust the recorder toward Bridget.

"Tell me, Dr. Bishop, how does it feel to know that the Butcher is a free man."

Shoving past Chase without saying a word, Bridget made a beeline toward Charlie, who was standing behind the crime scene tape next to Detective Larkin.

"Did you listen to my voicemail, Bridget?" Chase called after her, not bothering to hide his frustration. "If you didn't, you're gonna wish you had!"

Bridget ignored the warning as she ducked under the yellow tape and crossed to the porch, where Opal Fitzgerald had now joined Charlie and Larkin.

"This wasn't how I hoped to spend my Thanksgiving," Opal was saying as Bridget climbed the steps. "I set the timer for Cecil, so he knows when to turn off the oven. I just hope he doesn't burn down the house."

As the M.E. turned to go inside, Charlie pulled Bridget to the side and lowered her voice.

"They found a bracelet at the scene," Charlie said, her eyes grim. "You know the one I mean."

Bridget cocked her head.

"Is it the same as the others?"

"Looks like it to me," Charlie said, holding up her phone to show Bridget a close-up photo of what appeared to be Reagan's wrist.

Several thin leather strips had been tied together in an

overlapping knot to fashion a crude bracelet. Bridget felt another wave of nausea as she recognized the blood knot.

It had been Grady's signature in the past. His calling card.

"I've given the bracelet to the evidence team, and told them to keep the information to ourselves," Charlie said. "Just as we did before."

Nodding in numb acknowledgment, Bridget continued to stare at the photo on the phone.

"Do you have the messages that were sent to Reagan?" Bridget asked. "The ones from Max Bender?"

Charlie nodded.

"I already turned Regan's phone over to the evidence response team," Charlie said. "But I forwarded copies of the messages and the photo to myself."

Tapping on her phone, Charlie pulled up the string of texts that Bender had sent to Reagan, then handed it to Bridget.

As she scrolled through the messages, Bridget tried to piece together what she was seeing.

"So, Max Bender abducted Heather," she said.

"That's what it looks like," Charlie agreed.

"And his motive was to force Reagan into helping Grady escape from the courthouse."

Charlie nodded.

"Right again."

"Decker thinks Max Bender could be Grady's partner," Bridget said. "He even suggested this guy could have killed Tammy Vicker."

"Is that what you think?' Charlie asked.

"I'd say Bender's definitely involved with Grady somehow. But his partner? I'm not sure about that," Bridget admitted. "The texts may prove he abducted Heather, but we have no forensic evidence to show he killed Reagan."

She handed the phone back to Charlie.

"Did you track the number that sent these texts?"

"It's a burner phone," Charlie said with a grim nod. "All we know is that the caller was in Mount Destiny when he sent the messages."

"And Heather?" Bridget asked. "Do you think she's..."

"We've got to assume she's still alive," Charlie said, although her somber gray eyes told a different story. "We're working on a missing person alert and setting up a hotline. Hopefully, someone saw her and Ryder leaving the airport and noticed who they were with."

As Bridget turned to go, Opal Fitzgerald stepped out of the house, her face strained.

"I think I'm done here," she said. "Greg and I will take care of the autopsy as soon as we get back to the office, although we only have partial remains to work with."

"Her head...he took it with him?" Bridget asked, suspecting she already knew the answer.

Charlie and Opal both nodded.

"It looks just like the other Butcher crime scenes," Charlie said. "But we can't assume it's Grady. Not with everything else we know. We have to be sure."

"We'll make do with what that animal left behind," Opal

said, anger hardening her words. "If there's something to find that will help you guys catch him, I plan on finding it."

* * *

Leaving Charlie behind to manage the chaotic scene, Bridget followed the big van carrying Opal, her forensic technician Greg Alcott, and what was left of Reagan Rivera to the medical examiner's office an hour's drive away.

The place appeared to be deserted as Bridget parked her white Explorer and crossed the nearly empty lot.

She stepped into the quiet building, detecting the faint scent of chemicals and decay that permeated every room.

All but essential staff were at home for the holiday. She noted the reception desk was unmanned as Opal let her into the back where the autopsy suites were located.

As Bridget ducked into a small changing room to pull on protective coveralls, Greg pushed the rolling gurney into the autopsy suite and transferred Reagan's body to the dissecting table.

She watched as Opal layered on two sets of gloves, adjusted her mask, and signaled to Greg to activate the handheld voice recorder.

Lifting the white sheet, Opal folded it back to reveal what remained of Reagan's body and neck, eliciting an involuntary gasp of horror from Bridget at the grisly sight.

But the medical examiner seemed unmoved, and her expression remained stoic as she began to perform an external examination of the body and dictate her observations into the recorder.

"The body is that of a well-developed, well-nourished white female, approximately sixty-six inches and weighing one hundred thirty-eight pounds. Her appearance is consistent with the decedent's age of thirty-eight years."

Using a stainless-steel instrument taken from a nearby tray, Opal proceeded to examine and take measurements of Reagan's neck while Greg snapped photos from every angle.

"The decedent's head has been severed from the body at the neck. The decapitation was carried out above the thyroid cartilage. The wound appears to involve the C2-3 portion of the cervical spine."

Opal stood up straight and cleared her throat.

"An absence of hesitation marks indicates her attacker was quite strong and most likely familiar with human anatomy. The murder weapon is believed to be a very sharp cleaver, which was recovered at the scene."

She met Bridget's eyes.

"I think it's safe to say that the manner and cause of death will be listed as homicide by sharp force injury to the neck causing decapitation."

Bridget nodded weakly, watching as Opal moved on to perform an external examination of the rest of Reagan's body. She seemed to find nothing of interest until she got to Reagan's right hand.

As she was taking a swab from under each fingernail, Opal suddenly stopped and turned to Greg.

"We've got a hair here."

She sounded excited as she picked up a small pair of

forceps off the tray.

"It's caught in her fingers."

Unwinding the hair wrapped around Reagan's stiff hand, she held it up for Bridget to see.

The dark hair was at least three or four inches long.

"That's definitely darker and longer than Grady's hair," she said, picturing the killer standing in the courtroom, his light brown hair cropped short.

As Opal carefully placed the hair into a brown paper evidence bag, a question popped into Bridget's head.

Does Max Bender have dark hair?

She turned hopeful eyes to Opal.

"Is there a root attached?" Bridget asked. "Will we be able to get DNA?"

"There's a root," Opal confirmed with a grim nod. "So, a DNA profile is likely. But I'm not sure how quickly we can get the lab to work on it seeing it's Thanksgiving..."

Bridget was already backing out of the room.

"I'll call Vivian Burke," she said, tugging off her mask. "I'll ask her to test it today."

Hurrying back to the cubby where she'd left her purse, Bridget pulled out her phone and tapped on Vivian's number with anxious fingers.

The forensic examiner answered on the second ring.

"Let me guess, you're not calling to wish me a Happy Thanksgiving," Vivian said dryly.

"Sorry to bother you, but I need a favor."

Vivian laughed. The sound wasn't pleasant.

"Don't you always?" she said.

After an awkward silence, she relented.

"Fine...what do you need?"

"I'm not sure if you've heard, but Reagan Rivera's been killed," Bridget said. "We've recovered hair that may belong to her attacker and need a DNA profile as soon as possible."

She held her breath, waiting for Vivian's reply.

"I'm at my parents' house right now helping my mother prepare Thanksgiving dinner," she said. "They expect me to stay and help out all afternoon."

"Oh...sorry," Bridget said, her heart dropping. "Then I guess it'll have to wait until-"

Vivian cut her off with another sharp laugh.

"No, it won't," she said. "It'll give me the perfect excuse to leave early. I'll collect the specimen within the hour."

CHAPTER EIGHTEEN

Bender tapped his fingers nervously on the sedan's steering wheel as he once again drove toward Destiny Peak Overlook. He was getting used to the mountainous area and paid little attention to the scenic view on either side of him as he pressed down hard on the accelerator, suddenly impatient to complete his task.

I need to dump the bag and get home. Erica won't like waiting.

He didn't allow himself to think too long about the bag in the trunk. Or to remember what was inside.

After all, it was pointless to dwell on unpleasant things when there was nothing to be done about them.

Bumping down the narrow winding road toward the Iron Graveyard, he wondered why Lyle Grady had elected decapitation as his method of choice.

Can he really find the hassle and the mess satisfying?

Bender had now experienced the gruesome process twice, and he still couldn't understand the thrill. Why bother going to all that trouble if you didn't need to shut someone up or solve a serious problem?

Grady must be a true psychopath after all.

Bringing the sedan to a sudden stop, Bender climbed out

and circled to the back of the car. He sucked in a deep breath, then popped the trunk open.

He lifted his arm and pressed the sleeve of his jacket against his nose to block the terrible smell that rose to greet him as he looked inside.

The black garbage bag sat just where he'd left it.

Grabbing the heavy bag with his free hand, he used his elbow to slam the trunk shut, then began making his way along the path, well acquainted by now with the rocky, uneven terrain and the little twists and turns along the trail.

His mind moved ahead to the mine and the dark shaft, wondering what remained of the young woman who'd fallen in four days before.

The need to dispose of the bag would give him the opportunity to make sure Heather Winslow's final resting place was still undisturbed.

As he reached the yawning hole in the rock face, he looked around to scan the trees, making sure he was alone, then ducked his head and stepped inside, being careful not to trip over the iron rails that jutted out.

Immediately feeling suffocated inside the confined, airless space, he sucked in a deep breath, forgetting about the putrid smell from the bag before it was too late. The stench rose up around him, filling Bender's nose and mouth.

Dropping the bag on the ground, he put one hand on the rough wall and bent over, retching up the breakfast he'd eaten a few hours before.

He waited until the urge had passed, then stood and

wiped his mouth with the back of his hand.

Once he felt steady on his feet again, he pulled out the flashlight he'd brought with him and switched it on.

The bright beam of light lit up the cramped space and illuminated the tunnel that led further into the mine.

Stubbing the toe of his boot against the same iron rail that had tripped up Heather, Bender let out a soft curse and steadied himself.

He aimed the beam of light straight ahead, making out the edge of the shaft just to his left.

As he inched closer to the edge, he leaned forward to peek into the darkness below but could see nothing without the help of the flashlight.

Holding his arm out straight, he aimed the beam inside, illuminating the far side of the shaft, revealing an uneven rock wall supported by several buckled timbers.

The circle of light slid down the side of the shaft as Bender moved closer to the edge.

As he took another small step, the uneven ground seemed to shift under his feet, sending a cascade of rocks and dirt skittering into the darkness below.

Bender scrambled backward, tripping over the rusty rails in his haste to avoid sliding into the shaft, falling onto the ground beside the black garbage bag.

"Shit!" he yelled, rolling away and scrambling to his feet.

He tried to catch his breath without inhaling the nauseating fumes rising from the bag, not sure what to do.

He'd come with the intention of seeing Heather's body, but now he just wanted to get out alive.

Maybe he should have listened to all the dire warnings he'd heard about steering clear of abandoned mines.

Grabbing up the bag, he flung it forward with all his strength before he could change his mind.

Heather was down there, and she was dead. There was no way she could have survived the fall and lasted four days without food or water.

I'm just being paranoid. Time to move on.

Hurrying back to the mine opening, he thrust his head out into the cool, fall air and sucked in a long, sweet breath.

As he climbed up the path toward his car, his phone rang in his pocket. Digging it out, he saw Erica's name on the display along with the stunning image she'd recently started using as her profile picture.

Guilt rolled through him as he declined the call.

She was surely wondering where he was. It was Thanksgiving after all, and they'd been invited to eat dinner with her parents. It would be rude to be late.

And it wouldn't do for her to get suspicious. Not after everything he'd sacrificed for her.

If she ever even suspected what I'd done, she'd...

No, he wouldn't even think of that. He wouldn't let her find out. There was no way he was going to screw it up now.

He'd almost convinced himself that all would be well when he heard another buzz. This time the sound was coming from the burner phone in his pants pocket.

Tempted to ignore the call, he hesitated, then pulled it out.

"What the hell have you done?" Grady demanded. "Why

did you kill my lawyer?"

He didn't wait for Bender to respond before answering his own question.

"You're trying to pin this all on me, aren't you?" he said. "Just remember, if they find me and throw me back in Abbeyville, you're going to end up in the next cell."

"That's not how it is," Bender protested. "Reagan Rivera and her sister were unavoidable casualties. You said you wanted out of prison, right? So, I did what I had to do."

Grady sounded almost impressed when he spoke again.

"You killed Heather Winslow, too? The missing girl whose picture just went up on the news?"

"That was an accident."

His words were met with an ugly laugh.

"Well, your *accident* is all over the news," he said. "Every cop in the state is going to be out there searching for her, which means it's about time for me to hit the road."

Bender's stomach sank. He couldn't just let Lyle Grady leave. Not with everything he knew.

"But first, I need money and a new ID," Grady said. "Which means you have forty-eight hours to get me ten thousand in cash and a new ID. You can wire me more money once I'm set up somewhere far away."

Mind spinning, Bender tried to think.

"Okay, tell me where to meet you and I'll bring the cash," he said, his hand gripping the butt of his gun.

And when you arrive, you'd better be ready for a little surprise.

CHAPTER NINETEEN

Heather Winslow opened her eyes and stared sightlessly into the darkness that had swallowed her up. She wasn't sure how long she'd been there, drifting in and out of consciousness. She didn't know what day of the week it was, or if it was day or night.

The pain and the thirst were all that she knew.

But something had woken her. She'd heard a sound.

Was that a voice?

Lifting her head, Heather felt a sharp pain shoot through her neck and down her spine.

Have I broken my back?

The thought didn't panic her as it probably should have. It just floated through her mind, then dispersed to make room for the next, more important question.

Will he come back for me?

Fear fluttered at the edges of her memory.

Flashes of cold, piercing eyes over the muzzle of a gun. The spray of blood as Ryder tried to run.

A gasp escaped Heather's lips at the thought of Ryder.

Was it real? Is he dead?

Wincing, she rolled over on her side, ignoring the pain

that coursed through almost every part of her body.

Gritting her teeth, she used her right arm to maneuver herself up into a sitting position against the wall beside her.

Her left arm hung at an awkward angle by her side. Sharp pangs of agony shot up through her shoulder as she positioned it against her chest using her good arm.

She sat quietly in the dark, listening intently, not sure if she really had heard the man's voice, or if it had been a dream. Or even a delusion.

After ten minutes of complete silence, she reached down to check her legs, testing first the right, which felt sore but intact, and then the left, triggering a bolt of pain from her hip to her knee.

As she jerked her hand back, her fingers brushed against something hard in her pocket.

The key ring Dad bought me.

Forcing her hand into the front pocket of her jeans, she pulled out her keys, which she'd carelessly stuck into her pocket instead of her purse after going through security at the airport in Chicago.

Her fingers wrapped around a smooth, cylindrical object attached to the key ring. The miniature flashlight, not much bigger than the AA battery inside it, which her father had given her the last time she'd gone home.

"It'll come in handy in an emergency. And I know you still get scared of the dark sometimes..."

The memory of her father's teasing words brought a rush of hot tears to her eyes.

Holding the little flashlight in her shaking hand, Heather

pressed the tiny *ON* button, activating a narrow beam of light.

She blinked away her tears, trying to focus as her eyes adjusted to the sudden light, pointing the beam around her, gazing in muted horror at the rock walls all around her.

As she pointed the beam upward, she estimated that the walls rose up at least twenty feet, supported by a collection of split and buckled timbers.

Stricken by a sudden urge to get out, to escape, she grabbed for one of the timbers with her right hand and pulled herself onto her one good knee, determined to pull herself up and out of the dark, makeshift prison.

But as she pulled, her arm began to tremble with the effort, and she lost her balance. Toppling over on her side, she screamed out in pain as her broken arm hit the rock floor.

Writhing on the ground, she tried to tell herself that a broken leg and busted arm wouldn't kill her.

But the lack of water and food will.

The warning voice in her head stopped her tears. She couldn't afford to waste energy on useless emotions now.

She might only have a few days, or even hours left.

She needed to focus. Something had woken her from her heavy sleep. Whatever it was must have made her slumbering psyche imagine that it wasn't too late after all. That she could still be saved.

It was the man's voice.

Had he really been up there? Was he there even now?

But as she stilled her breathing and listened, there was

only silence above. Closing her eyes and concentrating hard, she tried to recall what she'd heard.

Yes, it was definitely a man's voice. And a thud.

Switching on her flashlight, she moved it slowly along the walls and then down to the floor.

She inhaled sharply as the beam stopped on a black garbage bag, which rested in the center of the shaft.

Was that what made the thudding sound?

Carefully, she inched toward the bag, wincing in pain as her broken limbs protested the movement, recoiling at the pungent odor coming off the bag.

Did the man come back? Did he throw down the bag?

She stopped still, suddenly wondering if it was some kind of trick. After all, why would he come back for her?

It isn't as if he would want to save me. Would he?

Now, as she looked at the bag, Heather felt a small glimmer of hope. It could have food and water inside.

She tried to ignore the voice that warned her to be careful.

That doesn't smell like any food you'd want to eat. Besides, he killed Ryder, remember? And what do you think he intended to do to you before you fell in here?

She shuddered to think.

But the rumble in her stomach and the dry pain in her throat made her reach for the bag.

Tucking the flashlight under her arm, she used her good hand to work open the drawstring and reach inside. Her fingers closed over something that felt strangely like hair, only it was sticky. Instinctively, she pulled her hand back.

Unable to stop herself, she bent over and looked down into the open bag. When she saw the two lifeless eyes staring up at her, she began to scream.

CHAPTER TWENTY

By the time Bridget arrived at her father's house, Paloma was already clearing the dining room table and wrapping up the Thanksgiving leftovers, her thin shoulders stiff and her mouth set firmly in a tight, disapproving line.

After leaving the medical examiner's office, Bridget had stopped by her house to pick up Hank and had ended up taking a shower and pulling on fresh clothes, not wanting to bring the smell of death and dismemberment with her.

"You're just in time for dessert," Bob said with a wink as Paloma set a sweet potato pie and a container of whipped cream on the table. "I'll go get some clean forks."

As her father hurried from the room, Paloma picked up a knife and began cutting the pie into small slices.

"Your father waited all day for you to get here," she said in a low angry voice. "He's not a young man anymore, you know. And after his stroke-"

Abruptly turning away as Bob came back into the room with a handful of forks, Paloma concentrated on sliding the slices of pie onto holiday-themed plates.

"Dad, have you been feeling okay?" Bridget asked as she

took a bite of the sweet, creamy dessert. "If there's something wrong, please tell me. I need to know."

Her father shook his head, looking confused.

"I'm doing fine," he assured her. "In fact, I went to the doctor last week for a check-up and he gave me a clean bill of health. I've even been considering getting back to work."

Choking on a bite of pie, Paloma set down her plate and reached for a glass of water.

"You can't be serious, Bob," she gasped, dabbing at her mouth with a *Happy Thanksgiving* napkin. "You've only just recovered. Anything could happen to you out there."

Genuine fear shone in Paloma's eyes, and for the first time in a long while, Bridget could relate to her stepmother.

She knew how scary it was to have someone you loved working a dangerous job. She'd grown up with a father who was a Major Crimes detective, after all.

And now I have Santino to worry about.

Bridget sighed as she suddenly thought of Aruba and the vacation they'd missed out on, wishing they had at least managed to have Thanksgiving dinner together.

Despite their good intentions and all their best efforts, so far they had spent the entire holiday apart.

After the pie had been eaten and Paloma disappeared into the kitchen to make coffee, Bridget turned to her father.

"I hate to eat and run," she said, throwing a guilty glance toward the kitchen door. "But I was kind of hoping to see Santino. He should be back from his mother's house soon..."

"You go ahead. I'll tell Paloma you said good-bye," he

said in a conspiratorial whisper. "And leave Hank here with me. You can pick him up tomorrow."

Giving the Irish setter a hug good-bye, Bridget hurried out to the Explorer and headed toward the city, but when she called Santino's number, he didn't pick up.

She left a voicemail saying she would call him back later and thought for a minute, then tapped on Gage's number.

They hadn't spoken since Reagan Rivera's murder and subsequent autopsy. It would be good to run the events of the day past Gage. Maybe they could even start a profile for the mysterious Max Bender.

"You aren't still working are you?" Gage asked as he picked up the phone. "Don't think we're going to pay you double time holiday pay."

"Aren't you the one who said my work with the BAU was priceless?" she teased.

Gage snorted.

"I doubt I used those exact words," he protested.

"Do you want an update on Reagan Rivera's homicide, or not?" Bridget asked as she merged onto the highway.

Checking her watch, she calculated the drive time to Stafford County.

"I could be at your house by eight o'clock," she offered.

"I'm on my way home now," he replied. "See you there."

＊ ＊ ＊

Bridget turned onto Mansfield Way just behind Gage's Navigator. She waited as he pulled into his garage, then parked behind him on the driveway.

As she stepped out of the Explorer, she waved to Russell, who had jumped out of the backseat, and then did a double take as Argus climbed out after him.

The behavior analyst had switched out his customary suit and tie for a Georgetown sweatshirt and faded jeans.

Seeing Bridget's surprise, Argus shrugged.

"Gage heard I don't have any family in the area, so he invited me over to his sister's house for Thanksgiving dinner," Argus explained, rubbing a hand over his stomach.

"That was nice of you," Bridget said as Gage appeared behind Argus in the driveway.

Gage raised both eyebrows.

"Nice had nothing to do with it," he said, leading the way into the house. "I thought if I have to suffer through another holiday meal at Anne's house, so should he."

As Bridget and Argus followed Gage into the kitchen, Russell headed for the stairs.

"I'm going up to my room," he called, rubbing his stomach as he'd seen Argus doing.

Before Bridget could take a seat at the table, she noticed Sarge sitting beside his empty food bowl. The cat looked decidedly unhappy.

Crossing to the counter, she picked up a box of kibble and poured some into his bowl, earning a disdainful glare.

"I can't stay long," she said, sinking into a chair next to Argus. "But I thought you'd want to hear the latest."

Gage sat across from her, propping his elbows on the table.

"I've talked to Charlie and seen the news," he said. "It sounds like it's been a hell of a day."

"It has been," Bridget agreed. "Especially for Dale Winslow. Poor man discovered one daughter's decapitated body, then learned his other daughter has been abducted."

She grimaced at the thought of Dale Winslow's pain.

The man had been so worried for his daughter when she and Charlie had interviewed him. He could never have imagined how much worse things were about to get.

But that's how it is when Lyle Grady is around. He destroys everything he touches.

Gage leaned back and cocked his head.

"Charlie mentioned messages on Reagan's phone," he said. "Is that how you found out about Heather?"

"The texts were from a man calling himself Max Bender," she said. "The name might sound familiar. Santino and Decker discovered a man by the same name had started visiting Grady at Abbeyville in the run-up to his hearing."

A frown carved two faint furrows on Argus' otherwise smooth forehead.

"Charlie said he abducted Heather in order to pressure Reagan into helping Grady escape?"

Bridget nodded.

"That's what it sounds like," she agreed. "And we still don't know where she is, or if she's alive. She hasn't been seen for almost four days. And there's been no sign of her boyfriend, either."

"And you went and viewed the autopsy?" Gage said.

"How did you talk Opal into doing an autopsy on Thanksgiving? I bet Cecil wasn't too happy."

An image of the medical examiner's angry face flashed behind Bridget's eyes.

"Opal wants to take Grady and his buddy Bender off the street just as much as we do," she said. "And after what we saw in that house, neither one of us had an appetite."

"So, who do you think killed Reagan?" Gage asked. "Lyle Grady or Max Bender?"

Bridget hesitated, picturing the scene at Reagan's house.

"If I based it solely on what I saw at the scene...at the autopsy, I'd have to say it was Grady," she finally said, thinking of the bracelet tied around Reagan's wrist. "Remember the blood knots Grady left on his other victims?"

The question seemed to take Gage by surprise. His eyes widened, and he nodded.

"There was a blood knot bracelet at Reagan's house?' he asked, sounding surprised.

"It was tied around Reagan's wrist," Bridget confirmed. "I mean, no one knew about Grady's signature outside the investigative team. So, you'd think it had to have been Grady, right? But then we found the hair."

Both Argus and Gage leaned forward.

"The hair?"

"Opal found a strand of hair in Reagan's hand during the autopsy," she explained. "It looked a lot longer and darker than Grady's did in the courthouse."

She shivered at the memory of Grady looking back in the

courtroom and his eyes meeting hers. The image was engraved in her mind. She could clearly picture his light brown, close-cropped hair.

"The good news is that it appears the hair was pulled out by the root, probably during a struggle, so it's likely the lab will be able to get a DNA profile," she said. "In fact, Vivian transported the DNA to the lab personally this afternoon and promised to expedite the profile."

She dug in her purse for her phone and scrolled through her email. With the FBI lab's rapid DNA technology, Bridget knew if could take as little as two hours to get a profile, although she wasn't sure what Vivian had meant by expediting it. Especially on a holiday.

Her heart sank when she saw no email from Vivian.

"No news yet," she said, dropping her phone on the table.

"How about I call and light a fire under her?" Gage said.

Taking out his phone, he tapped on Vivian's number, activated the speaker, and set the phone next to Bridget's.

Vivian answered on the second ring.

"Happy Thanksgiving!" he said. "Thought I'd call and-"

"Cut the crap," she snapped. "I know why you're calling. Luckily, most of the lab staff are workaholics or loners. Which means, I've already managed to get the DNA results."

Bridget's pulse jumped at the forensic examiner's words.

"The DNA profile we extracted from the hair in Reagan's hand did not match Lyle Grady's profile."

Vivian paused as if for dramatic effect.

"But it does match the DNA recovered from under Tammy Vicker's fingernails. It's all in the report, which I'll be sending out shortly. Now, I've got to go."

The connection dropped.

Bridget stared wide-eyed at the phone, momentarily stunned into silence.

After a long beat, she looked up at Gage and Argus.

"So, whoever killed Tammy killed Reagan Rivera, too."

"And based on the texts recovered from Reagan's phone, I'd say Max Bender has to be our number one suspect."

Bridget nodded, not sure how to feel about the information. If Grady had killed Reagan, they would know who they were looking for, but now...

"We don't know who Max Bender is or where he is," she said with a frown. "And we don't know what he'll do next."

"The answer has to be in the data," Argus insisted. "We just have to add in this new information and-"

"And that could take days if not weeks," Bridget insisted.

She met his eyes, imagining both he and Gage were thinking the same thing she was.

Who else will have to die while we try to figure this out?

The question was still running through her head an hour later when she pulled off the Arlington exit and headed toward Santino's apartment.

It was nine o'clock by the time she knocked on his door.

"Happy Thanksgiving," he said, pulling her inside. "I was beginning to worry. I wasn't sure you'd make it."

"I wasn't either, after the day I've had."

Bridget sniffed the fragrant air.

"But I'm here now," she said. "And I don't want to talk about work."

"I couldn't agree more."

Santino led her into the living room where a fire was already ablaze in the fireplace.

"My mother forced me to take some leftovers home and I'm heating them up now. We can open some wine and have a picnic by the fire."

Bridget rested her head on his shoulder and nodded.

"Sounds perfect," she said. "Who needs Aruba, anyway?"

CHAPTER TWENTY-ONE

After Bridget and Argus had gone, Gage scooped up Sarge and held him against his chest, stroking the cat's soft fur as he opened the refrigerator and peered in at the leftovers his sister Anne had insisted he take home.

Poking at a congealed casserole, he moved on to open a small container, wincing at the soggy cranberry sauce inside.

The sound of Russell's video game came from the other room, causing a familiar sense of guilt to wash over him.

The teenager had been up in his room playing video games ever since they'd gotten home from the incredibly awkward holiday dinner. The whole time Russell had sat without joining in the conversation as he pushed around the food on his plate.

Why'd I take him to Anne's house anyway? What was I thinking?

His younger sister had disapproved of him taking in Russell from the start and she took every possible opportunity to make her feelings known.

Over dinner, she'd been thrilled to hear that Kyla Malone

was back in town, making it clear she thought Kenny's son should be with his aunt.

But Gage wasn't about to make any decision just to get his overbearing sister off his back.

Checking his messages, Gage was tempted to return several missed calls from Kyla, then decided he'd do it later after he'd had a chance to unwind.

He needed time to think.

He needed time to figure out what would be best for Russell. That was what mattered. Not what Anne wanted, or Kyla wanted, or even what he wanted.

This was about what Russell needed.

But as he stood in the living room, he saw headlights flash outside the window. He walked over and looked out just as Kyla's rental car pulled into the driveway.

Irritation surged through him at the unwelcome intrusion.

He checked his watch, then jerked open the front door and stepped onto the porch, already rehearsing the royal telling off he would deliver. Then he heard a soft voice call his name.

"Gage?"

Kyla was already climbing out of the car.

She held up a white bakery box.

"I bring a peace offering," she said. "It's a chocolate pecan pie. Kenny and I always begged my mother to make her pie at Thanksgiving, so I thought..."

Her voice wavered, and she paused to steady it.

"I thought now that Mom and Kenny are gone, maybe

Russell would enjoy this," she said, the tremble in her voice nearly breaking Gage's heart.

A tear slipped from her eye, despite her rapid attempt to blink it away, and Gage strode forward and took the bag in one hand and her arm in the other.

"Come on in," he said, steering her toward the door. "I was just wishing I had something sweet to eat."

He pushed through the door and called out in a booming voice that sent Sarge pelting into the other room.

"Russell! Your Aunt Kyla is here! She's got pie!"

Eager footsteps pounded down the stairs, and then Russell was bounding around the kitchen, his quiet, sullen mood replaced with a wide grin.

Gage pulled out plates and forks and cut huge pieces of the sticky, gooey pie, then poured them all glasses of cold milk.

He relaxed back in his chair, enjoying the sweet dessert as Russell filled Kyla in on his new school and the new friends that he'd made so far.

After Gage had finished the last bite on his plate, he stood and carried it to the sink. Kyla jumped up to help him clear the dishes, sending a pile of folders cascading to the floor.

As she bent to pick them up, Gage heard a startled gasp.

Looking around, he saw her staring down in horror at the scattered contents of the Backroads Butcher case file. A photo taken at Tammy Vicker's crime scene lay face up on the floor.

Gage rushed forward to cover the photo of the reporter's

decapitated body before Russell could see it.

He plucked it up and slid it back into the folder with the rest of the documents, then turned to see Kyla still standing frozen in place.

"Russell, you go on up and brush your teeth," Gage said, waving away the boy's objections. "Aunt Kyla and I need to talk about a few things."

Reluctantly, Russell headed toward the stairs. Once he was gone, Kyla drew in a deep, shaky breath.

"Hasn't my nephew been exposed to enough violence and death already?" she said in a low voice. "I understand you have a job to do, but-"

She hesitated as Gage's phone began buzzing on the table.

Gage looked down at the display, his eyes widening as he saw Roger Calloway's name.

"That's the Special Agent in Charge of the Washington Field Office," he said apologetically. "I really need to take it."

Grabbing up the phone, he walked into the living room to answer the call. If the SAC was calling after nine on a holiday, it couldn't be good.

"Have you seen the news?" Roger demanded. "The press is claiming the Bureau's letting a serial killer run around killing people. They're saying the Butcher is back, and that he killed Reagan Rivera. It's gone national."

Gage forced himself to stay calm despite Calloway's accusatory tone.

"That's not true. It's irresponsible reporting," Gage

objected. "DNA at the scene doesn't match Grady, so-"

"I don't need a lecture on how unfair the world is," the SAC snapped irritably. "What I need is for you and your team at the BAU to provide my team at the Washington Field office with a profile on Reagan Rivera's killer."

Sensing movement behind him, Gage looked over his shoulder to see Kyla standing in the hall.

"The media is stirring up the public," Calloway thundered on. "It's reaching fever pitch, and-"

"We're already working on it," Gage interjected, turning away, raising his own voice in an attempt to be heard. "I've even brought in Bridget Bishop to help."

It took another five minutes to convince Calloway they were doing everything possible and to get him off the phone. By the time Gage returned to the kitchen, it was empty.

Hurrying to the front door, he opened it and looked out at the driveway, but Kyla's rental car was gone.

Feeling something soft rub against his legs, Gage looked down to see Sarge standing in the doorway beside him.

Scooping the tomcat up with a sigh, he went back inside.

* * *

Gage took a long sip from his glass of merlot and leaned back on the sofa. The late news was on, and thus far reports on Reagan Rivera's murder and Heather Winslow's disappearance had dominated all the local channels.

A faint knock sounded on the front door just as a high-school photo of Heather Winslow appeared on the screen.

Switching off the television, Gage jumped up and crossed to the foyer, hoping Kyla had come back to finish their discussion.

But when he looked through the peephole, he saw a flash of red hair. Argus was back.

"I added the initial data on Reagan Rivera's murder into the cluster analysis algorithm I'd created during the Backroads Butcher investigation," the analyst said as soon as Gage opened the door. "The results showed a statistically significant probability that–"

"Argus, it's almost midnight, and a holiday, remember?" Gage interrupted, looking at his watch. "Don't you ever stop...or sleep?"

He lifted a hand to stop the flood of words spilling from Argus's mouth, then turned toward the hall.

"At least cut the jargon and dumb it down for me a little."

He pushed his way into the kitchen, sinking into a chair by the window. Argus trailed him into the room like an anxious puppy. The analyst dropped his laptop bag on the table and pulled out a creased folder.

"All you really need to know about the algorithm is that it highlights connections or similarities between victims and crimes."

Argus spoke slowly as if talking to a child.

"And in this case, the algorithm found that all the homicides related to our investigation had one important similarity: the killer's signature. Even in the two homicides where DNA was matched to someone other than Grady, the same signature was left behind."

Gage cocked his head, trying to follow along.

"The Butcher's signature was only revealed to the press and the public at Grady's trial," Argus added. "Which was *after* Tammy Vicker was killed."

Gage thought back to the media circus that had played out around the investigation and trial.

"From what I remember, pretty much everyone knew that the Backroads Butcher abducted his victims off a backroad and chopped off their–"

"No, no, no...I'm not talking about his M.O.," Argus interjected, lifting his arm, and gesturing to his wrist. "I said his *signature*."

Gage blinked when he saw the blood knot bracelet tied around Argus' wrist.

He shook his head to dislodge the memory of the looped and twisted strips of leather that had been tied around Tammy's delicate wrist when she was found.

Only a handful of people working on the investigation had been told about the bracelets, and the information hadn't been released to the press or the public.

The only others who'd known about them prior to the trial had been certain family members who'd been asked if they could identify the bracelets as a personal item.

But none had known where they'd come from.

"A bracelet similar to this one was found on every victim," Argus said, rubbing a finger over the twisted leather. "The strips were tied into the same style of knot.

It's Grady's signature. It's the way he marked his victims."

"Right," Gage said, conceding the point. "We tried to keep the bracelets out of the news. It was a high-profile case from the start, so we figured we might get a few false confessions. We wanted to have something only the killer would know."

Memories of the panic in the community started to seep back into Gage's mind. He'd almost forgotten the mass hysteria that had surrounded the Butcher case.

The discovery of a stream of headless bodies discarded along the quiet backroads of Virginia had been national news.

"Right. Information about the Butcher's signature was purposely held back," Argus said. "Only a few people in the investigation knew, and they were sworn to secrecy."

"Okay, let's assume the blood knot is Grady's signature. How does that help us identify Max Bender? How does it prove who killed Tammy Vicker and Reagan Rivera?"

Argus produced a disappointed frown as if Gage was being purposely thick-headed.

"Tammy's killer must have known about the Butcher's signature when he left a bracelet on her wrist. Which means he had this information *before* it was released to the press or the public at the trial."

Gage felt his stomach tighten as he realized what Argus was saying.

"So, our guy left the bracelet to make it look as if Grady committed the murders," Gage murmured. "Which means he had access to confidential information in the Butcher investigation before we arrested Grady."

His words earned a smile from Argus.

"That's right. He could have been working the case, or-"

Gage held up a hand to stop Argus.

"Don't tell me you think an agent or a cop was involved," he said, shaking his head. "Believe me, that line of investigation won't earn you any friends in the Bureau. Not in a high-profile case like this one."

"I'm not here to make friends," Argus shot back. "I'm here to find the truth, wherever it leads."

The resolve in Argus' voice told Gage it would be pointless to argue. He wouldn't listen to anything but the data.

"Fair enough," he said with a sigh. "But this is serious. If we start investigating fellow agents and officers, we need to have more justification than just your algorithm."

Seeming not to have heard him, Argus reached into his bag and pulled out a folder.

"We won't just need to investigate the agents involved," he said. "There are other ways the unsub could have gotten the information about the blood knots."

He opened the folder to reveal a spreadsheet.

"Using my algorithm, and the old case files, I've compiled a list of people who potentially knew about the bracelets," he said. "People Grady might have confided in. His family, friends, and people he worked with at the time."

Gage felt his shoulders stiffen as Argus continued.

"With the first few victims, their next-of-kin was shown the bracelet when they identified the victim's body," Argus said. "So, they are on here, too. It's possible-"

"Reverend Abernathy," Gage said as his eyes fell on a name near the top of the list.

His pulse instantly kicked up a notch.

"I told you and Bridget that man wasn't in his right mind. If he knew about the bracelet..."

Mind whirling, he began to pace the room.

Just because Abernathy was a preacher didn't mean he was above suspicion. Gage had seen enough bad men hiding behind religion to dispel that myth.

And just because Abernathy lost his children to murder, doesn't mean he isn't capable of killing someone else's child.

Gage had seen his share of broken and abused victims turn their pain into rage and hate. Half the criminals and killers he'd interviewed had once been victims themselves.

Hell, who knows what I would be willing to do if someone killed Russell and carried off his head?

The thought started his feet moving back to the living room. Back to his phone.

"I need to call Charlie. She needs to set up a task force meeting for first thing tomorrow morning."

He checked his watch, hoping she was still awake.

"We need a plan to question the reverend."

"What about the rest of the list?" Argus asked.

Gage nodded grimly.

"Yes, we'll recommend that everyone on the list is interviewed," he agreed. "But your data is telling us that a family member might be involved, and my gut is telling me the reverend's not right in the head. Sounds like a combination we can't ignore."

He was already picking up his phone.

"Now, go get some rest. I'll see you tomorrow morning."

CHAPTER TWENTY-TWO

Charlie held the phone to her ear and tried to suppress a yawn. She was finding it hard to focus on Gage's muddled explanation of Argus' latest algorithm. The one thing she did understand was his request to call an emergency task force meeting first thing in the morning.

Looking at her watch, she saw it was now midnight.

"Well, it is short notice," she said, trying to keep the sarcasm out of her voice. "But I was planning to pull the team together tomorrow in any case. I'll add Argus' algorithm to the top of the agenda, and I'll see you then."

She ended the call before he could respond, too tired to talk about work or algorithms or anything else.

As she walked into her bedroom, Charlie stopped in the doorway, and stared at the empty bed, wishing Hale was there to tell her everything would look better in the morning.

He had a way of making her believe the words were true.

But he'd already checked into a hotel near the hospice, planning to stay close by for as long as Bea Allen held on.

Turning off the light, Charlie crossed to the bed and climbed under the covers, hoping to erase the stress and fatigue of the day with at least a few hours of sleep.

But as she lay in the dark and closed her eyes, her mind returned to the hospice, and the look on Hale's face when she'd stopped by to see him and Bea on her way home.

He had been sitting by the bedside reading aloud and hadn't noticed her when she'd walked into the room.

Her heart squeezed in her chest as she remembered the deep, soothing sound of his voice and the weariness in his eyes as he'd closed the book and motioned for her to follow him out into the hall.

"I didn't know you were an Agatha Christie fan," she'd said, craning her neck to read the title as the door swung shut behind him.

"I am now," Hale had replied with a half-smile, holding up the tattered copy of *Appointment with Death.* "This is the fourth one I've read to her so far. Bea has converted me."

Charlie had lingered as long as she could, hating to leave him, but knowing she had no choice. Bea could pass at any time, and Hale had vowed to be by her side when she did.

He hadn't been there for his own mother when the time had come, and he wasn't about to suffer through that kind of grief and regret again.

Turning onto her side in the empty bed, Charlie plumped the pillow under her head, trying to get comfortable. But the cold sheets and suffocating darkness seemed to close in on her like a tomb.

With a sigh of frustration, she threw off the covers and slid out of bed. Wrapping her robe around her, she returned to the living room, switched on the television, and poured herself a glass of wine.

It's a holiday, after all. Time to celebrate, right?

As she sank onto the sofa, switching the channel to the local news, Heather Winslow's high-school yearbook photo appeared on the screen. There was no mention of her handsome, young boyfriend.

They still hadn't been able to reach Ryder Forbes' parents in Fiji, so for the time being they'd been obligated to keep his name and photo out of the press.

Charlie sighed, feeling sorry for the couple, who would be in for a dreadful shock when they got back from the island.

Draining her glass, she reached again for the bottle.

* * *

Charlie was operating on two hours of sleep and three cups of coffee the next morning when she arrived at Quantico.

Making her way to the BAU conference room that Gage had reserved for their emergency meeting, she saw Bridget standing just inside the door.

"I guess you got my meeting request," Charlie said, setting her bag down at the head of the conference table. "I wasn't sure anyone would come, seeing that I sent it at two in the morning."

"You look tired," Bridget said, stopping to study the tell-tale circles under her eyes. "Is it Hale? Has his friend taken a turn for the worse?"

Swallowing hard, Charlie nodded.

"The doctor said Bea could pass at any time, so Hale's staying at the hospice until...well, until the end."

She still felt a little awkward about her teary-eyed conversation with Bridget the night before. She wasn't used to losing control of her emotions at work, but she knew the psychologist would understand.

"It must be very hard for him," Bridget said quietly. "He'll need you when it's all over."

The image of Hale's tired, handsome face at the hospice the night before hovered in Charlie's mind, but she pushed it away as Argus came into the room.

Noting his wrinkled shirt, mismatched tie, and bloodshot eyes, Charlie suspected the analyst hadn't gotten any more sleep than she had.

"I know Gage told you about my theory," Argus said, pulling out a sheet of paper. "This is an initial list of people who potentially knew about the blood knot bracelets."

He lowered his voice.

"Gage has some crazy idea that Reverend Abernathy may be involved, but I'm thinking our guy could be one of Grady's friends or family members, or even someone who worked on the investigation."

"You mean, like a cop or an agent?" Charlie asked.

Her chest tightened at the idea. She'd had to investigate and even arrest fellow agents in the past. It wasn't something she'd ever hoped to repeat.

"Could be anyone who knew about Grady's signature," Argus said. "That information was purposely held back and wasn't in the news. It didn't come out until the trial. By then, we were no longer keeping it under wraps. We had our guy."

"But we can't dismiss the theory that Grady had a partner, can we?" Charlie said. "Maybe someone who was there with him during Tammy Vicker's murder?"

Argus and Bridget both shook their heads.

"That doesn't really fit Grady's profile," Bridget said. "He worked alone, I'm almost sure of it."

She frowned as if still considering the possibility.

"And I don't think he knew who killed Tammy during his first trial," she said. "Or if he did know, I'm guessing he had no way to prove it without admitting he'd killed the others."

Wagging his head, Argus quickly agreed.

"If he'd had a partner back then, I feel sure he'd have pointed the investigation in their direction," he said. "There's no way Grady would have stayed quiet and taken the hit for someone else."

Charlie thought of Lyle Grady's sullen face and shuddered. Did any of them really know what the Butcher was capable of doing if cornered?

"I'm thinking Grady only figured out who killed Tammy, or at least how to prove it, recently," Bridget said. "It must have been around the time Reagan Rivera took on his case. Around the time Max Bender showed up at Abbeyville."

"So why did Max Bender go to Abbeyville?" Charlie wondered aloud. "What did he and Grady talk about?"

She looked expectantly at Argus, hoping he had an answer.

"That's the million-dollar question," he said. "Unfortunately, I don't have an algorithm for that."

"So, all we've got to go on is your theory then," Charlie said, regarding him with a dubious expression. "We have to assume Tammy's killer knew about the blood knot bracelets?"

Bridget and Argus looked at each other and nodded.

"Well, Gage's idea that Abernathy could be involved sounds farfetched to me," Charlie said. "But of course, we'll have to follow up since he's on your list. We'll look into Abernathy and the other victims' family members, but that still leaves Grady's known associates, and the people working the investigation."

She studied the list.

"Looks like we're all on here," she said, glancing up at Argus. "Including you."

"Yep, my name is on there," he said, sounding almost proud. "Which is why I've already given Vivian Burke in the FBI lab a DNA sample."

He rubbed a hand over his red hair.

"She was very thorough. Took a blood, saliva, and a hair sample. I think she'll confirm I'm not a match to the killer." he said. "And I've made sure that everyone I talked with about the bracelets is on that list."

Charlie grimaced at the thought of asking everyone on the long list to give a DNA sample and provide names of anyone they had talked to about the Butcher's signature.

"I guess I better ask Calloway for some extra agents," she said. "Getting information out of everyone on here will be hard enough. Getting DNA will be near impossible."

CHAPTER TWENTY-THREE

Bridget glanced at the conference room door, surprised to see Santino standing in the hallway. He hadn't mentioned he'd be at Charlie's emergency task force meeting that morning, and she was glad to see that he and Decker had managed to make it over to Quantico in time.

"As you all know by now, Lyle Grady's lawyer, Reagan Rivera was found dead in her Mount Destiny home yesterday morning," Charlie said, standing at the front of the room. "An autopsy was performed in the afternoon, and her death has been ruled a homicide by decapitation. DNA evidence found during Reagan's autopsy was not a match to Grady."

She paused, giving Santino and Decker a chance to find seats and settle in at the end of the table, then continued.

"While the DNA wasn't a match with Grady, it did match DNA obtained from the Tammy Vicker homicide," Charlie said. "Which means it's likely that the same unsub killed both women."

Bridget glanced toward Santino, interested in his reaction to the revelation, but he didn't seem surprised.

"At the crime scene, we recovered Reagan's phone, which had incriminating texts from a sender using the name Max Bender," Charlie said. "The texts indicate Heather Winslow, Reagan's sister, has been abducted and is in danger. Accordingly, we've issued a missing person alert and have set up a hotline, as I'm sure you've seen on the news."

Gesturing to the smartboard behind her, she lifted a small, white remote. An image of Heather Winslow's missing person poster appeared alongside a headshot of a handsome young man with brooding eyes.

"Heather was last seen with her boyfriend, Ryder Forbes. We haven't been able to contact his next of kin, so his disappearance hasn't yet been announced to the press."

Charlie exhaled heavily as she surveyed the room.

"Thus, our mission has been expanded," she said. "In addition to Lyle Grady, we're now also looking for Heather's abductor, Max Bender, the prime suspect in the deaths of Tammy Vicker and Regan Rivera."

Clearing her throat, Charlie turned to Bridget and handed her the little remote.

"Based on this new information, we've asked the BAU to start working on a profile for Max Bender," she said. "Bridget is here to share what they've got so far."

Bridget carried a folder to the front of the room.

"Our first goal is to find out everything we can about Max Bender," she said. "So far, we don't know very much. Thanks to Santino and Decker, we do know the alias he's using, and that he used stolen information to obtain a driver's license, which he presented at Abbeyville State Prison. If he's used this alias elsewhere, it could lead us to him."

She opened the folder on the table and scanned the document inside, not sure how much help it would be.

Glancing at Argus, she decided to start with the most crucial evidence they had: Grady's signature.

"While it will take time to come up with a complete profile," Bridget said, "we do know that our unsub was familiar with the Butcher's signature prior to the public release of that information at trial."

She pointed toward the smartboard which displayed a close-up image of the blood knot bracelet found on Justine Abernathy's wrist.

"Most of you will remember the leather bracelets left on each victim," Bridget said.

She caught Shannon Larkin's eye.

"For those new to the case, it's enough to say that a very similar bracelet to the one on the screen was found on each of the Butcher's suspected victims. The bracelets were fashioned out of leather strips and tied into an intricate knot, known as a blood knot."

Clicking on the small remote in her hand, Bridget moved to the next image.

Before she could continue, Decker spoke up.

"How would the unsub have known?" he asked. "Are you thinking there was a leak in the investigation? Someone running their mouth for the benefit of the press?"

Bridget hesitated. Before she could respond, Charlie

jumped in.

"We'll certainly be looking into that possibility, Decker," she said. "But please, give Bridget a chance to finish."

The big blonde man nodded and sat back in his chair, turning his eyes back to the smartboard.

"Argus compiled an initial list of people who knew about the bracelets," Bridget said. "It includes relevant investigating agents and officers, known associates of Lyle Grady, as well as certain family members of the victims."

"It'll be our job to interview each of the people on this list. We'll need to find out if they told anyone about the bracelets," Charlie chimed in. "If so, we will talk to each of the people they told, and so on. And for the men on the list, we'll need to ask for a DNA sample, so that we can eliminate them as a suspect."

"Why just the men?" Larkin asked.

"The DNA samples taken during the autopsies for Tammy and Reagan confirm that the killer was a man."

Decker leaned over and muttered something in Santino's ear. She tried to read Santino's expression, but he didn't give anything away.

"Interviewing fellow agents and grieving family members is always difficult," Charlie said. "You'll need to be tactful, but also persistent. This isn't just about seeking justice for Tammy and Reagan. It's about saving lives. Whoever killed these women is still out there."

Santino sat forward and cleared his throat.

"I hate to state the obvious, but some of us are on this list," he said. "Doesn't that present a conflict of interest?"

"I've asked Calloway to assign some extra agents from the Washington field office to help with that," Charlie assured him. "They will manage the interview and follow-up for anyone on the list that is in this room. I'm sure we will all cooperate fully."

She paused and looked toward Decker, as if expecting a protest, but he remained silent.

"Okay, then," she said. "Check your assignments and let's get started."

Santino stood and pointed toward a name and address midway down the list.

"Decker and I are heading over to West Virginia this afternoon to follow up on a possible sighting of Grady," he said. "So, we can talk to Michelle Ewing's mother. Her place is just over the state line."

Bridget winced at the mention of Patsy Ewing. The single mother had been devastated to lose her only daughter, Michelle during the Butcher's deadly spree. Her aguish during the trial had been palpable.

The memory brought a sudden rush of anger as Bridget thought of all the pain Lyle Grady had left in his wake.

And his reign of terror isn't over yet.

"Okay, I'll add Patsy Ewing to your list, Santino," Charlie agreed as everyone began to gather their things. "Let me know how it goes."

"Who's assigned to Reverend Abernathy?" Gage asked.

"I am," Charlie said quickly. "Bridget and I will go over to Mount Destiny this afternoon, and we'll stop by the church. Now, if you'll excuse me, I need to update

Calloway."

As Bridget slid her laptop back into her bag, she felt Santino come up beside her.

"You okay?" he asked in a low voice. "You seem upset."

"I was just thinking about Michelle Ewing and her mother," Bridget said, unable to summon a smile. "Please give Patsy my regards when you talk to her."

Santino studied her tense face, then nodded.

As he turned away, Bridget fought the impulse to reach out and pull him back.

She knew he and Decker were unlikely to make it back until the following day, and she wanted to tell him to call her later. Wanted to remind him to be careful.

She'd grown up with a detective as a father, and she knew from all his stories that law enforcement never knew what might happen when they showed up unannounced to conduct an interview.

Her father had been shot at, shouted at, and even had dogs set on him. And Santino would be approaching a grieving family. Who knew what might happen?

But there was nothing to be done about it. All she could do was watch as Santino turned and walked away.

CHAPTER TWENTY-FOUR

Santino checked the GPS again, then turned his red Chevy onto a narrow country road lined on either side with a thick collection of weathered trees and the occasional gravel and dirt path leading into the dark, overgrown woods beyond.

"You sure we're not lost, man?"

Decker scratched at the pale stubble on his chin.

"Cause it sure looks like we're in the middle of nowhere."

Tapping on the brakes, Santino pointed to a neat, two-story house with a wide porch and a sloped roof that sat just off the road, half-hidden from view by an ancient oak tree.

As the pickup pulled onto the driveway, Santino tried to recall the few details he could remember about Michelle Ewing's homicide. Like all of Grady's other victims, the schoolgirl had suffered a violent and terrifying end.

As Santino brought the Chevy to a stop, he looked toward the porch where a woman stood in jeans and a thick sweater.

He instantly recognized Patsy Ewing from the trial.

The last four years hadn't been kind.

The woman wasn't yet middle-aged, but it looked to Santino as if she had been worn down by too much grief.

As the men climbed out of the truck, Patsy beckoned them forward as if she'd been expecting their visit.

"That sure was quick," she said as they drew closer.

"What do you mean by *quick*?" Santino called, exchanging a glance with Decker.

The woman moved to the top of the stairs.

"Well, I just called the police less than ten minutes ago and here you are," she said. "That seems quick to me."

"We aren't police," Santino said. "We're with the U.S. Marshals Service. We're here about Lyle Grady."

Patsy froze in place, and her face hardened.

"I thought when that man escaped he might come here in person," she said, staring Santino straight in the eyes. "I was kind of hoping he would, you know? I'm ready for him."

Moving one hand toward the wooden banister, she picked up a rifle that had been propped against the post.

Decker grabbed for his Glock, but Santino waved him back without taking his eyes off Patsy.

"Now, you don't want to go and do anything like that, Ms. Ewing," Santino said, slowly walking forward. "Killing a person changes you. I wouldn't recommend it."

"Oh, I want to do it, alright," she said, but she was already lowering the rifle. "Of course, if that box did come from *him*, it means that he was too much of a coward to show up. He probably knew I'd be waiting."

She stepped aside to reveal a cardboard box on the porch.

"It got delivered today. The regular mailman brought it."

Santino eyed the box, seeing right away that it had already been opened, although the flaps covered the contents.

"It's a skull," she said as he started up the steps. "Probably just a prank. You'd be surprised how heartless some of these online trolls can be. One of them must have found my address."

But something in the woman's eyes told Santino she didn't think the skull was a prank.

"You put the rifle down and I'll take a look," he said.

Looking down at her hand, Patsy stared at the rifle for a long beat, then propped it back against the post.

As Decker moved up closer behind him, Santino stepped warily toward the box, expecting something to jump out at him at any minute.

Leaning over, he pulled back one of the flaps, and then the other. Peering over his shoulder, Decker let out a high-pitched whistle.

The skull inside was real, as was the bracelet resting beside it. Two strips of leather tied into a blood knot.

"That's no prank," Decker said, dropping to his knees next to the box. "This is the real thing."

"Don't touch it," Santino warned, putting a hand on Decker's shoulder. "Leave it right there until the evidence response team arrives."

Decker sat back on his heels and whistled again, this time under his breath.

"Lyle Grady sure is one crazy mother-"

"That's enough," Santino said, cutting him off with a warning look as Patsy swayed on her feet.

"Ma'am, we're gonna need the FBI to collect this. They can test it in their lab to find out if these remains belong to your daughter," he said. "And while we're waiting, would you mind if I ask you a few questions?"

* * *

Santino and Decker sat with Patsy in the kitchen as they waited for the FBI's evidence response team to come and collect the skull.

"Has Lyle Grady contacted you since he was incarcerated, or after he escaped custody?" Santino asked.

Patsy shook her head.

"I haven't heard a peep from that monster," she said. "I send him a letter every so often asking him what he did with my daughter's head. Guess I won't have to do that anymore."

A tear trembled at the edge of her eye but didn't fall.

"The bracelet in the box. Did that look familiar to you?"

This time Patsy nodded.

"That was on Michelle's body when I went to see her in the morgue. The medical examiner said it was on her wrist when she was found, but I'd never seen it before. I found out during the trial that the Butcher had put it on her."

"Did you ever tell anyone about the bracelet?" Santino asked. "I mean, before the trial?"

"Well, no one but that reporter," she said. "The one who

went and got herself killed."

Santino froze.

"You mean Tammy Vicker?"

"That's right," Patsy agreed. "She came by a few months after they found Michelle's body. Started asking questions and showing me pictures. Now that I think about it, she had a picture of that bracelet, too."

Plucking a tissue from a box on the table, she blew her nose and wiped at her eyes.

"She just kinda pushed her way in," Patsy said, sounding angry at the memory. "I was awful mad. I asked how she'd gotten the pictures."

"What did she say?"

Patsy sighed as if it made her tired just to think of it.

"She told me she had an *inside source.*"

Her mouth tightened as she said the words.

"That's how she said it. Like she was in some kind of movie or something," Patsy said. "Then she had the nerve to ask me for an on-camera interview. Well, I told her where she could go."

Leaning forward, Decker propped his big elbows on the kitchen table and narrowed his eyes.

"Did this *inside source* have a name?" he asked.

Patsy shrugged.

"She didn't say. Or if she did, I can't remember. All I can remember is being shocked when I saw later that she'd ended up being the Butcher's last victim."

"Did you ever tell any of the investigators that Tammy Vicker had come by here?" Decker asked.

She looked surprised.

"No one ever asked," she said. "At least, not back then."

"What do you mean...not back then?"

A flash of remembered annoyance filled her face.

"Well, this man came by here a while back. He was taking pictures of the house and trampling through my bushes. When I asked him what he was doing, he said research."

She rolled her eyes.

"Turns out he's one of those true crime podcasters. I never listen to that stuff, but my sister's always going on about it."

Santino had a sinking feeling that he knew who she must be talking about.

"The guy said he was making a podcast about the Backroads Butcher and wanted to interview me on the next episode. I refused, of course, although I did end up answering some of his questions. He was a persistent man."

"Was his name Chase Grafton?" Santino asked.

A slow simmer of anger had already started up in his chest.

"That's right," Patsy said. "His podcast is called *Chasing Killers*, I think. He claimed it was number one on the charts."

"Did he ask you about the bracelet?" Santino asked.

Patsy hesitated.

"No, not that I can remember," she finally said. "But he did ask me if I'd ever met any of the other victims and that made me think about Tammy Vicker."

"What'd you tell him?" Decker asked, sounding impatient.

Patsy's back stiffened.

"Well, I told him she came by. I told him what I told you."

"Can you remember anything else that Tammy said?" Santino asked. "Anything at all. It could be important."

Patsy hesitated, then shook her head.

"I'm sorry," she said. "I was such a mess back then, it's a miracle I remember her stopping by at all seeing that I was drunk half the time and out of my mind the other half."

She tried to smile as she dabbed under her eyes.

"Grief will do that to you, you know," she said softly.

"Yes, ma'am, it will," Santino agreed. "I lost my wife a few years back, so I can imagine what you've gone through."

Patsy's face softened in sympathy. As she reached out and laid a hand on his arm, Santino felt Decker's eyes on him.

He didn't make it a practice to talk about his personal life at work. Only a few colleagues knew about Maribel and their unborn child.

"I'm so sorry," Patsy said. "Can I ask how she died?"

A familiar ache pulsed inside Santino's chest at the remembered image of Maribel's lifeless body.

"She was murdered."

His throat constricted around the words, but somehow

saying them to this woman made the truth easier to bear.

She had lived with the same pain he had endured for years. She was one of the few people that could truly understand what he was going through.

They'd both faced their worst nightmare. And they'd managed to keep going. That was something.

"I'm so sorry," Patsy said again.

Then a van pulled into the driveway.

Santino jumped up to greet the FBI special response team that had arrived to collect the skull, hoping it would provide a clue as to where Grady was and who'd been helping him.

CHAPTER TWENTY-FIVE

L yle Grady slept fitfully in the driver's seat of the old delivery van, hidden from the world by the thin, rusted walls of a defunct storage facility outside Providence Gap. Streams of light filtered through the dented metal roof, casting mottled shadows on the van's windshield.

Slowly opening his eyes, Grady stretched and looked around, then smiled as he remembered where he was.

Years ago, after Bridget Bishop had unmasked him as the Butcher, he'd hidden the Mount Destiny Delivery Express van in one of the abandoned storage units, secured the flimsy door with a lock, and had gone on the run.

Eventually, the U.S. Marshals had caught up to him and he'd been carted off to his dismal cell in Abbeyville.

But he'd never completely given up hope of getting out, and he'd figured the old van would still be there if he ever returned for it. After all, who would think there was anything of value inside the derelict building or the battered van?

Adrenaline had coursed through his veins like lightning when he'd opened the storage unit earlier that week to see the van sitting there just as he'd left it, his secrets safe inside.

And while the van's engine hadn't turned over right away, he'd fully expected some work would be needed.

Now, after only four days and a few stolen spare parts, he'd gotten the old van running again.

Sitting up straight in the driver's seat, he gripped the steering wheel and squeezed hard, glad to be back behind the wheel where he belonged.

His eyes landed on Officer Pickering's phone. It was on the dashboard where he'd thrown it earlier, although he'd turned it off just in case the feds thought to track it.

He'd been tempted to ditch it altogether but decided it may come in useful in the future if he needed a back-up.

Digging in his pocket, Grady pulled out his burner phone, liking the smooth feel of it in his hand.

Of course, it wasn't the phone the man calling himself Bender had left for him in the silver Honda outside the courthouse. He wasn't a total fool.

Within an hour of his escape, Grady had dumped both the phone and the car Bender had provided.

He knew Bender couldn't be trusted.

Just like the name he was using, every other word out of the man's mouth was a lie.

And soon, if Grady had his way, everyone would know it.

Tapping in the number Bender had given him, he held it to his ear, then cursed as the call rolled to voicemail.

"You've got twenty-four hours left to get me the money and ID," he growled into the phone. "I'll call tomorrow to arrange the time and place, and you'd better pick up, or the next call I'll make will be to the FBI hotline I keep hearing about on the radio."

Ending the call, he threw the burner phone onto the dashboard next to Officer Pickering's device.

Catching sight of his own angry face in the grimy rearview mirror, he forced his face muscles to relax.

"You're a lucky bastard," he muttered to his reflection. "Six months ago, you had no chance of being a free man ever again. And now here you are."

He thought back to the day everything had changed.

That day six months ago when out of the blue, he'd had a visitor. Someone who had unwittingly offered him his freedom, and the chance for a whole new future.

And tomorrow, I'll have enough money to hit the road again.

The thought of being back on the road in his van sent a surge of excitement through him. Who knew where he would go and what he would do?

There was a big world out there to explore.

So many roads to drive. So many young women needing a ride.

Grady looked in the rearview mirror again and smiled. His new adventure would have to wait just a little while longer.

First, he had an errand to run.

He crawled out of his seat and into the back of the van, stepping over the blanket he had laid out, and kicking aside the discarded food wrappers and beer bottles he'd collected over the last few days.

Rummaging through a stack of boxes against the wall,

Grady found the photo box he'd been looking for.

As he opened it, several photos fell out.

One landed face up on the van floor. It showed Tammy Vicker standing under a streetlamp, her bright blonde hair brassy in the artificial light, her arms around a man who had his back to the camera.

Grady studied the photo and then stuffed it back in the box before rifling through the others.

He found one that showed the man's face clearly and held it up to the light from his phone to get a better look.

This is it. This is the money shot.

He laughed as he pictured the same photo displayed for all to see on the nightly news.

Slipping the photo into the back pocket of his pants, he gathered the rest of the photos and stuffed them back into the box. He hesitated before he replaced the cover, staring down at a close-up shot of Tammy's face.

The reporter had gotten what she deserved, even if he hadn't been the one to give it to her.

She'd been asking too many questions and getting so very close. He'd impulsively followed her from the television station after work one night and seen her meet the man.

After that, he'd never been able to get close enough to grab her. She'd always been with her camera crew or with the mystery man she was obviously seeing on the side.

After her murder, Grady had suspected right away that her secret lover must have been the one to kill her.

But who would have believed him?

The pictures by themselves didn't prove murder. And besides, the incriminating photos had been locked in the van with his other treasures, out of reach.

Putting the lid back on the photo box, he returned it to the pile, then crossed to the old wooden steamer trunk he'd wedged into the corner.

The trunk had belonged to his grandfather. When he'd found it in his mother's attic, full of musty linens and yellowed photographs, he'd known just what to do with it.

Slowly opening the lid, he looked inside, savoring the rush of power and pleasure that rolled through him when he saw the two skulls neatly arranged along the bottom.

There had been seven to begin with, but after mailing out five surprise packages, these were the only two left. The most important ones.

He'd saved the best for last.

Reaching into the trunk with both hands, he pulled out his final delivery, holding the skulls side-by-side.

There would be no packaging or mailing these.

No, this time, I'll make a personal delivery.

CHAPTER TWENTY-SIX

Bridget sat in the passenger's seat of Charlie's Expedition, speeding toward Mount Destiny. She stared out the window at the passing cars with brooding eyes, wondering for the millionth time that day where Heather could be.

Is she still alive or has she suffered the same fate as her sister?

Flyers for the missing girl were already going up on every corner, and the pretty coed's face had appeared on every broadcast that morning, along with a plea for any information to be called into the hotline.

But so far, they had no idea where she could be, and still didn't know the true identity of the man who'd taken her.

There was only one thing that she and Charlie could do to help Heather. They needed to find Max Bender.

So, why are we on the way to interview Reverend Abernathy?

Looking over at Charlie, Bridget sighed.

"Don't you think this is a waste of time?" she said.

Charlie shrugged.

"Gage is convinced the reverend's unbalanced, although I can't see him killing anyone. But he could have told someone about the blood knot," she said. "Maybe even someone at the mental hospital he was in. And Gage made me promise to put him at the top of our list, so..."

"So, we're wasting a whole afternoon," Bridget replied.

She looked over at Charlie's fixed expression and sighed, sensing she wasn't going to talk her way out of the task.

"You may be right," Charlie conceded. "But we promised Gage that we'd talk to Abernathy. So, let's just get it over with and we can move on to the next person on our list."

Opening the folder on her lap, Bridget ran her finger down the list of names.

"After Abernathy, we've got Alistair Kennedy," she said with a notable lack of enthusiasm. "Driving to the Mount Destiny Courthouse to question him seems like a waste of resources, as well. Might as well take time to interrogate Judge Hawthorne while we're at it."

Charlie didn't laugh at the idea as Bridget had expected.

"Unfortunately, the judge is on our list, too," she said, reaching over to tap on a name further down the page.

"After Michelle Ewing's body was found, we got a tip on a known sex offender in the area and submitted a search warrant request. Hawthorne signed it. The blood knot bracelet, or any materials that could be used to make it, were listed in the warrant as items to be seized if found."

Dreading the thought of interrogating the disagreeable judge, Bridget felt her phone buzz in her pocket.

It was Santino.

Bridget put him on speaker phone.

"We had an interesting talk with Patsy Ewing," he said. "Turns out that just before Tammy Vicker died, she attempted to interview Patsy and asked her about the blood knot bracelet. She claimed a *close inside source* on the investigation told her about it."

Bridget and Charlie looked at each other with wide eyes.

"That's not all," Santino said. "We also found out Chase Grafton went out to West Virginia to see Patsy about six months ago. Just about the time he started visiting Grady."

The podcaster's name elicited a scowl from Bridget.

"What did *he* want with Patsy Ewing?" she asked.

"Chase said he was planning a podcast series on the Backroads Butcher and was conducting research," Santino said. "During his visit, Patsy told him about her meeting with Tammy. She also mentioned that the reporter had been close to someone on the investigation."

"Maybe *that's* how Chase convinced the Butcher to grant him an interview," Charlie said, switching lanes to pass a slow-moving minivan. "He used Tammy's claim that she had an inside source."

The thought of Chase Grafton's involvement irritated Bridget. She wondered what else the serial killer had shared with Chase during their meetings.

Maybe I shouldn't have deleted all of Chase's voicemails.

"Sorry, but I've got to go," Santino said. "Decker's waiting for me. You two be careful."

Bridget looked down at the phone as he ended the call. She thought a minute, then navigated to the podcast app. She studied the screen with a thoughtful frown.

Chasing Killers was still at the top of the true-crime list.

Her eyes scrolled down the available episodes, stopping

on one that had been released several weeks earlier, not sure what she was hoping to hear.

Tapping the *Play* icon, she motioned for Charlie to listen as Chase Grafton's smooth voice flooded through the car.

"Welcome listeners, I'm your host Chase Grafton and this is the Chasing Killers podcast. Today's episode features new information about convicted serial killer Lyle Grady's quest for a retrial.

The light in front of Charlie's Expedition turned red, and Charlie brought the big SUV to a stop as Chase continued.

Recently, the man known as the Backroads Butcher has made some pretty startling claims about the original investigation into his alleged crimes.

Bridget rolled her eyes at the word *alleged*. Did the podcaster really believe Grady's guilt in the other seven murders was in doubt?

"Today I'll be talking to Reagan Rivera, a defense attorney who has gained fame in the last few years by challenging wrongful convictions in courtrooms around the country."

A sudden thought popped into Bridget's mind, prompting her to pause the episode and turn to Charlie.

"What if Grady told Chase about Max Bender during their interview?" she asked. "What if he told him who Bender really is?"

Charlie kept her eyes on the road, considering the idea.

"We shouldn't jump to conclusions," she said, even as she deftly switched lanes and prepared to make a U-turn. "But I think we need to talk to Chase and find out what Grady told him. The interview with Abernathy will have to wait."

Bridget was already searching for Chase's number.

He answered on the first ring.

"I've been wondering when you would call," he said, sounding smug. "Let me guess. You'd like to ask me about Lyle Grady?"

Bridget swallowed back a sharp reply.

"Where are you?" she asked. "We need to meet."

* * *

Chase Grafton was pacing back and forth in the lobby of the Culver County courthouse when they arrived, his trusty recorder in hand.

"Thanks for meeting me here," he said, gesturing to the old building as if he owned the place. "I've been here most of the day conducting research for an upcoming episode of *Chasing Killers*."

He raised one eyebrow and grinned.

"I'm thinking of calling it *The Butcher's Big Escape*."

Bridget refused to give him the satisfaction of a reaction.

"Why did you go to see Lyle Grady in Abbeyville?" she asked bluntly. "What did you two talk about?"

"If you'd bothered listening to my podcast, you'd know that I've been interested in the Backroads Butcher case ever since I saw one of Tammy Vicker's special reports on it," he said. "Then, after she was killed and added to his list of victims, I was hooked."

He shivered dramatically.

"It's all too creepy," he said. "First you report on a killer, and then he shows up and kills you? That's wild, right?"

Not waiting for Bridget's response, he went on.

"Anyway, last year I produced a series of episodes on Elliot Fisher and found out he'd been Lyle Grady's cellmate."

Bridget knew about Elliot Fisher. He'd spent ten years in jail for killing a little girl who had lived down the block from him. He was exonerated of the crime after DNA taken during autopsy had been matched to a family friend.

"Elliot told me Grady claimed he'd been framed," Chase said. "He was convinced there was a DNA sample stored in the FBI lab that could prove it."

Noting that the door to one of the courtrooms had swung open, releasing a flood of spectators, Bridget guided Charlie and Chase toward a side alcove.

"So, you decided to get involved based on Grady's claim of innocence?" Charlie asked, looking dubious.

"I'm not a fool," he snipped. "I know half the people in Abbeyville insist they've been framed. But when I heard that Reagan Rivera was thinking of taking on his case...now, that got my attention."

He lifted a hand to adjust his beanie.

"That's when I decided to do a little digging of my own," he said. "I spoke to anyone related to the initial investigation who would talk to me."

He flashed a smile at Bridget and Charlie.

"Neither of you would take my calls."

Ignoring the jibe, Bridget kept her voice neutral.

"But you managed to speak to Patsy Ewing, right? Was she the one who told you Tammy's information came from someone close to the investigation?"

Chase seemed taken aback, but he nodded.

"Yes, Patsy was very forthcoming," he admitted. "She'd gotten the impression that Tammy was in a relationship with someone who had access to the case details."

His voice had lost some of its smugness.

"After that, I made it my business to find out everything I could about Tammy's life during the months leading up to her death," he said. "I interviewed her family, coworkers, and friends. Turns out Tammy had been seeing a new man."

Pausing as if for dramatic effect, Chase cleared his throat.

"Did you find out who this mystery man was?" Charlie asked, clearly annoyed that Chase Grafton seemed to know more about Tammy than she did. "Did you get a name?"

The light in the podcaster's eyes dimmed.

"No," he admitted. "She never introduced him to anyone that I could find. And when she was suddenly killed, no one seemed to think the information about Tammy's love life was important. The press and police announced that she was the latest Butcher victim, and everyone bought it."

"But you thought the man she'd been seeing could have been the one to kill her?" Bridget asked.

Chase shrugged.

"I thought it was worth looking into," he said. "Seeing that the police never did. Only, I was tired of hearsay. I wanted to get the truth straight from the horse's mouth."

"And that's when Grady agreed to talk to you?" Charlie asked. "After you told him about Tammy's mystery man? What did he have to say?"

Lifting his chin, Chase smirked.

"He said he was innocent, of course. So, I did what the FBI should have done. I kept digging for more information. Finally, I reached the bottom of the barrel and talked to his lawyer."

"You spoke to Lonnie Millford?"

Bridget resisted the urge to roll her eyes.

"Yep," Chase said. "And before you say it, I already know the guy's about as sharp as a bag of slime. But he's full of interesting details."

He lowered his voice and leaned forward as if preparing to share confidential information.

"Lonnie told me the FBI lab couldn't get enough DNA from the sample under Tammy's fingernails to test, so it was deemed inconclusive. Judge Hawthorne wouldn't let him even mention it during the trial. Sounded to me like the judge might have been biased."

"None of that is new information," Charlie said.

Her impatience was palpable.

"Not to you, maybe," Chase replied with a snort. "But Regan Rivera found it all very interesting. And once she got the FBI lab to retest Grady's DNA, she was convinced he hadn't killed Tammy Vicker. The rest is history."

"The murder of Officer Pickering, and Grady's attempt to flee justice for the eight murders he has been convicted of, is certainly *not* history," Bridget replied, unable to hide her outrage any longer. "The fact that Grady is on the loose in this community presents a very real and *present* danger."

Moving forward, Charlie stood directly in front of Chase, obviously unconcerned about invading his personal space.

"What do you know about the circumstances leading to Lyle Grady's escape from this courthouse, Mr. Grafton?" she asked, her voice as sharp and cold as ice. "Is there something we should know about that as well?"

"Just what are you trying to say?"

Chase's eyes had widened in exaggerated indignation.

"I'm saying Grady had help at the courthouse, and you seem to know an awful lot about what was going on leading up to his hearing."

"This is classic," Chase said, throwing his hands in the air. "The FBI nabs the wrong killer and then tries to blame the guy who figured out their fuck-up!"

Pushing past Charlie, he charged down the corridor toward the exit, leaving them to stare after him.

"I'd like nothing more than to go after that arrogant prick and arrest him," Charlie muttered under her breath.

"Too bad being a callous jerk isn't actually a crime," Bridget said, managing a wry smile.

As she stepped out of the alcove, she nearly collided with a harried-looking woman in form-fitting yoga pants. The woman didn't seem to register Bridget's presence as she strode past her without breaking stride.

Bridget watched the woman disappear through the exit, then turned to look down the hall leading to the administrative offices.

"I think Judge Hawthorne's chambers are down there," she said, her mind flashing back to the list in her folder. "We might as well check him off while we're here."

But Charlie wasn't listening. She'd already dug her phone out of her pocket and was tapping in a text.

Moving down the hall on her own, Bridget scanned the names next to each door. She stopped outside Judge Hawthorne's chambers.

The door was open. A young man in a suit and tie stood at the desk in a tiny reception area. He looked up as he slid a laptop into a black leather backpack and scooped up an armful of folders.

"If you're looking for the judge, he already left for the weekend," the man said. "I was just heading out myself."

Bridget shook her head, deciding he must be one of the law students who clerked for the judge.

"Okay, thanks anyway," she said, somewhat relieved.

After her combative conversation with Chase Grafton, she wasn't sure she was in the best frame of mind to question the notoriously grumpy judge anyway.

She'd started to turn away when the man spoke again.

"You're Bridget Bishop, aren't you?" he asked as he zipped his bag. "I saw a video of your testimony against Lyle Grady. It was during a lecture on the use of expert witnesses."

Slinging his backpack over his shoulder, he moved toward the door, obviously in a hurry.

"My professor said your only mistake was being too emotional on the stand," he told her, stopping to close and lock the door behind him. "But I thought you played it just right. You certainly convinced *me* that Grady was a monster."

The clerk didn't wait for a response. He scurried away leaving Bridget gaping after him, not sure if she should be flattered or offended.

Played it just right? Does he think it's all some kind of game?

She was still frowning when she saw Charlie walking toward her, her phone back in her pocket, a questioning look in her gray eyes.

"Judge Hawthorne is gone," Bridget said, gesturing to the door behind her while trying to look disappointed. "So, looks like we missed our chance to talk to him until Monday."

"Nonsense," Charlie replied. "We'll go to Hawthorne's house tomorrow. That should rattle his cage."

She turned back the way they came.

"But for now, let's grab something to eat. I'm famished. And after that, we need to finish what we set out to do before we got sidetracked by Chase Grafton."

Bridget sighed, sure that she already knew what Charlie was going to say.

"We need to talk to Reverend Abernathy."

Swallowing back her objections, which had already been heard and overruled, Bridget followed Charlie to the exit.

She slowed as they neared the door, her heart plummeting.

A missing person poster with Heather Winslow's face had been affixed to the glass. Thoughts of the college coed darkened her already black mood.

Who took you, Heather? And where are you now?

CHAPTER TWENTY-SEVEN

Bender stepped outside, then quickly closed the back door behind him as a high-pitched voice called out from the bedroom. Pulling out his burner phone, he opened the special app he'd installed to track the phone he'd left for Grady. There were no red dots, no signals to track.

The phone must be turned off or deactivated. Same for the tracker he'd left on the silver Honda.

"Honey?" Erica called again from inside, only this time she sounded closer.

Shoving the burner back in his pocket, he trampled through the bushes onto the sidewalk, resisting the urge to accelerate into a slow jog.

He kept his hood up and his head down as he made his way down the street and into the corner store.

Searching the shelves, he grabbed two mini bottles of vodka and headed for the counter.

The television behind the clerk was tuned to the nightly news. A pretty young reporter stood in front of the Culver County Courthouse.

Bender froze in horror, but when the reporter spoke, he

realized his eyes must be playing tricks on him.

The reporter on the television wasn't Tammy Vicker.

Of course, she's not Tammy, you idiot.

He dug in his pocket for cash as the reporter droned on.

"Shocking news from West Virginia today as the mother of Michelle Ewing, the third of the Backroads Butcher's victims, received a package in the mail containing a skull."

Dropping cash in front of the clerk, Bender didn't wait for the change or a bag. He scooped up the bottles and dropped them into his jacket pocket with angry jerking movements that prompted the customer behind him to take a step back.

He spun on his heel and pushed his way back out onto the street, ignoring Heather Winslow's face on the Missing Person poster taped to the door.

Twisting off the top of the first tiny bottle, he wondered what the hell Grady was trying to do.

Had he sent the package to Patsy Ewing? Had her daughter's skull really been inside it?

With one long gulp, Bender emptied the clear, liquid contents into his dry mouth, then opened the other bottle and repeated the process.

Warmth slid down his chest and into his belly, softening his anxiety and relaxing the tense muscles of his back and arms.

Throwing the empty bottles into a nearby trashcan, he continued back the way he'd come, confident Erica wouldn't smell the odorless alcohol on him or taste it on his mouth.

He needed to be cool and collected when he got back.

He couldn't allow Erica to sense that anything was wrong.

Everything he'd done had been for her. He couldn't screw it up now. Not when he was so close to getting rid of Lyle Grady and the threat he represented for good.

But the nasty voice in his head wouldn't be silent.

Are you crazy? Grady's not going to just let this go. He's going to try to wring you for every penny he can get, and then he's going to hang you out to dry.

Standing outside the back door, he hesitated, wishing he'd gotten a fifth of vodka instead of the piddly little bottles.

His fear and anger had already burned through the alcohol, and he felt unpleasantly sober.

Leaning his head against the rough stone wall, he exhaled deeply and counted to ten, willing the anxiety to leave, summoning the icy calm resolve that had served him well so many times before.

I'll do what I have to do, no matter what it takes. Just as I did with Tammy Vicker. Just as I did with Heather Winslow and Reagan Rivera.

Lyle Grady might prove more cunning and resourceful than the women he'd taken so easily by surprise, but he would beat the deranged killer at his own game.

He squared his shoulders, steeling himself for what was to come. Knowing what he had to do.

It wouldn't be pleasant, but it was a necessary evil.

And by the time I'm finished, everyone will think the Butcher is up to his old tricks, and Grady won't be alive to say otherwise.

CHAPTER TWENTY-EIGHT

Reverend Abernathy turned the corner onto Central Avenue and headed north toward the center of town. As he made his way up a steep incline toward the Mount Destiny Food Bank, his breath came in shallow gasps and his legs began to tremble under his cassock.

He resisted the urge to stop and rest.

The cardiologist had insisted that he get some light exercise every day in hopes of slowing down the congestive heart failure that threatened to send him to his grave before he'd had the chance to fulfill his vow.

But his earthly job wasn't finished yet, no matter how weary his old bones felt as he plodded on, and the fear of failing his children kept his feet moving despite the breathless pain in his chest.

The news he'd seen about the skull being mailed to Michelle Ewing's mother had given him a strange sense of hope. It was an emotion he hadn't felt in a long while.

Perhaps the end is near. Perhaps my mission is almost over.

After losing Justine and Virgil Junior to the Butcher, the reverend had vowed to hang on long enough to find the missing remains of his children. He'd promised to make them whole again so that they could rest in peace within the family mausoleum beside their mother.

Abernathy's children had both still been alive, still whole, when he'd first received his dire medical diagnosis.

At the time, the doctor had given him less than a fifty percent chance of still being alive in five years, and the reverend's faith and his children had been the only things preventing him from falling into a downward spiral of despair.

But after the Butcher had taken his children from him, the reverend had learned the hard way that his own death wasn't the worst thing that could happen to him.

The worst had happened the night Lyle Grady slaughtered Justine and Junior on a dark backroad only a few miles from where he now stood.

And now the worst had happened to another man.

Dale Winslow's eldest daughter had been killed and the youngest had gone missing. The possibility that she'd been abducted was high. The probability they'd find her alive was not.

Abernathy had made the long trek to offer his support and guidance. He was one of the few who could even begin to understand what Dale was going through.

Stopping outside the old building, the reverend paused to catch his breath.

He caught the glow of candlelight through the window.

The vigil for Heather Winslow had already started when he stepped inside the roomful of somber faces illuminated by candlelight.

Abernathy's eyes scanned the crowd, stopping on a drawn, hollowed-eyed man with limp, silvery gray hair, and a thick, overgrown mustache.

The reverend immediately recognized the look of anguish in Dale Winslow's bloodshot eyes. He'd seen it every day in his own mirror for years.

Ever since the Butcher had killed Justine and Junior, leaving him mad with grief and rage.

Making his way through the crowd of bodies, Abernathy did nothing to draw undue attention, but his shock of white hair and tall, thin body drew all eyes in his direction.

By the time he stood in front of Dale, the room had gone quiet. Every ear strained to hear what the father of two murdered teenagers would say to the man who had already lost one daughter and was looking for the other.

"I too, have suffered the pain of losing both my children," Abernathy began, his voice low. "I pray that you-"

"Heather isn't dead," Dale spit out before the reverend finished his sentence. "So don't talk about her like she is."

The thick odor of alcohol hung in the air around Dale as Abernathy studied the man's sallow face.

"My baby's alive and she's going to come home," Dale added, raising his voice as he backed away. "I'm not like *you*. I still have a child. *I'm* still a father."

Turning away, Dale stumbled toward the back door, his steps uneven and his head down.

Abernathy followed after him, using one bone-thin arm to stop the door from closing behind Dale as he stepped out into the alley behind the building.

Night had fallen, casting a dark, moonless chill over the narrow strip of asphalt that separated the food bank from the warehouse behind it.

"I meant you no harm," the reverend said quietly.

He couldn't make out Dale's face but saw his shadowy silhouette leaning against a black metal dumpster.

"As a father, your hope is your strength, so you're right to hold on to it," he said, resting a thin, gnarled hand on his chest. "We sacrifice everything, even our hearts for our children. In the end, hope is all we have left."

"And when that's gone?"

Dale's words were soft and slurred but they cut through Abernathy like a knife.

"I really don't know," he admitted, closing his eyes. "Mine hasn't failed me yet."

"But your children...they're both dead."

Abernathy inclined his head.

"In this world, yes," he agreed solemnly. "But I still have hope for another, better place. That hope keeps me upright."

Silence followed the statement.

"I wish I could say I believed in something more," Dale finally muttered. "But after my wife died, I lost what little faith I had. And now that Reagan is gone, and Heather is..."

His voice faltered.

"Heather is in God's hands now," Abernathy said. "I pray that He will deliver her safely home."

"God didn't take my girl," Dale growled, banging a fist

against the dumpster. "The man who did may be evil, but he's just a man. And if I ever find him, he'll be a dead one."

* * *

Reverend Abernathy walked slowly up South Calvary Road toward the Mount Destiny Church of Redemption.

Looking up toward the darken sky, he searched in vain for even a sliver of light.

It must be a new moon. Time for beginnings...or is it endings?

Finally, Abernathy reached the shelter of the church steps. Lamplight illuminated his white hair and deeply lined face.

As the old man stuck his key in the lock, he was surprised to find it had been broken.

He pushed the door open, expecting someone to jump out at him, but all was still. As he moved up the aisle, he could see that someone had disturbed the altar.

Slipping his hand into the wide pocket of his cassock, Abernathy felt only the smooth cover of his prayer book and realized he'd left his cell phone in the rectory.

He was always forgetting the device, never quite becoming used to carrying it around. Realizing he was empty-handed, the reverend started to back away.

He'd call the police, or maybe even the FBI agent. The blonde woman with the kind gray eyes who'd given him her card at the courthouse after Grady had escaped.

But before he could get his tired legs moving again, his eyes fell on the altar.

He cried out and lunged forward.

His legs, already tired from the walk home, buckled underneath him.

For one horrifying moment, he thought he wouldn't be able to get up again. Then slowly he reached for the pew beside him and pulled himself up to a standing position.

Forcing himself to take small, steady steps, he made his way to the altar and stared down.

Two white skulls had been placed in the middle of the long altar table.

The reverend reached out a hand to touch one of the skulls, then froze at the sound of soft footsteps behind him.

Closing his eyes, he began to pray.

CHAPTER TWENTY-NINE

Bridget stepped out of the Expedition and gazed up at the white spire of the Mount Destiny Church of Redemption with trepidation. The last time she'd come to the church to question Reverend Abernathy, he'd been carrying a hidden gun in his robes, and his mental state had been hard to read.

While she wanted to say he was a normal grieving father struggling to come to terms with his loss, there was an underlying sense of brokenness about him that unsettled her.

Bridget's experience as a criminal psychologist had taught her that emotional stress and trauma often resulted in mood disorders and unpredictable behavior. And there was no denying that the reverend had suffered his share of trauma.

Which means there's no telling what we might find inside.

Charlie started up the wide steps, then looked back at her.

"Are you ready for this?" she asked with a sudden, concerned frown. "You look pale."

Hesitating, Bridget studied the outline of the big building

against the sky. Night had fallen quickly, and the new moon above them provided no light.

"I'm good," she lied, moving toward the steps. "Let's go."

Unable to dispel the strange sense of foreboding that had washed over her as soon as she'd seen the church, she followed Charlie to the big double doors and pushed inside.

Her eyes had yet to adjust to the dim light in the sanctuary when she saw a tall figure staggering toward her.

"Reverend Abernathy?" Bridget called.

"He brought them home to me!"

Abernathy's voice was thick with emotion, and as he moved closer, she saw his eyes were bright with tears.

"Brought who home?" Bridget asked, reaching out to steady the older man as he swayed in front of her.

Feeling the terrible trembling in his arm, she wondered if he could be suffering another breakdown.

But then he spoke again, gesturing to the altar behind him.

"My children," he said. "He brought my children home."

Bridget looked past him, her eyes lighting on two skulls, which had been carefully arranged on the altar side by side, one slightly larger than the other.

"Over there, Charlie," she said softly, stepping around Abernathy to move forward, one hand on her gun. "Grady must have done this. He must have been here."

She saw Charlie pull out her Glock and walk quietly forward, scanning the aisles, the pews, and the altar.

As Bridget approached the altar from the opposite side,

she looked down at the skulls in muted horror, trying to keep her mind focused on securing the building.

She couldn't allow her emotions to take over. Not yet. Not until she was sure Grady was gone.

Tearing her eyes away from the empty orbital sockets of the smaller skull, she turned toward the sacristy.

Inching forward, she put one foot on the bottom step and then the other. Glancing down, she saw the muddy footprint just as she sensed movement ahead.

Looking up, she saw Lyle Grady standing in the shadows, a gun in his hand, hate blazing in his eyes.

Before she could lift her own weapon, Grady aimed the gun squarely at Bridget and tightened his finger on the trigger.

Time seemed to freeze as Bridget braced herself for the impact. Then Abernathy was in front of her, lunging forward with a defiant yell as the gunshot cracked through the church like lightning.

"No!" Bridget screamed as the reverend's body dropped to the floor beside her. "No!"

She swung her Glock toward Grady as a second shot rang out from behind her.

Charlie fired two quick shots into the shadows, aiming at Grady's retreating figure.

A yelp of pain was followed by a slamming door.

"I'll go after him," Charlie shouted, already halfway to the door. "You call 911. Ask for an ambulance and back-up. Tell them Grady was here."

Grabbing for her phone, Bridget punched in 911 and held

it to her ear as she knelt beside Abernathy's motionless body.

"A man's been shot at the Church of Redemption on South Calvary Road," she said when the operator's voice sounded at the other end of the connection. "We have an agent in pursuit of the shooter. We need an ambulance and backup right away."

She stuck the phone back in her pocket and leaned over to check the reverend's pulse. As she felt for his carotid artery, she noticed the pool of blood under his head.

Gingerly turning him over onto his back, she cried out as his head lolled toward her, revealing a gaping wound over his wide, staring eyes.

Pain and regret rolled through her.

It was too late for her to do anything now. Abernathy had saved her life, but she wouldn't be given the chance to do the same for him.

As sirens began to wail in the distance, Bridget bent over Abernathy's still figure and gently closed his eyes.

CHAPTER THIRTY

The drive from Stafford County seemed to take forever as Gage fought Friday night traffic westward toward Mount Destiny. When he turned onto South Calvary Road, the street outside the church was already lined with police cars, a fire truck, and the M.E.'s van.

Parking his Navigator along a side road, he walked around the block and jogged up the steps, ducking under the yellow crime scene tape without being stopped.

He pushed through the doors, careful to stay on the path the responding officers had outlined along the aisle.

Opal Fitzgerald knelt near the altar, her head bowed as if in prayer, as she examined Abernathy's body.

As Gage moved closer, he noticed Bridget sitting in the front pew by herself. She looked up with red-rimmed eyes as he sat down beside her.

"He saved me," she said in a small voice. "Reverend Abernathy stepped in front of me and...and now he's dead."

"This is Lyle Grady's doing, not yours," Gage reminded her. "The man was coming here to terrorize Abernathy. He'd have likely killed the poor man whether you'd come along or not. So, don't take his death on your shoulders."

Bridget didn't look convinced, but she fell silent as Gage swallowed back his own pang of guilt.

After all, he'd been the one who had thought the Reverend might be capable of murder. It made him look pretty foolish now that the man had sacrificed his life to save Bridget.

He heard a familiar voice talking to Opal and looked up to see Charlie walking toward them.

"You missed the excitement...again," she said.

"So, where's Grady now?" he asked.

Charlie shrugged.

"I shot at him after he did that," she said, gesturing to Abernathy's body. "I hit him, but he managed to get away."

Her eyes narrowed at the memory.

"He's wounded at least. I'm not sure where the bullet went in, but he was dripping blood on his way out of here."

"Did you see where he went?"

She nodded and raised her eyebrows.

"He was in a delivery van...*the van.*"

Gage stared at her, not sure he understood.

"The same van he used before?"

"Yep, the same van," she agreed.

He gaped at her, wondering how Grady had managed to get his old van back.

"From the look of the blood trail leading out of the church, Grady's blood loss was substantial," Charlie said. "And we haven't been able to find a bullet yet. Could be inside him."

The information was promising. From the sound of it,

Grady wouldn't get far before he'd have to seek help. Even if he managed to stem the blood loss, he'd likely need medical care eventually to treat the wound and remove the bullet.

"Well, if there's any luck in this world at all, he'll bleed out before he can hurt anyone else," Gage said.

Charlie raised her eyebrows.

"Unfortunately, we can't rely on that as our plan of action," she said dryly. "We'll put out an updated APB, letting all units know to be on the lookout for the van, and that Grady is armed, wounded, and very dangerous."

"Are we okay to take the body now?"

Gage turned to see Opal Fitzgerald and Greg Alcott.

"Sure, Opal, if you're done here and have everything you need, go right ahead," Charlie said

The M.E. and her assistant loaded Abernathy's thin body onto the gurney. Once he'd been covered with a sheet and the straps had been secured, they rolled him down the aisle and through the door.

After Abernathy was gone, Gage noticed that a small book had fallen to the floor beside the altar where the CSI team was working.

He moved forward and looked down at it.

It was a child's prayer book.

A name had been written in childish handwriting on the front cover.

Justine Abernathy.

Gage crouched down and used a single finger to open it.

A small photo had been tucked behind the front cover.

He picked up the photo and stared at it.

It showed a family of four.

The Abernathy family before tragedy had taken its toll.

The reverend looked younger and stronger in the photo.

One arm was hung over the shoulder of a handsome young man who had the reverend's smile, and the other around a lovely teenage girl with light brown hair falling over her shoulder. The girl stood next to a laughing woman who could only have been her mother.

"At least they're all together again," Gage said to no one in particular as a knot formed in his stomach.

He stood and checked his watch, thinking of Russell.

The boy would be wondering where he was.

Looking down at the family photo in his hand, Gage pulled out his phone and started to tap on Russell's number, mentally calculating how long it would take him to fight his way through traffic back to Stafford.

But he hesitated when he saw Bridget slumped in the pew.

He couldn't leave her like this.

Not after she'd been seconds from death and was showing signs of having a serious case of survivor's guilt.

Impulsively, he tapped on Kyla's number.

It was the fourth ring, and Gage was about to give up, when she answered the phone sounding breathless.

"Kyla?" he said, unable to disguise the relief in his voice. "I'm sorry to bother you on a Friday night."

He suddenly wondered if she was out on a date.

It's the weekend after all, and she's a beautiful woman.

"Is Russell okay?" she asked, sounding worried.

"Yes, he's okay," Gage said. "But something's come up at work and I was hoping you could spend some time with Russell until I get home."

There was a moment of silence, and then Kyla sighed.

"Sure," she said softly. "I'm on my way."

CHAPTER THIRTY-ONE

As the sun came up on Saturday morning, Lyle Grady sat in his van twisting two leather straps together before deftly tying them into a blood knot, trying to ignore the throbbing wound on his arm. Holding up the finished product, he decided it would have to do.

Rolling the bracelet onto his wrist, he winced as a fresh jolt of pain shot up his arm.

The gunshot wound would have to be taken care of soon since he was pretty sure the bullet was lodged inside.

While Grady had managed to wrap it up and stop the bleeding overnight, it was painful and tender to the touch, and would soon become infected if left to fester.

He couldn't afford to wait around any longer playing cat and mouse games with Bender.

Time to expedite my plans.

As he'd made his final preparations the night before, Grady had decided there was only one way to make sure Bender would do exactly as he was told.

I'll have to grab the bastard by the heart.

Jumping out of the van, he pulled up the door to the storage unit and stared around at the abandoned property, making sure he was still alone, figuring it would be the last time he'd ever see the old place.

As he climbed back into the driver's seat, he was relieved to hear the engine rumble to life.

Wincing, he threw the gear into reverse, then slowly backed out and headed toward Mount Destiny, keeping under the speed limit, knowing if he got stopped by a state trooper, he'd be back in Abbeyville by sundown.

He slowed as he approached the outskirts of town.

Taking out his phone, he followed the GPS directions to a small beauty salon set back from the road, then double-checked the name on the sign.

Yes, that's the one I saw in her post this morning.

A thrill of anticipation rushed through him as he parked the van behind a dumpster in the beauty salon's parking lot, pulled up his hoodie, and shoved sunglasses over his eyes.

Grady was still sitting there twenty minutes later when the woman walked out of the salon wearing designer jeans that showcased her yoga-toned legs and a cashmere sweater.

Her curly brown hair had been freshly highlighted with golden streaks, her nails freshly painted a classic red.

Waiting for her to take one more selfie in front of the salon, Grady climbed out of the van.

As she used her remote to unlock the door to a sporty red BMW, he stepped up behind her and stuck a gun in her back.

"Hello, Erica," he muttered into the fragrant mass of

curls that covered her ear. "Don't scream or I'll shoot you dead."

Forcing her to walk to the BMW, he popped open the little trunk and shoved the woman inside, keeping the gun trained on her with his one good arm.

Her eyes widened as his hood slipped back.

"You're...the Butcher," she stammer.

"That's right," he sneered, enjoying the fear he saw on her face. "And you're my ticket out of here."

Slamming the trunk shut, he slid into the little car's driver's seat and started the engine.

With a triumphant laugh, he pulled back onto the road.

* * *

Grady stuck to the speed limit as he drove the BMW toward the edge of town. Finding a warehouse that appeared to be closed for the weekend, he parked the car behind it.

He surveyed the area to make sure he wasn't being observed, then got out of the car. Circling around to the back, he opened the trunk.

Erica was still trussed up just as he'd left her.

Holding up his burner phone, Grady snapped a photo, making sure to capture the blood knot bracelet tied around her delicate wrist.

He slammed the lid shut again and tapped out a message. He would send it to Bender along with the picture.

If you want her back alive, get me the ID and cash today.

He already knew that Bender would comply.

The man would do anything for the woman, that much was obvious. Why else would he have killed Tammy Vicker?

The man had been so desperate to hide their affair that he'd been willing to commit murder.

Grady emitted a scornful laugh at the thought.

In his opinion, the proverb that claimed pride went before a fall was all wrong. Love was the real killer.

It made strong men weak.

Luckily, it wasn't an affliction he'd ever had to deal with.

Of course, he'd felt something for Justine Abernathy. Nothing so corny as love. He wouldn't even have called it lust.

But it had been all-consuming just the same, leaving him unable to think of anything else.

She'd gotten into his head. Taken over his mind, almost as if he'd been possessed. There had been only one way to regain control, to take back his power.

Snatching her off her front porch when she'd signed for a bogus delivery had been easy. Although, when her older brother had heard her screams and given chase in his pick-up truck, he'd had no choice but to kill him, too.

The pure surge of emotion he'd felt when he'd held Justine's life in his hands had been addictive.

He imagined it was the same mind-blowing rush junkies felt when they were shooting up. He'd never felt anything so intense. But then, he'd never felt much of anything before that day, other than anger and discontent.

Later, after he'd been caught and convicted, the

250

psychologist at Abbeyville had diagnosed him with antisocial personality disorder, saying it made it hard for him to have empathy for others, or to control his impulses.

Most inmates in the maximum-security unit had the same diagnosis. It seemed to be a one-size-fits-all disorder.

Grady figured there were plenty of people on the outside who had the same. The man calling himself Bender was one of them. But he'd taken a different path in life.

And the man who'd helped him figure out the truth about Bender could be another.

Taking out his phone again, Grady tapped in another text. This time to Chase Grafton.

I know who killed Tammy Vicker. You get me $10,000 and I'll give you his name. You and your podcast will be famous.

CHAPTER THIRTY-TWO

Bridget woke up to the sun shining in the window and Hank softly nudging her hand. She rolled over with the intention of going straight back to sleep, then heard a man's voice somewhere in the house.

As she sat up and opened her eyes, sudden memories of the night before, and of Reverend Abernathy's violent death, came crashing in on her.

She hadn't gotten home until late, and she now recalled that Santino had insisted on staying over.

He hadn't wanted her to be alone in the house. Not after he'd heard about the shooting and found out the disturbing details of Grady's narrow escape.

After pulling on a pair of faded jeans and a warm green sweater, Bridget followed Hank into the kitchen.

Santino had already brewed coffee and was spreading strawberry jam on toast when she walked in.

"I've got to take Hank out," she said, not meeting his eyes. "And then I'm going to drop him off at my dad's house."

Santino stopped her before she could walk out the door and took her hands in his.

"Have some coffee and toast," he said. "You need to eat."

When she didn't answer, he sighed.

"Starving yourself won't bring Reverend Abernathy back," he chided softly. "You can't blame yourself for what happened to him."

"Who should I blame then?" Bridget asked, finally meeting his eyes. "I was there with a gun, but I still let Grady shoot an innocent man in cold blood."

She pulled her hands out of his grip.

"I'm allowed to feel shitty about it, okay?"

"Okay," Santino said, lifting both hands in surrender. "You're right. It's a lot to deal with, which is why I think you should go see Faye Thackery. She's helped you come to terms with trauma before. I can make an appointment for you if..."

His words died away as he saw the flush of anger fill Bridget's cheeks.

"I may have allowed Lyle Grady to kill Abernathy, but that doesn't mean I'm officially helpless," she protested. "I don't need you to make an appointment for me, or breakfast, or anything else."

Knowing she was being ungrateful and childish, she forced herself to stop and suck in a deep breath.

"Now, I'm going to take Hank for a walk. Then I'll drop him off at my father's house."

She hesitated, knowing Santino wasn't going to like what she was about to say.

"After that, I'm going with Charlie to continue our

interviews," she said. "Judge Hawthorne is next on our list."

"You're planning on working today?"

Santino sounded incredulous.

"Of course, I am," Bridget said. "Just like you. Neither of us can afford to sit at home while Grady and Bender are both out there ready to kill again."

Santino opened his mouth to protest, then closed it again with a sigh of frustration.

"Decker's expecting me any minute," he admitted, shaking his head. "The news about Reverend Abernathy's death has prompted a flood of calls to the tipline and there are a few that sound promising."

"You go on," Bridget urged. "Once I drop off Hank, I'll meet up with Charlie. And don't worry, I'll be fine."

* * *

Bridget drove her old Explorer past Judge Hawthorne's palatial home and parked along the curb.

As she shut off the engine, her phone buzzed on the seat beside her, displaying Gage's number.

"I just called to check on you," he said. "Last night you seemed pretty upset when you left. It really wasn't your-"

"Thanks, Gage, but I really can't talk right now," she said, cutting him off. "I'm outside Judge Hawthorne's house waiting for Charlie."

Glad for the excuse to avoid another conversation about her guilty conscience, she checked her watch, wondering where Charlie was.

"You really think the judge could have something to do with all this?" Gage asked.

"I doubt it, but the man is on Argus' list," Bridget pointed out. "Which means Argus' algorithm is telling us it's possible. And right now, I don't want to leave any stone unturned."

"Just be careful," Gage said. "After what happened last night, we know Grady is wounded and on the run. That'll make him even more dangerous than usual."

Bridget looked in her rearview mirror as she ended the call, feeling jumpy.

After several cars had passed behind her and a delivery van had come and gone, she decided to go up to the door and make sure the judge was home.

Charlie can join us inside when she arrives.

Walking up to the door, Bridget surveyed the immaculate exterior and lush landscaping.

She hesitated briefly, then knocked, surprised when Judge Hawthorne flung open the door only seconds later wearing what looked to be golfing attire.

"Oh, it's you," he said, appearing momentarily confused. "I thought you were Erica."

Bridget plastered on a smile.

"Sorry to bother you, Judge Hawthorne. I'm Bridget Bishop with the-"

"Yes, I remember you," he interrupted, his forehead creasing into an irritable frown. "What do you want?"

"I'm working with the FBI. We're investigating Lyle

Grady's escape and several related homicides," she said. "I was hoping to ask you a few questions. My colleague, Agent Day, will be joining me shortly."

The judge's frown deepened.

"What could I possibly tell you about Grady, other than he's a psychopath?" he asked. "But then, *you're* the one who told *me* that when you were on the witness stand at his trial."

"Please," Bridget said, trying to hold on to her polite smile as she sensed the judge's growing frustration. "We just have a few questions about your role in the original investigation. It shouldn't take long."

Hawthorne looked past Bridget, surveying the road.

"My wife and I have company coming for lunch," he said, stepping back into the house. "So, this will need to be quick."

He led Bridget down a long hall.

Their soft footsteps on the marble floor were the only sounds she could hear as she followed the judge's broad back deeper into the house.

Waving her toward a plush sofa, Hawthorne remained standing while she took a seat.

She stared up at him as he loomed over her with a reproachful expression.

"What exactly is this about, Dr. Bishop?" he asked.

"As I said, it's about Lyle Grady. It seems that certain information regarding his crimes may have been shared with someone outside of the investigation."

The judge looked confused.

"You're saying there was a leak?"

Before Bridget could answer, she heard voices coming down the hall.

"Darling, were you expecting a visitor?"

A slim woman in an elegant white caftan strode into the room, followed by Charlie Day.

Bridget jumped to her feet at their arrival.

"Oh, you already have a guest," the woman said, coming to a sudden stop. "Who is this?"

Her critical gaze traveled from Bridget's chestnut curls to the black blazer she'd pulled on over her sweater, then down to her low-heeled shoes.

"This isn't a reporter, is it, dear?" she asked.

"No, I'm with the FBI's Behavioral Analysis Unit," Bridget said. "Sorry to interrupt on a Saturday but Agent Day and I have a few urgent matters to discuss with Judge Hawthorne."

The woman didn't take Bridget's offered hand.

"Well, please hurry it up," she said, throwing an icy glare in the judge's direction. "My husband and I are expecting our daughter for lunch."

Without another word, she spun on the heel of her ballet flat and exited the room.

"Judge Hawthorne, you signed a search warrant related to the original Backroads Butcher investigation," Charlie said, speaking in a brisk voice. "The investigators were hoping to find a specific item. Something the Butcher left at his crime scenes as a sort of signature. Do you remember that?"

"It's been a few years, but yes, I remember authorizing a search for some sort of jewelry, I believe. Why? What does this have to do with-"

"It was a leather bracelet tied into a blood knot," Charlie said, her eyes hard. "Did you ever discuss that warrant or the object we were looking for with anyone outside the direct investigation?"

"Of course not," he said, bristling. "I'm not a fool."

"This is important, Judge Hawthorne," Charlie cautioned him. "It could be a literal matter of life and death. Please think back. Was there ever an occasion that you shared this with anyone outside the team? Perhaps even socially?"

Hawthorne stiffened in outrage as he shook his head.

"Not even your wife or daughter?" Bridget asked.

"Absolutely, not," he snapped. "Are you crazy? I would never expose them to such things."

He marched toward the door.

"Now, if you'll excuse me, I need you to go," he said. "And rest assured, the Bureau will be hearing from me about this."

Bridget's phone buzzed in her pocket as she and Charlie followed him to the foyer.

Glancing down, she saw a text from Chase Grafton.

Lyle Grady wants to sell his story. You interested in buying?

She stared at it for a long beat, then turned to the judge.

"Just one more thing, Judge Hawthorne, and then we'll go," she said, gripping the phone so hard her hand hurt. "We want you to sign an emergency warrant."

The judge gaped at her in confusion.

"We need to track a cellphone," she said. "I think we've identified someone who can lead us to Lyle Grady."

CHAPTER THIRTY-THREE

Bender flung his phone onto the passenger's seat of the black sedan and squeezed his eyes shut, but it was too late. The image of Erica tied up in the trunk of her BMW had already been burned into his mind.

Grady had taken her.

The only woman he'd ever loved. The only person who mattered to him in this whole, hateful world.

Bender shoved his foot down hard on the accelerator, sending the sleek sedan careening toward the highway, wanting to get out of town as fast as possible, seeking the kind of shelter only the mountains could provide.

As he risked a glance at the phone, the thought of his beloved Erica at the mercy of the Butcher tore a roar of outrage from his throat.

"I'll kill him!"

Banging his hand down hard on the steering wheel, he yelled again, his voice reverberating through the car.

"I'll blow his fucking head off!"

The deafening shout left his throat aching and sore, and his hand throbbed from the blow against the steering wheel.

But the pain drained away some of his anger and fear, allowing him to rein in his emotions, allowing him to think. There had to be a way to save Erica and eliminate Grady.

Maybe if I just give him what he wants...

Of course, the idea was ludicrous. Even laughable.

The man known as the Backroads Butcher would never willingly let Erica go. Not alive, and not without a fight.

But I could make him think I'm going along with his plan. That I'm following his instructions and all he has to do is show up.

Speeding toward Destiny Peak Overlook, Bender's plan began to solidify in his mind.

First, he would lure Grady down to the Iron Graveyard. He'd tell the serial killer he had the money and the new identity he'd demanded.

He'd say he was ready to exchange both for Erica, but that he wanted to see her alive before the exchange took place.

Then, once Grady arrived, Bender would kill him.

Leaning over to open the glove box, Bender pulled out a heavy, long barrel Glock and laid it on the passenger's seat next to the phone.

This wasn't the time to mess around with knives or meat cleavers. The job he had in front of him would take something much more powerful, much more precise.

As long as I don't miss and shoot Erica.

Suddenly, Bender wondered what he would tell Erica once this whole nightmare was over. How could he explain what had happened and the violence she would surely witness?

The next thought stole his breath away.

What if the Butcher has already told her everything?

Stark fear filled Bender at the thought of Erica knowing all his dirty secrets. She would hate him...leave him.

But no, Grady won't risk telling Erica anything until he has his money and ID safely in hand. Will he?

The urge to kill the Butcher, to eliminate the threat he posed once and for all, overwhelmed Bender. It was all he could do not to scream out in rage again.

Instead, he lightened his foot on the accelerator and slowed the car, remembering his DNA was on file now as part of the Tammy Vicker and Reagan Rivera investigations.

If I'm stopped and arrested for anything, they'll collect my DNA. Once that happens, it's all over.

Pulling off the highway at the rest area just before the Destiny Peak Overlook, Bender parked the sedan and pulled out his phone.

He had to be very careful. There could be no wrong moves.

And most importantly, he couldn't stop until the Butcher was dead. Not after everything he knew.

And not after he'd taken Erica.

Even if Grady did turn Erica over unharmed, there was no way he could allow the man to just walk away.

His only chance to get Erica back, to get his life back, was to kill Lyle Grady. And if he played his cards right, he might even be able to turn the whole situation to his advantage.

All I have to do is make it look as if I caught Grady trying to conceal the evidence of his crimes in the Iron Graveyard.

If Bender could make everyone believe that Grady had been the one to push Heather Winslow into the shaft, and the one who had shot Ryder Forbes, he would never be suspected of being involved.

And once the black garbage bags were discovered in the shaft, along with the final pieces of Reagan Rivera and Tammy Vicker, everyone would naturally assume the convicted serial killer had killed them, too.

If Bender happened to swoop in and save Erica by shooting down the Butcher, he'd come out looking like a hero.

Satisfied with his plan, Bender picked up the burner phone and tapped in a message.

I've got your money and ID, and I'll be waiting for you at Destiny Peak Overlook in one hour.

CHAPTER THIRTY-FOUR

C hase Grafton's phone began to buzz as he slowed his blue Honda hybrid and made the turn toward Destiny Peak Overlook. Checking his watch, he brought the car to a halt, then pulled out his phone and studied the name and number on the display with a smug smile.

He'd always known the day would come when Bridget Bishop would come crawling to him.

He had tried to get the psychologist's attention for years, going so far as to date her best friend and interview her neighbors and acquaintances.

Now, after years of being ignored and ridiculed by the uptight profiler, *she* was the one desperate to speak to *him*.

Unable to resist, he tapped *Accept* to answer the call.

"Where is Grady?" Bridget demanded. "If you know, you need to tell me now, before he kills anyone else."

"It's the U.S. Marshal's job to track down fugitives, not mine," he said. "Although from what I've heard, your boyfriend couldn't even find the man who killed his own wife, so I doubt he can find Lyle Grady."

He smiled at Bridget's soft gasp of surprise, then plowed on before she could respond.

"Of course, if you grant me an exclusive interview, I may be able to point you in the right direction."

"I'm sure you know obstruction of justice is a criminal offense under both federal and state law," Bridget said. "At a federal level, it can earn you up to ten years in prison."

Chase scoffed.

"And I'm sure you've heard of freedom of the press," he said. "I know plenty of lawyers who are ready to defend my first amendment rights, so your threats don't scare me."

"I may not scare you, but Lyle Grady should," Bridget shot back. "As should the man who helped him escape. The same man who killed Reagan Rivera to hide that fact."

Staring down at his phone, Chase tried to process what Bridget was telling him.

"Are you saying Grady didn't kill Reagan Rivera?" he finally asked, reaching for his recorder. "You're saying he has some kind of a partner?"

"I'm saying Grady isn't the only dangerous man in Mount Destiny that you need to worry about," Bridget replied. "Someone killed Reagan Rivera and abducted Heather Winslow. And you're making a deadly mistake if you think you won't be next if you happen to get in his way."

Movement in the trees ahead caught Chase's eye. His pulse quickened as Bridget's words replayed in his head.

You're making a deadly mistake if you think you won't be next.

Straining to see past the shadows ahead, he frowned and gripped the phone to his ear. Had Grady already arrived? Or was someone else there?

"Sorry, but I've got to go," he said abruptly, tapping the display to end the call, his mind spinning with questions.

Does Grady have a partner? Has he been playing me all along?

Of course, Bridget could be mistaken, or maybe even trying to dissuade him from covering the story.

But something in her voice had convinced him she was telling the truth. Underneath her irritation, she'd sounded worried, maybe even scared.

So, if Bridget was right, and Grady hadn't killed Reagan Rivera, who had?

A possibility flitted through Chase's mind as he recalled Grady swearing up and down he hadn't killed Tammy Vicker.

The killer had claimed someone framed him for her murder, although he had never revealed who he suspected.

And for some reason, Chase had believed him, despite knowing that Grady was a psychopath who'd killed at least seven other people.

But why would Tammy's killer help Grady escape? And why kill Reagan Rivera? Was it because she was trying to exonerate Grady? Or was she getting too close to the truth?

If that was the case, then anyone who was seen as a possible ally of Grady's could become a target.

A chill rolled through Chase's body, but he shrugged it off.

He was at the overlook to meet Grady.

He'd driven straight over, taking less than thirty minutes to arrive after he'd gotten Grady's last message.

He knew he probably should be scared of the serial killer,

but he felt that he and Grady had an understanding.

The man was a monster, that was true. A psychopath who killed women for the thrill of it. But during his interviews with Grady, the two of them had gotten along quite well.

Besides, Grady needed him.

The man was a fugitive who wanted money, as well as revenge over those who had tried to lock him away for the rest of his life.

Chase could give him a little of both.

He'd brought as much cash as he could scrape together, and he was ready to give Grady a chance to share his side of the story with thousands of diehard *Chasing Killers* listeners.

That was the kind of bait Grady wouldn't be able to resist. It would give the killer a chance to take a final shot at all his enemies and expose Tammy's true killer.

If Grady believed he would then ride off into the sunset with a bag of Chase's cash, he would definitely buy in.

Of course, Chase wasn't planning to let that last part happen. He didn't particularly want a serial killer roaming around the country spending his hard-earned money.

And he figured it couldn't hurt his ratings if he was given credit for bringing in the infamous Backroads Butcher.

Just look how much press Bridget Bishop got the first time around. The case made her famous.

He was about to tap in a message to Bridget with the meeting location when the driver's door was wrenched open.

A hand reached in and grabbed him by the shirt and

dragged him out of the car.

Chase's phone fell out of his hand and tumbled into the grass under the car.

He looked up to see Grady holding a gun in one hand.

The bored, disdainful look Grady had worn in Abbeyville during their visits was gone. The killer's eyes were bright and wild, and spittle flew from his mouth.

"Where's the cash?" he yelled.

"It's in the trunk," Chase said, his heart hammering hard in his thin chest.

Grady stomped to the back of the car, shoving Chase in front of him, forcing him to open the trunk.

It contained a gym bag with several thick stacks of twenty-dollar bills.

"That's not ten thousand dollars," Grady said in a dangerous voice. "Are you trying to rip me off?"

"It was all I could come up with," Chase gasped.

He kept his eyes on the gun.

"I...I can get you the rest tomorrow."

"I won't be here tomorrow," Grady said.

He glared down at the gym bag.

"And from the looks of it, neither will you."

Trying to think fast, Chase lifted his hands.

"Come on, man, I'm just a podcaster. I don't have that kind of money lying around," he cried. "But I do have thousands of listeners. And they'll want to hear your side of the story. I'll tell them whatever you want them to know."

Grady's scowl deepened. As his finger tightened around the gun, Chase squeezed his eyes shut and prepared to die.

Then the killer's grip loosened.

He pulled Chase off the path toward a bright red BMW, then released him and popped the trunk open.

The stench from inside made Chase's stomach clench.

Lurching to the side, he bent over, spewing out his lunch.

Grady laughed as he laid the gun down and reached into a cardboard box. He grinned as he pulled out a human head.

Before Chase could react, a tormented cry came from behind him. Both men whirled around as a shot rang out.

Grady dove for cover, losing his grip on the head, which fell into the grass with a sickening thud.

He rolled along the ground, clutching his arm in agony as a man stepped out from behind a black sedan, which was half hidden by the overhanging trees.

With another cry of rage, the man pulled the trigger again.

Chase screamed as Grady's head exploded. Blood and tissue sprayed through the air, coating his face and body, as well as the area around him.

The podcaster stood frozen, watching in amazed horror as Grady's body slumped against the ground.

The Backroads Butcher was dead.

Jerking his head up at the sound of footsteps on gravel, Chase saw the man from the dark sedan walking toward him.

Inching backward, he was about to scream again in panic, when he suddenly recognized the man's face.

With a sigh of relief, Chase faced the shooter.

As blood spatter dripped from his beanie, he pulled it off his head and let it drop to the ground beside him.

"You scared me to death," he said, shaking his head. "I thought you were one of the bad guys. What are you doing here?"

"I came here for my wife," the man answered in a hoarse voice. "But I'm too late. She's dead, and so are you."

Lifting the gun, he aimed it at Chase and pulled the trigger.

CHAPTER THIRTY-FIVE

Bridget sat forward in the passenger's seat of Charlie's Expedition as the faded sign for Mount Destiny Overlook came into view. A red arrow on the sign pointed hikers and sightseers toward a narrow side road that was nearly obscured by a thick layer of leaves from the surrounding oak and maple trees.

"Okay, take the next right," said the deep voice coming from Charlie's cellphone on the dashboard.

Special Agent Luis Cortez had been playing navigator for them ever since Judge Hawthorne had reluctantly signed the emergency warrant to track Chase Grafton's phone.

"The road winds down the mountain for quite a way, but you're close to the phone signal now, so you may want to slow down and keep an eye out."

Slowing the Expedition to a crawl, Charlie scanned the road ahead, then suddenly stepped on the brakes as they came upon a sleek black sedan parked under a tree.

"We see a car," Charlie said for Cortez's benefit. "Can't see the full license plate from here, but it's a Virginia tag."

Bridget's pulse jumped as she spotted a blue Honda hybrid, parked at an angle further down the road.

"That's Chase Grafton's car," she said, then pointed to a lanky figure standing beside the Honda. "And there's Chase. I almost didn't recognize him without his beanie."

"We've got the subject in sight," Charlie said, reaching for the phone. "We should be good from here."

Cortez replied immediately.

"Negative, Agent Day, I'll stay on the line until you give the all-clear. In the meantime, I'll let the MDPD know you may need backup."

Charlie reached for the door handle, but Bridget shot out a hand, holding her back.

"Hold on, there's someone with him."

A man in a dark hoodie stepped out of the shadows cast by the sprawling tree. As they watched, the man lifted a long barrel gun and pointed it at Chase's forehead.

Bridget recoiled as the man appeared to pull the trigger, but the gun didn't fire. She exhaled in relief.

Did the gun jam? Or maybe he ran out of ammunition.

With a frustrated shout, the man smashed the gun over Chase's head, sending the podcaster crumpling to the ground.

Charlie grabbed her phone, speaking rapidly to Cortez.

"We've got an armed male up ahead and another man down. Go ahead and call for that back-up...and throw in an ambulance while you're at it."

She turned to Bridget, who had already pulled her Glock from its holster.

"You sure you want to do this?"

"I'm sure," Bridget said, suddenly impatient, not

wanting to let Chase's assailant get away. "Come on, before he reloads. Let's go!"

Shoving the phone into her pocket, Charlie flung open the door, stepped out of the SUV, and pointed her Glock at the man in the hoodie.

"Stop right there!" she yelled. "Armed FBI!"

The man spun toward them as Charlie darted forward, taking cover behind a thick oak tree.

Following Charlie, Bridget kept her eyes on the man, whose face was still hidden by shadows.

Unsure if he had managed to reload his gun, she stayed low to the ground, using the tree trunks as shields, keeping her Glock in the ready position.

"FBI!" Charlie yelled again. "Put your weapon down!"

The man ducked behind the blue Honda, then jumped up and sprinted down the path, heading toward the base of the mountain.

Bridget ran to the Honda and knelt next to Chase, who was covered in blood and had a nasty gash on his head.

As she checked his pulse, Bridget was relieved to feel a strong and steady beat under her fingers.

"I think he's okay," she said as Charlie ran up behind her.

But Charlie was looking past the Honda with wide eyes.

Following her gaze, Bridget let out an involuntary scream.

Lyle Grady's body was sprawled on the leaf-strewn ground, half his head blown away.

"Grady's dead," Bridget murmured in shock as Charlie

pointed to something on the ground a few yards further.

"Over there," she said. "What *is* that?"

Bridget moved forward, her Glock still out in front of her, her knees trembling as she approached the object.

As she stood over the severed head, she blinked hard twice, not sure what, or who, she was seeing.

"That looks like Grady's work," she said, turning away. "Only Grady is dead, so..."

She looked down the path toward the base of the mountain, her heart hammering in her chest.

"So, that must be Bender," Charlie said.

Bridget nodded.

"I think you're right," she agreed. "Let's go get him."

CHAPTER THIRTY-SIX

A bird cawed overhead as Charlie jogged down the path, her eyes wide and alert as she looked for the figure in the hoodie amongst the trees. He'd had plenty of time to reload, and she knew he could step out from behind a tree at any time and get off a shot before she knew what hit her.

Is that really Max Bender?

Picturing the man's silhouette, Charlie thought that something about him seemed familiar. Had she seen him somewhere before?

Footsteps sounded in the grass, and she spun around to see Bridget coming up behind her.

The psychologist's eyes were wide, and Charlie could see the slight tell-tale tremor of the gun shaking in her hand.

Bridget's fear was understandable. But it made Charlie anxious, and she thought of Hale with sudden longing.

She'd always felt secure when he'd been there to have her back in dangerous situations. He'd helped save her life more than once, and she'd returned the favor a few times as well.

They made a good team.

A branch cracked a few yards ahead and Charlie jerked her arm up and let off a shot.

Tree bark splintered and flew into the air as a deer jumped and bounded away.

Bridget spoke up from behind her.

"I think I know where he's going," she said in a hushed voice. "My father and I used to look for abandoned mines whenever we went hiking in the Appalachians or the Shenandoah Valley."

She nodded toward the winding trail.

"If I remember correctly, there's an old mine at the base of this mountain. The locals used to call it the Iron Graveyard."

Charlie felt a shiver roll through her at the name.

She nodded and kept walking, but a sense of dread washed over her at the thought of going into the mine. She hated dark, confined spaces. And there would likely be a desperate man inside waiting to take a shot at her.

Again, the thought of Hale filled Charlie's mind.

Regret mixed with her fear.

Why did I waste so much time being scared and pushing him away? I should have enjoyed every minute we had together.

Forcing her mind back to the trail in front of her, Charlie focused on the uneven path and the surrounding forest, well aware that even a moment's distraction could give the man in front of them the opportunity to attack.

A flash of silver in the underbrush caught her eye. She stopped and squinted down, not sure what she was seeing.

"What is it?" Bridget whispered at her elbow, then

followed Charlie's gaze. "Is that a *suitcase*?"

Charlie nodded and stepped into the underbrush.

As she pulled the small silver suitcase toward the trail, she saw a long, dirty-white duffle bag lying a few yards further into the forest.

"I think we've got something here," she called out, turning back to stare at Bridget. "And it doesn't look good."

Trampling over fallen leaves and broken branches, Charlie crossed to the duffle bag and stared down at it.

"Ryder Forbes," she said aloud, reading the baggage tag as Bridget stepped up beside her, still holding her gun out and nervously eyeing the surrounding forest.

Bridget's eyes widened at the name.

"Should we open it?" she asked, swallowing hard.

With a resolute nod, Charlie bent over and pulled back the zipper, releasing a swarm of flies into the air.

Stumbling backward in her haste to escape the mass of buzzing insects, Charlie managed to stay upright only by grabbing onto Bridget's arm.

Both women turned and hurried back to the trail.

"There's nothing we can do for him now," Charlie said, not quite sure if she was talking to Bridget or herself. "We've got to keep going or we'll lose Bender for sure."

Bridget nodded and they hurried on, but as the trail began to flatten out, she stopped and ducked behind a tree, pulling Charlie with her.

"There it is," she said.

As she saw the black hole of the mine entrance yawning open before them like the entrance to a tomb, Charlie's mouth went dry.

"I think he's in there," Charlie said, inching forward. "I thought I saw something move, but I'm not sure."

"What do we do now?" Bridget whispered. "Should we go inside, or wait for back-up?"

Charlie met Bridget's scared, blue eyes and tried to think.

Did he go into the mine to hide? Or did he continue on the path?

She was suddenly possessed by a terrible certainty that if they went into the mine, they would never come out.

"I'll make this easy for you," a deep voice said as the muzzle of a gun jabbed into Charlie's back. "You two are going in the mine. Now, drop your guns and get moving."

Glancing back, Charlie gaped in surprise.

Alistair Kennedy stared back at her, his hand fisted around the Glock in her back, his normally blue eyes as wide and dark as black holes in his ashen face.

"*You're* Bender? But...*why?*"

The words escaped her in a breathless rush, forced out by the incomprehensible revelation that the prosecutor who had helped to convict Lyle Grady was also the man who had helped him escape.

"Everything I did, I did for Erica," he said in a hoarse croak. "But he killed her. The Butcher killed my wife."

CHAPTER THIRTY-SEVEN

The nightmarish image of Erica's severed head hovered behind Alistair Kennedy's eyes as he watched the women drop their weapons and walk toward the mine. How had he let it happen? How had it come to this?

"Why did you do it?" Bridget asked. "Why did you kill Tammy Vicker?"

"I made a mistake," he muttered. "One little mistake."

It hadn't been his fault. Not really.

He'd been working long hours on the Backroads Butcher case. He'd been overwhelmed and tired.

He'd allowed the reporter to seduce him.

She'd been young and beautiful, and so very eager.

And he hadn't been used to the attention and flattery.

He hadn't been used to anyone but Erica.

Erica had been his first love. His college sweetheart. And he'd considered himself unbelievably lucky to have somehow convinced her, the beautiful daughter of an influential judge, to marry him.

He had kept his wife on a pedestal, never quite daring to believe she was his even as he lived in fear that she would leave him.

And her father had taken him under his wing, securing Alistair an internship in the Commonwealth Attorney's office and mentoring him through his career, successfully shepherding him into his current role as lead prosecutor in Mount Destiny.

His life had seemed perfect until the Backroads Butcher case had thrown the whole area into a panic.

The town had been inundated with a swarm of aggressive reporters, the most persistent being Tammy Vicker, and Alistair had been drawn into the investigation, updated on every development in preparation for a future trial.

When Tammy had approached him asking for a story, he'd been unable to ignore the unspoken invitation.

Their affair had lasted less than three weeks, but by the end, Alistair's attraction for the reporter had turned to panic as Tammy started making threats he couldn't ignore.

"She tried to ruin my marriage," he said.

Anger caused his hand to tighten around the gun.

"I had to stop her. So, I decided to make it look as if the Butcher had struck again. I left the stupid blood knot bracelet and I cut off her head."

He shoved Bridget toward the dark hole of the mine, trying not to picture Grady holding up Erica's head.

Trying not to think of what he'd lost.

"My plan would have worked if that bitch hadn't managed to scratch me," he said, pushing Charlie toward the darkness.

"Don't do this, Alistair," Bridget said.

She stopped and turned to face him.

"You can end all this now. As you said, it was all a mistake. You weren't in your right mind. You can end this before anyone else gets hurt."

"It's too late."

Shaking his head, Alistair lifted the gun.

"*I'm* already hurt. And *Erica* is hurt," he ground out between clenched teeth. "Now it's *your* turn, Dr. Bishop."

CHAPTER THIRTY-EIGHT

B ridget flung herself into the cold darkness of the mine as Alistair pulled the trigger. The gunshot exploded into the small cavern, sending bits of dirt and gravel flying around her feet.

Ears ringing, she tripped over the rusty rail tracks that led into the mine and fell. Splintered wood and metal tore at her knees, ripping away fabric as she struggled to her feet and felt along the stone wall.

Using the wall as her guide in the blackness of the mine, she stumbled forward, staying low and moving as quickly as possible, hoping against hope that Charlie had used the distraction to escape back into the woods.

I haven't heard another gunshot. That's a good sign, right?

The air felt still and thin as Bridget made her way further into the mountain. Sensing the immense weight and mass of the mountain above her head, she leaned against the wall struggling to catch her breath.

Although she'd never suffered from claustrophobia in the past, she felt the stirrings of panic as she imagined being crushed or trapped in the suffocating darkness.

Forcing herself to stand still, she listened.

Her heart jumped in her chest as she heard heavy breathing and soft footsteps coming closer.

Instinctively, Bridget started moving again, her hands feeling the way along the rough wall, her feet heavy and clumsy with fear.

She stopped as the toe of her shoe connected with something hard on the ground. Bending over, she felt along the edge of a metal object, her fingers softly outlining what seemed to be a rusty pickaxe or hatchet of some kind.

Assuming it must be one of the many tools the miners had left behind when the place had been shut down, she picked it up and held it in her trembling hand as the footsteps and breathing drew closer.

As she braced for an impending attack, images of her life, or at least the important parts, flashed through Bridget's mind. Her mother's voice. Her father's face. Santino's smile. Hank's dark, trusting eyes.

The little voice in her head pulled her back to attention.

Focus and wait. You'll know when it's the right time to strike.

Bridget inhaled softly, trying to hold her breath.

Suddenly she saw a light and a shadow behind it.

Alistair was holding his cellphone in one hand, using the flashlight app to create a circle of light in the dark.

Bridget flattened herself against the wall.

She could see that he still had the gun in his other hand.

Lifting the pickaxe over her head, she waited until he was only a few feet away, then brought it down with all her might.

The handle shattered as the blade smashed against the

side of Alistair's head, knocking him into the stone wall.

His phone skittered across the uneven floor and his gun slid under an abandoned mining cart.

Instantly, Bridget scooped up the phone, using the light to guide her back toward the entrance, stumbling on the uneven path as she retraced her steps.

Seeing the soft glow of light up ahead, she cried out in relief, knowing if she could just get outside, she could find a place to hide. She'd be safe.

She hurried forward, then stopped still as she saw the body sprawled on the ground just inside the mine opening.

"Charlie!"

Distant voices sounded from outside the mine as she rushed forward and cried out again.

"In here...we're in here!"

Hearing footsteps behind her, Bridget spun around to see Alistair looming over her, his head bleeding, his eyes crazed, the broken pickaxe blade in his hand.

He lifted the blade, but before he could bring it down, a shot rang out. Jerking to a stop, he staggered backward, shock taking over his face as he began to fall.

Then he was gone, disappearing into the vertical shaft with a surprised, high-pitched scream that ended abruptly when he hit the ground below.

Bridget stared numbly at the empty space where he'd stood as voices and footsteps crowded in around her.

A flashlight lit up the dark.

Bridget turned to see Santino and Decker beside her, and then Hale was there, pushing past them.

"Where's Charlie?" he asked.

His usual five o'clock shadow had grown into a patchy beard, and his tired eyes showed signs of too many late nights spent beside Bea Allen's hospital bed.

Bridget raised anguished eyes to him, then looked toward Charlie's motionless body on the ground.

Hale rushed forward and sank down beside her.

"Don't do this to me, Charlie," he whispered as he leaned over her, frantically feeling for a pulse. "Don't you go, too."

Tears welled in Bridget's eyes as Hale's shoulders sagged. He looked back at her, his face ashen.

"Is she..."

"She's got a pulse," he choked out. "Call an ambulance."

* * *

Bridget waved to the paramedics as they appeared on the trail lugging a red trauma bag and a hand-carried stretcher.

"She's in here," she called, motioning them toward the opening in the rock and then following them inside the mine, which was illuminated by a portable crime scene lamp.

Charlie was still unconscious as Hale moved aside to allow the paramedics to perform an initial examination.

But as they began to load her onto the stretcher, she came to and looked up at Hale, who hovered over her.

"Why are you here?" she murmured. "You're supposed to be at the hospice with Bea. What..."

Her voice faltered as she saw the grief on his face.

"She's gone?"

Hale nodded.

"She passed this morning," he said. "It was quiet and peaceful, just as she wanted."

He sighed and took Charlie's hand.

"But as soon as I left her room, I got a call from Luis Cortez. He told me you were tracing a target toward Destiny Peak and needed back-up. So here I am."

Stepping back, Hale allowed the paramedics to lift the stretcher and carry Charlie out of the mine, then followed after her.

Bridget crossed to Santino, who stood by the vertical shaft, and dropped her head onto his shoulder.

"What about Alistair?" she asked.

They both leaned forward and looked over the edge but could see nothing in the darkness below.

"You'll need this to see anything," Decker said, pulling a military-grade flashlight from his holster and shining it toward the bottom of the shaft.

Alistair Kennedy's body was sprawled on the uneven ground below, his head twisted at an unnatural angle.

"Doesn't look like there's any rush to get him out of there," Decker said. "But I saw some rope in your truck..."

He moved the light around the visible area of the shaft, then hesitated, lingering on several black garbage bags.

"I don't want to know what's in those bags," he said with a grimace. "I have a feeling-"

His words were interrupted by a moan. A weak voice drifted up to them.

"Help..."

Decker jumped at the sound and almost lost his footing.

"Holy crap," he cried out. "Someone's down there."

"I'll get that rope," Santino said, already moving toward the mine opening. "And I'll call another ambulance."

Soon Santino returned along with two officers wearing Mount Destiny Fire & Rescue uniforms.

"Cortez was one step ahead of us, as usual," he said as the officers carried in a portable stretcher and began to unwind a thick coil of orange rescue rope.

Using a makeshift pulley system, they slowly lowered Decker down into the shaft.

Bridget watched with wide eyes as he lifted a thin figure from the shadows and placed it on the stretcher, then tied on the rope.

"Okay, lift her up," Decker called.

Santino and the two officers pulled up the stretcher and carefully lowered it onto the ground beside Bridget.

A disheveled young woman with dark hair and emerald, green eyes blinked up at her.

"Heather Winslow," Bridget murmured. "You're alive."

CHAPTER THIRTY-NINE

G age pushed his way through the revolving doors of the FBI Field office in D.C. and waited for Argus and Bridget to join him in the marble foyer. He was surprised to see both Charlie Day and Tristan Hale waiting for them just past security.

"I didn't expect a welcome party," he said, trying not to stare at the white bandage on Charlie's forehead.

"Thought I should warn you that Roger Calloway will be sitting in," Charlie said, rolling her eyes ever so slightly. "He's usually too busy to join any of my meetings, so it came as something as a surprise when I saw his response."

She led the trio to the elevator, pushing the *Up* button as Hale crowded in behind them.

"I'm mainly here for moral support," Hale said when they were all standing inside. "I really don't know much about the case, other than the way it ended."

Throwing him a withering look, Charlie sighed.

"Ignore him," she said. "He's just fishing for another compliment. Ever since he swooped in and helped take down Alistair Kennedy, he's been milking the humble hero routine for all it's worth."

Bridget flashed a smile as she looked from Charlie to Hale.

"Well, I for one am extremely grateful," she said. "I wouldn't be standing here now if you and Santino hadn't come to the rescue."

A pleased flush rose in Hale's cheeks as the doors dinged open to reveal a long hallway. Gage and Bridget followed Charlie toward a conference room near the end.

Several rows of office chairs had been arranged facing a podium, which stood in front of a wide smartboard.

Gage saw that most members of the Backroads Butcher Task Force were in attendance, as well as a handful of agents he didn't recognize.

He took a seat next to Bridget, leaning over her to greet Santino and Decker on her other side.

Looking back over his shoulder, he saw Detective Larkin sitting in the last row, wedged between Opal Fitzgerald and Vivian Burke.

Overall, it looked like a full house.

As the room grew quiet, Gage turned back to see Roger Calloway saunter into the room wearing his usual pin-striped suit and inscrutable expression.

The special agent in charge stopped to speak quietly to Charlie before selecting a seat in the front row. He kept his eyes on the podium as Charlie tucked a strand of hair behind her ear, inadvertently drawing attention to her bandage.

"Okay, everyone, let's get started," she said. "I'm sure we're all ready to officially wrap-up the second Backroads

Butcher Task Force and move on.”

Most heads nodded in agreement, including Gage’s.

“Our SAC has requested a high-level walk-through of the case we’ll be turning over to the prosecutor,” she continued.

Opening a thin folder on the podium in front of her, she took a sip of water and cleared her throat.

“After this meeting, Agent Hale and I will deliver our evidence and findings to a special prosecutor who will decide if any additional charges are to be filed in relation to the circumstances surrounding Lyle Grady’s escape and the series of homicides that took place thereafter.”

“Both Lyle Grady and Alistair Kennedy are dead,” Decker boomed out. “So, who’s been charged?”

Gage glanced at Charlie, eager to hear her answer.

“All your questions will be answered in due course,” she said. “Now, we’re here to walk through the case. We’ve been asked to provide a clear accounting of what happened, as supported by the evidence.”

Turning to the smartboard, she lifted a small remote and clicked. A professional headshot of Tammy Vicker appeared. The reporter’s vivacious smile and bright blonde hair looked strangely out of place in the cheerless room.

“Tammy Vicker’s homicide was originally attributed to the Backroads Butcher based on several similarities to the Butcher’s previous crimes.”

Charlie clicked again on the remote, prompting Gage to wince as a grisly crime scene image appeared.

“She was found wearing a leather blood knot bracelet,

which was known to be the Butcher's signature," Charlie explained. "And she'd been decapitated, which was another key part of the Butcher's M.O."

Another click produced a full-body photo of Alistair Kennedy in a suit and tie.

"Now, thanks to our colleagues in the FBI lab, the DNA evidence found under Tammy Vicker's fingernails has been matched to Alistair Kennedy, the Commonwealth prosecutor on the Butcher case."

Charlie gestured to where Vivian Burke was sitting. The forensic examiner acknowledged her with a nod.

"Both blood and tissue cells were collected from Tammy's body during autopsy," Vivian confirmed. "We compared that sample to tissue collected during Alistair Kennedy's autopsy. There's no doubt it's a match."

"Unfortunately, at the time of the original trial, technology didn't allow the DNA to be tested," Charlie added. "Which is why Lyle Grady was tried and convicted for Tammy's murder along with the seven other homicides."

She moved to the next slide, which displayed photos of all eight victims Grady had been convicted of killing.

"We considered the case settled until about six months ago," she said. "I've asked Bridget Bishop to help me walk you through the series of events leading up to and following Grady's escape."

Standing at Charlie's words, Bridget walked to the front of the room and stepped behind the podium.

"About six months ago, while Lyle Grady was serving his

time in Abbeyville, he received a visit from Chase Grafton, a true crime podcast host who was producing a new series focused on the Backroads Butcher murders."

Gage wasn't surprised to see a faint grimace of distaste pass over Bridget's face as she spoke the podcaster's name.

"It seems the research for his show had uncovered Tammy Vicker's connection to someone close to the investigation," she explained. "And Chase hoped to use this information to win Grady's trust."

She looked back at the smartboard, which now displayed a promotional shot of Chase Grafton wearing his red beanie.

"Turns out Grady wasn't surprised by the information. He told Chase that he knew who Tammy's true killer was, only he'd been unable to prove it since there hadn't been enough blood and tissue to get a viable DNA profile."

"But Chase's visit got Grady thinking. Especially after his old cellmate Elliot Fisher was exonerated of murder through new DNA technology."

Reagan Rivera's face now appeared on the smartboard.

"Grady was able to convince Reagan Rivera to take on his case. Reagan immediately arranged for the tissue under Tammy's fingernails to be retested., and when a DNA profile was obtained that didn't match Lyle Grady, Judge Hawthorne scheduled a hearing to consider her petition for a retrial."

Sucking in a deep breath, Bridget met Gage's eyes.

"During the hearing, Grady killed a guard and escaped from the attorney-client conference room via a fire escape."

Gage's breath caught in his throat as he recalled standing

beside Bridget in the courthouse. The image of Officer Pickering's lifeless body flashed before his eyes.

"Grady went on the run and was at large for five days before we re-captured him," Bridget said. "We now know Grady had planned the escape in advance. He must have realized he'd never be released, even if the conviction for Tammy's death was overturned. Escape was his only real chance of freedom."

She motioned to Charlie, who again clicked the remote.

"That's where Alistair Kennedy comes in," Bridget said.

Behind her, a photo of a man and woman in an embrace appeared on the smartboard.

"We now know he killed Tammy to stop her from telling his wife they'd been having an affair. Grady had actually seen them together. He'd been watching Tammy before his arrest, perhaps worried that she was getting too close. We found several photos in Grady's van, including this one of Alistair and Tammy together."

Gage studied the photo with a mystified frown.

How could Alistair cuddle up to the reporter one day, and then brutally cut her down in cold blood the next?

"We've since reviewed communication between the two men, and it's clear Grady used what he knew to blackmail Alistair into helping him escape," Bridget said.

"It's also clear that Alistair's knowledge of the courthouse layout and security helped him manage to hide a knife for Grady," Bridget added. "And he used Reagan Rivera, too, since she had access to a private conference room reserved for attorneys and their clients."

"But why would Reagan Rivera agree to help Grady escape?" Calloway asked, speaking up for the first time.

"She was coerced," Bridget said. "Alistair abducted her sister Heather to use as leverage. Heather's boyfriend, Ryder Forbes, was collateral damage. Alistair couldn't very well leave him as a witness, so he killed him."

Calloway frowned.

"But he didn't kill Heather?"

"No, although he likely thought he had," she replied. "He took her to an abandoned mine below Destiny Peak. She tried to run and fell into a vertical shaft."

Skipping forward a few slides, Bridget stopped on a crime scene photo of the old mine.

"He must have known Reagan would contact the feds once she realized Heather wasn't going to be returned, so he killed her, too. He attempted to make it look as if Grady was responsible."

She moved on to an image of a stiff hand with its fingers curled into a fist. A leather bracelet had been tied into a blood knot at the wrist.

"However, a strand of hair was collected from Reagan Rivera's hand during autopsy. We were able to obtain a DNA profile that has since been matched to Alistair."

Bridget worked her way through several more slides, describing Reverend Abernathy's murder and her own narrow escape, before moving on to Erica Kennedy's abduction.

Calloway fell quiet again, his arms folded over his chest.

"After almost a week on the run, Grady was desperate for

money and a new identity, which Alistair had promised him," Bridget said. "In order to apply pressure, he abducted Alistair's wife, Erica Kennedy, who also happened to be Judge Hawthorne's daughter."

"And we don't think Judge Hawthorne was aware of his son-in-law's involvement in all of this?" Calloway asked, suddenly looking alert.

"Not until his daughter turned up dead," Charlie chimed in. "As far as we know, Hawthorne had nothing to do with his son-in-law's activities. It's possible Alistair persuaded the judge to grant a hearing in the first place, but we have no proof of that."

A throat cleared in the back of the room, and all eyes turned to Hale.

"Charlie and I have interviewed Hawthorne several times and found nothing that implicated him," he said. "Of course, we couldn't get much out of him. He's still pretty torn up."

Calloway's face creased into a frown as Hale explained.

"You see, we still haven't found his daughter's body, although her head was found at Destiny Peak."

An awkward silence followed.

Eventually, Calloway turned back to Charlie and Bridget.

"Destiny Peak...is that where Grady was taken down?" he asked. "How exactly did you know he'd be there?"

"Chase Grafton called me and told me he was going to meet Grady to exchange money for an exclusive interview," Bridget said. "I obtained a warrant to track his phone."

The SAC cocked his head.

"Why would Chase Grafton call you?" he asked.

Bridget hesitated, and Gage could see she was struggling to answer the question. It was hard to fathom what had driven the podcaster's dogged pursuit over the years.

"I'm not really sure," she finally admitted. "But in subsequent interviews, Chase claims he was planning to turn Grady in after he'd gotten what he wanted from him. He said he thought I'd be interested in coordinating that effort."

Her answer seemed to satisfy Calloway. He leaned back and resumed watching as Bridget moved through the last few slides, covering Grady's death by Alistair's bullet, their discovery of Ryder's body, and the pursuit through the mine.

"Agent Hale showed up with Deputy Marshals Santino and Decker in time to stop Alistair from adding me and Agent Day to his list of victims."

Bridget shot a grateful glance toward the men in the back.

"Alistair was shot once in the chest," she said. "He fell into a vertical shaft and died instantly."

She gestured toward the smartboard.

Gage expected to see an image of Alistair's recovered body, but instead, he saw a thin figure being carried up the mountain on a stretcher.

"We found Heather Winslow alive at the bottom of the shaft," Bridget explained. "She was in the hospital for a few days to treat her dehydration and to set a few bones, but she's made a miraculous recovery. At least physically. Her mental and emotional healing will take some time."

"So, that's it?" Calloway asked, preparing to stand. "Both Lyle Grady and Alistair Kennedy are dead, and there are no outstanding crimes to investigate? No charges pending?"

"Not quite," Charlie said, returning to the photo of Chase Grafton in his red beanie. "We did make one arrest for obstruction of justice."

A hard edge entered her voice.

"Currently, Mr. Grafton's out on bail pending trial and sentencing. The special prosecutor will decide if additional charges are needed for his role in all of this."

Giving a curt nod, Calloway checked his watch and stood.

Before heading to the door, he stopped in front of Charlie.

"Good job, Agent Day," he said, sticking out a thick hand. "I have to say I'm impressed. And glad to see you back at work so quickly. You're a real asset to the Bureau."

He turned to Gage, leaving Charlie standing still and stunned behind him.

"It's good to see you, Gage," he said in a gruff, man-to-man voice. "Your team really came through for us on this one. Glad to have Bridget back in your unit. You were a fool to let her go."

Gage glanced toward Bridget, wondering if she'd heard the remark. He considered telling the SAC that Bridget was only acting as a consultant, then decided not to burst the man's bubble. He'd find out the truth soon enough.

As Calloway and the other attendees began to file out of

the room, Gage stood beside the white board, staring at the closing slide Charlie had put up.

She'd created a photo montage of the victims and families impacted by Lyle Grady and Alistair Kennedy.

Gage's eyes were drawn to a picture of a younger, smiling Reverend Abernathy standing with his wife and children under a crystal blue sky.

The photo had obviously been taken long before the man's whole world had been torn apart by Grady's evil deeds.

It's scary just how quickly heaven can turn to hell.

Pushing away the disturbing thought, he turned to leave but stopped short when he saw Bridget standing behind him.

She looked past him to the photo of Abernathy.

"His memorial service is this afternoon, you know," she said softly. "Faye said I should go. She thinks it'll provide closure."

"And that's the holy grail of therapy, is it?" Gage asked with a sigh. "Are we all just in need of closure?"

"Closure, peace...whatever you want to call it...whatever lets you sleep at night," Bridget said.

Her words conjured images in Gage's mind. Shifting shadows in his bedroom the previous night. Reproachful apparitions that had refused to let him sleep as he'd lain awake staring at the shadows on his ceiling.

"Well, whatever you call it, I could sure use some of it," Gage said. "Maybe I'll pay my respects to the reverend, too."

* * *

The steps of the Mount Destiny Church of Redemption swarmed with parishioners somberly dressed in black.

Making his way through the throng behind Bridget, Gage entered the sanctuary. He was greeted with the heavy scent of lilies and the deep, soothing sounds of a familiar hymn.

He searched the room until his eyes found the source of the music. A young woman sat on a bench in front of an old wooden organ. Flowers had been woven into her long hair, which fell down her back in soft waves.

As if she felt his eyes on her, the organist turned and looked back. When she saw Bridget, she smiled and nodded a greeting, before turning back to her hymn.

"You know each other?" Gage asked.

"That's Zadie Monroe, a childhood friend of Justine's," Bridget said. "You don't remember her? She's the one who told me about Grady. We may never have caught him if it wasn't for her."

Gage moved closer, watching as the young woman's fingers danced over the keys, her slim back swaying slightly to the mournful melody.

"That's Zadie?"

He tried to match the young woman in front of him with the shy teenager he remembered. How had she grown into a woman so quickly?

His surprise at the girl's transformation was accompanied by a thought that Justine Abernathy would have been the same age as Zadie if Grady hadn't cut her life short.

A pang of nostalgia rolled through Gage at the opening notes of another hymn. He hummed along to *Old Rugged Cross*, one of his mother's favorites, as he followed Bridget down the aisle.

Silently, they joined the line of mourners moving slowly past a large photo of Reverend Abernathy on the altar.

After a moment, Gage realize the man in front of him was Dale Winslow. He started to speak, then realized that Dale's head was lowered in what appeared to be silent prayer.

As they neared the memorial photo, Gage stepped closer, clearing his throat. Dale raised his head and their eyes met.

"You're the FBI guy, aren't you?" Dale said.

"One of them," Grady replied. "Although that's not why I'm here. I came to pay my respects, just like everyone else."

"He was a good man."

Dale's voice cracked on the words.

"He didn't deserve to die. He didn't deserve any of it."

Gage thought he could hear self-recrimination and bitterness behind Dale's words. After all, the man had survived Grady's evil, Abernathy had not.

"*No one* deserves what the Reverend went through," Gage said, following Dale as he stepped away to allow the next in line to pay their respects. "You both suffered a terrible loss."

But Dale had already started walking toward the exit, his head down and his shoulders slumped.

Impulsively, Gage followed him down the aisle and into the narthex.

"Wait, Mr. Winslow," he called softly.

He wasn't sure what he planned to say if Dale turned around. But he didn't like to think of the broken man carrying guilt that wasn't his to bear.

He'll need to be whole and healthy for Heather's sake.

Perhaps Gage would give him Faye Thackery's number. The therapist might be able to help both father and daughter.

But Dale continued around the corner without looking back. Several mourners were walking in the same direction.

"What's back there?" Gage asked Bridget as she stepped up beside him. "Where are they all going?"

"The mausoleum," Bridget said, her voice somber. "It's where Abernathy's wife and children are. I imagine he'll be interred beside them now."

Comforted at the idea of the reverend being reunited with his family, he followed Bridget around the side of the church.

They followed a winding path through a gate, coming to a stop in front of a white granite building that looked to be about the same size as a garden shed.

An ornate iron gate blocked the narrow door leading into the structure, keeping out the small group of mourners who had gathered around.

Bridget gasped softly beside Gage as they stood side-by-side gazing up at an engraved inscription above the entrance.

"For whoever would save his life will lose it,
But whoever loses his life for my sake will save it."
Luke 9:24

"I should feel guilty, knowing he died in my place," Bridget said. "But standing here now, all I feel is peace."

As Gage smiled down at her, his pocket buzzed, breaking the silence. He dug for his phone and checked the display, instantly shattering the moment of calm reflection.

The automated text message was from Russell's school.

Your student was not in school today. Please send a written excuse with your student upon their return.

Checking his watch, Gage saw that it was well past time for Russell to have gotten home. Where had he been all day?

He quickly tapped on the boy's number, but his phone rang without answer before rolling to voicemail.

Hey, you've reached Russell's phone. You know what to do.

Gage's heart sank as he listened to the message.

The problem was, he *didn't* know what to do.

He'd only been a foster father for little more than a year. He was in no way qualified to be solely responsible for another human being, especially a teenager who'd gone through as much pain as Russell had endured.

Ending the call without leaving a message, Gage raced to his Navigator and jumped inside. As he sped east toward Stafford County, he tried to call Russell's number again, but the boy still didn't pick up.

Fear suddenly coursed through Gage like a tidal wave.

Something terrible must have happened. What if he's been kidnapped or maybe run over by a reckless driver?

As he pictured Russell's thin body lying in the street, he pushed his foot down hard on the accelerator.

He couldn't imagine losing the boy now. Not after everything they'd been through.

If anything happens to Kenny's son, I'll never forgive myself.

Eyes flicking to his watch again, he suddenly wished he'd made friends with the neighbors. He needed someone to check on Russell before he got home.

Snatching up his phone, he tapped on Kyla's number, remembering that she'd been staying at a hotel nearby.

She answered on the second ring.

"Russell missed school today. I don't know where he is..."

Within seconds Kyla had agreed to drive over to the house on Mansfield Place to see if he was home.

"I'm on my way. I'll call you as soon as I arrive."

When his phone buzzed ten minutes later, Gage hesitated as his own words from earlier replayed in his mind.

It's scary just how quickly heaven can turn to hell.

Swallowing hard, he jabbed his thumb on the display.

"He's here," Kyla said, sounding relieved. "He was playing basketball with a friend."

She was sitting on the steps petting Sarge when Gage finally pulled into the driveway, although she'd sent Russell inside and the other boy home.

"Playing hooky isn't the worst thing he could have done," she said as Gage climbed out of the car. "We've both done worse, I'm sure."

Her smile faded as she saw the look in his eyes.

"Wow, you were really scared, weren't you?"

Nodding weakly, he allowed her to take his hand and lead him to the front steps. She sat down next to him and waited.

Once he'd caught his breath, he looked up and met her eyes. They were kind eyes. Kenny's eyes.

"I was thinking maybe when you move back to D.C., you could stay here," he said, surprising himself. "I've got plenty of room. Together, we could give Russell what he really needs. We could give him a family."

Kyla's startled expression told Gage his suggestion had taken her off guard.

"It's hard for me to admit, even to myself," he added softly, his eyes searching hers. "But I'm not sure I can manage it on my own. Not the way Russell deserves. I could really use some help."

For a long beat, Kyla considered his words. Then a soft smile lifted the corners of her mouth.

"I think I can do that," she said.

Relief washed through Gage as he jumped to his feet.

"That's good. It's *great*, actually," he said, scooping Sarge up from the top step. "Let's go tell Russell."

CHAPTER FORTY

Bridget pulled her old Explorer into Faye Thackery's driveway just in time for her four o'clock appointment. The psychotherapist held sessions in her home-based office, and Hank immediately recognized the neat little bungalow as they pulled up outside, sticking his head out the open window and wagging his tail in anticipation of the treats Faye always offered.

As she let Hank out of the backseat, the Irish setter ran around to the office entrance on the side of the bungalow, letting out a single bark to let the therapist know he'd arrived.

Throwing open the door, Faye beckoned them inside, her short, silvery hair pushed back with a wide headband, and her elfin face creased into a wide smile.

"I hope you like pumpkin spice lattes," she said, holding up two cups from the coffee shop in town. "I was coming back from the store and couldn't resist."

Handing one of the fragrant cups to Bridget, she reached into her pocket and pulled out the treat Hank had been expecting, before leading them into her cozy session room.

As Faye got out her notebook and pen, Bridget settled into

a comfortable chair across from her.

"So, you said you've got big news?"

Faye's eyes were bright and expectant as Bridget nodded.

"Are wedding bells and a white dress involved?" Faye asked.

At the look of surprise on Bridget's face, she waved the comment away with a tiny hand.

"To be honest, I recommend the freedom and independence of the single life, anyway," she said. "And I should know, considering how many times I've been married."

"No, I'm not getting married," Bridget said, feeling her stomach tighten at the news she was about to share. "But I am making a pretty big life change. And it's partially up to you. You've helped me work through my...issues."

Taking a small sip of the latte, she set her cup on the table and exhaled.

"I'm going back to the BAU full-time," she said. "No more private practice for me. It's official."

Faye blinked at her.

"Wow, that is big news," she said. "I certainly wasn't expecting that. Not after everything that's been in the news about Lyle Grady and that prosecutor over in Mount Destiny."

A shadow fell over Bridget's face at the mention of the murderous men who had caused so much pain to so many.

"Grady's death, and all that led up to it, is part of the reason I feel I have to go back."

Her words caused a small frown to crease Faye's forehead.

"You *have to* go back? I don't like the sound of that."

Not sure she knew how to explain her decision, Bridget took another sip of the sweet drink, stalling for time.

She'd been in a contemplative mood ever since she'd left Reverend Abernathy's memorial service the day before.

The man had suffered unimaginable loss and grief, but he'd lived his life in the service of others, and in the end, he'd given his life to save another.

It was the kind of legacy few left behind, and it had made Bridget question what her own legacy would be.

After a restless night, she'd known what she had to do.

"I guess it's about what I really what to achieve with my life," Bridget finally said. "Regardless of my fear and anxiety, I want to spend my life making a difference."

Faye raised her delicate eyebrows.

"And private practice...that doesn't make a difference?"

Bridget shook her head.

"That's not what I meant. Of course, if I stay in private practice, I'll certainly help people and make a difference in their lives," she conceded. "But I've experienced firsthand that evil walks among us. At the BAU, I'll be working to stop it."

She met Faye's eyes, willing the therapist to understand.

"I have the chance not only to change lives but also to save them," she said. "It's a chance very few people are given."

"Well, it sounds as if you've made up your mind," Faye said. "You haven't chosen an easy road, but that doesn't mean it's not the right one."

* * *

Bridget stepped out of Faye's office and followed Hank to the Explorer. The rest of her session had gone well, and she felt ready and eager to share her big news with Santino.

As she ushered Hank into the backseat, a beat-up Volvo pulled into the driveway.

Turning around, Bridget saw Dale Winslow step out, circle around to the passenger's side, and open the door.

Seconds later, Heather Winslow emerged.

As she moved slowly toward Faye's office, Bridget noted the sling on Heather's arm and the brace on her knee.

"Dr. Bishop?" Heather called when she saw Bridget standing beside the Explorer. "I've been meaning to call you. To thank you for everything you did for me and Ryder."

The young woman's voice faltered on her boyfriend's name.

"You're very welcome," Bridget said, moving forward to save Heather the extra steps. "And I'm so sorry about Ryder."

"There's going to be a memorial service," Heather said shyly. "His parents are arranging it...if you'd like to come."

Bridget nodded and smiled.

"I'd like that."

She saw Dale shifting behind his daughter, looking at his watch. His hair was neatly combed and his face clean-shaven.

"I hate to rush you two," he said. "But Dr. Thackery will be waiting for Heather."

Heather rolled her eyes and smiled at Bridget.

"Ever since I've been home, he's been acting like a nervous nursemaid," she said, then turned to her father. "I can go in without you. Just be here to pick me up in an hour."

Without another word, she began limping up the path.

"It looks like she's doing well," Bridget said as Dale watched his daughter's progress with worried eyes.

"The doctors say she'll make a full recovery, at least physically," he said. "But mentally and emotionally? That's still to be determined."

"Bringing her here is a good start," Bridget said. "Faye's the best there is when it comes to treating trauma."

"That's what Agent Gage said when he called yesterday and gave me the doctor's number," Dale said. "I was surprised she agreed to see Heather so soon. I just hope it helps with the nightmares. She needs to get some sleep."

As he ran a hand through his hair, Bridget detected the scent of clothes detergent and Old Spice cologne.

Perhaps caring for his daughter was providing the worried father with his own version of therapy.

Climbing into the Explorer, Bridget turned toward the highway, deciding to head straight to Santino's apartment. It was time to share her big news.

* * *

Santino's handsome face was pensive as he opened the door.

"I wasn't expecting you until later," he said, shoving his phone in his pocket. "Has something happened?"

"Yes, it has," she said, stepping past him into the apartment with Hank on her heels. "And I thought I should tell you before you hear it from anyone else."

His subdued expression didn't change as he closed the door behind her and crossed to the sofa.

"Okay, what is it?" he asked. "What's your big news?"

"Well, you know I left the Bureau after the Backroads Butcher case because I felt...burned out," Bridget said, then shook her head. "No, that's not the right word. It was more than that. I wasn't just exhausted, I was...*broken*."

She reached out and took his hand, her eyes finding his.

"But over the last year or so, I've started to heal," she said. "And now that Grady is dead...well, what I'm saying is, I'm ready to try again."

Santino raised his eyebrows.

"Ready to try what again?"

"I'm going back to the BAU," she said, swallowing hard. "I've spoken to Gage, and he's willing to have me back."

She braced herself for Santino's reaction, not sure what to expect, then relaxed as his mouth lifted into a pleased, knowing smile.

"I was wondering how long it would take you to figure out where you belong," he said, cocking his head. "Chasing bad guys is in your blood. There's no denying it."

"I was hoping you'd say I belong with *you*," she teased, drawing him closer, wanting to feel the warmth of his body against hers. "After all, it's the one place I always feel safe."

A shadow passed over Santino's face.

"You don't need me to keep you safe," he said, gently pulling her arms away from his neck. "You're a capable federal agent. Just think of all the scrapes you've managed to get yourself out of."

"I've always had help," she replied, suddenly worried by his distant attitude. "You, and Charlie, and–"

"Of course, we all need help," he said distractedly. "But that doesn't mean we're helpless."

He stood and turned away.

"Santino...is something wrong?"

She reached out to touch his arm, hurt when he pulled away.

"Actually, I have news to share, too. Something I should have told you about a while ago."

When he turned back, the serious expression on his face scared her. Possibilities whirred through her head.

Is he seeing someone else? Is this when he tells me he just wants to be friends? Or maybe he's been relocated to California. Long-distance relationships never work...

A knot of dread formed in Bridget's stomach as she waited for him to speak. She should have known what they had was too perfect to last.

"It's about Maribel," he finally said, swallowing hard. "About how she died. You know I don't like to talk about it, but I might not have a choice...not if Chase Grafton has his way."

He sighed and pulled out his phone.

She looked down to see a text from Chase on the screen.

Anger flooded through her as she noted Santino's stricken expression.

"He's been threatening to do a podcast and...well, it's time I face up to it anyway."

Suddenly, Bridget recalled the podcaster's taunting words.

Your U.S. Marshal boyfriend couldn't even find the man who killed his own wife. What makes you think he can find Lyle Grady?

Bridget raised a hand to Santino's strong, stubbled jaw.

"You don't have to tell me anything you don't want to," she said, speaking quickly. "Whatever happened in the past won't change the way I feel about you now."

Santino met her eyes, his face creasing into a pained smile.

"I know," he said simply. "But it changes how I feel about myself. You see, what happened to Maribel isn't really over. Not for me. Maybe it never will be."

His voice faltered, but he cleared his throat, forcing the words out.

"And now Chase Grafton is going to drag it all back out in the open," he said, running a hand through his dark hair. "You see, the man who killed Maribel is still out there, and I still haven't forgiven myself for letting him get away."

The knot in Bridget's stomach twisted at his words.

"I tried for years to find her killer," he admitted. "The search dominated my life. I was obsessed, I guess you could say. I thought maybe I'd gotten over it, but..."

The catch in his voice broke her heart.

"I know it's not fair to you," he said quietly. "But I can't move on until he's brought to justice."

"Then I'll help you," she heard herself saying without stopping to consider what she was promising. "If we work on this together, I know we can find him."

Santino shook his head.

"I did everything I could back when it happened, and–"

"Things are different now. There's new technology, new databases, new methods," Bridget said, not sure if she was trying to convince Santino or herself.

He shook his head again, but this time, there was the tiniest glimmer of hope in his eyes.

"We figured out who killed Tammy Vicker after all this time," she continued. "We can figure this out, too."

She stood and moved toward Santino, pulling him to her, wanting to comfort him, to save him.

She knew how toxic guilt could be, and how much damage it could do if left to fester.

And Santino had suffered too much already.

"You're not in this alone," she murmured in his ear. "You have me and all the resources of the BAU on your side."

Hank snuffled at their feet as if reminding them of his presence.

"Looks like even Hank wants in on this one," Bridget said, reaching down to ruffle the Irish setter's fur. "He may not be much of a guard dog, but he's excellent at offering emotional support."

Santino couldn't hold back a laugh as Hank gazed up at him with adoring eyes as if to back up Bridget's statement.

"You're starting to convince me," Santino said. "But it isn't going to be easy."

Bridget's heart skipped a beat as their eyes met and held.

"Nothing worth fighting for ever is," she replied softly. "But I'm pretty sure you're worth it."

The End

Start Melinda Woodhall's
Veronica Lee Thriller Series beginning with
Her Last Summer as reporter Veronica Lee
investigates the death of a celebrity writer. When
Veronica begins the search for a heartless serial
killer, she becomes the unwilling subject of her
own deadly story.
Read on for an excerpt of:
*Her Last Summer: A Veronica Lee Thriller,
Book One*

HER LAST SUMMER
A Veronica Lee Thriller, Book One

Chapter One

Portia Hart's four-inch heels clicked against polished marble as she entered the hotel suite's foyer, dropped her bag on the floor, and pressed a switch on the wall. Recessed lighting illuminated the luxurious suite's elegantly appointed sitting room. She didn't notice the man standing in the shadows as she crossed to the big window and looked down at the dark river below.

Catching sight of her reflection in the glass, she pushed back a strand of silky blond hair and inhaled deeply, then smiled and turned her head.

"I know you're here," Portia called out in a playful voice. "I can smell your cologne. It's the one I picked out for you in St. Barts, so you can stop playing around. I've been on my feet for hours and..."

Her voice faltered as Xavier Greyson appeared in the bedroom doorway. Folding leanly muscled arms over his smooth, bare chest, he rested against the doorjamb and let his lips curl into a wicked smile.

"I thought I'd surprise you and come early," he said, raising an eyebrow, "but if you'd rather I leave and come back tomorrow-"

"Oh no, you're here now and I'm not letting you go anywhere." Portia stepped forward, lifting her face to his. "I thought I'd have to spend the whole night up here all alone."

Allowing her to pull his head down for a lingering kiss, Xavier raised a hand and entwined it in her long, blonde hair. He tugged her head back and gazed down into her adoring eyes.

She really is a beautiful woman. And so very trusting.

He bestowed a gentle kiss on her forehead and released his grip. Ignoring her cry of protest, he moved back into the bedroom.

"First things first, my dear." His voice was soft but firm. "As you were saying, you've been on your feet for hours. You need a warm bath and a stiff drink."

Portia followed him through the bedroom into the suite's opulent bathroom where a crystal chandelier hung over a massive, freestanding tub. She gasped in pleasure; the tub was already full of hot water. Puffs of steam drifted up, turning the room into a warm, dreamy haze.

"That water looks divine." She turned to him and raised a perfectly arched eyebrow. "And the tub's deep enough for two."

Her whispered words sent a ripple of regret down his spine. For a split second, he was tempted to delay his plan and join her in the tub.

What harm will another hour do?

He dismissed the thought as quickly as it had come. He couldn't afford a further delay. The book signing had lasted longer than he'd anticipated, and the hardest part was yet to come.

No, the plan is in motion. There's no turning back now.

"I think you just might be right." Xavier reached out and untied the silk sash of her dress with a practiced hand. "So, why don't I go ahead and pour us some wine while you slip out of those clothes."

Leaving Portia to undress, Xavier padded back into the living room and crossed to the bar. An open bottle of the hotel's most expensive Merlot sat beside two crystal wine glasses. He reached into the pocket of his jeans, extracted a tiny plastic bag, and considered the fine white powder within.

This will make it all a bit easier. For both of us.

He shook the powder into the bottom of one glass and then stuffed the bag back into his pocket.

"I was getting lonely in there."

Portia's voice startled him, and he jumped as her arms circled his waist. Her bare feet had made no sound on the marble floor.

Pouring a long splash of wine on top of the powder, Xavier exhaled and turned to peer down into Portia's eager face. He noticed that she'd changed into one of the hotel's bulky cotton robes.

"I ordered the best Merlot they had," he murmured,

trying to gauge the look in her eyes as he handed her the wine, "to celebrate your book hitting the bestseller list again."

Portia shrugged her shoulders as if to say the achievement was no big deal, but a blush of happiness stained her cheeks. Xavier filled the other glass and lifted it to clink against hers. He wondered if she had noticed the slight tremor in his hand.

His heart faltered as he saw the smattering of white powder on the rim of her glass, but Portia seemed oblivious; she brought the glass to her lips and drank deeply.

"Now, let's see about that bath," she said, carrying her drink out of the room. "The water's getting cold."

Looking around the living room one last time, Xavier reviewed his plan. He didn't feel good about the delay, but he had no choice. He'd just have to get the next step over quickly and move on.

Relieved to see the robe discarded on the floor, a genuine smile played around his mouth as he took in Portia's long, slender figure reclining in the luxurious tub.

She is an exquisite woman. One of my better finds, I have to admit.

He shook his head to clear it.

"I'm feeling a little dizzy." Portia's words were slurred as she squinted up at him. "I think the water's too...hot."

Xavier took a deep breath and moved forward, steeling himself for what had to come next. The uneasy sensation was back. Something didn't feel right, but what could it be? Had he forgotten something? Or was he just getting weak and soft?

"You're just tired," he said, circling the tub and placing his well-manicured hands on Portia's shoulders. "I'll scrub your back."

"No, I really...don't feel well. I want to get out. I don't-"

A gush of hot water stopped her words as he forced her shoulders down, triggering a sudden flash of panic. She flailed her arms and kicked her feet, sending a wave of water over the side of the tub.

Anger flooded through Xavier as he struggled to hold Portia down, feeling the scalding water soak through his jeans.

The bitch got my jeans wet. How am I supposed to get out of here now?

He gripped her shoulders with mounting frustration. A black t-shirt and hoodie were hanging safely in the closet, but all his other clothes were packed and waiting for him in the car.

He hadn't planned on leaving the hotel looking like a drowned rat. His appearance would definitely raise questions. Especially since the after-dinner crowd had likely dispersed by now. A lone man walking out in soaking wet jeans would be noticed.

A stinging pain brought his attention back to the woman struggling under the water. Portia had stuck up one desperate hand to claw at his wrist, while her other hand now gripped the edge of the tub. Xavier grimaced as her long fingernails dug into his skin.

Stifling the curse that hovered on his lips, he tightened

his aching hands in frustration and pushed Portia lower in the water.

I should've waited for her to pass out. I should've followed the plan.

Her eyes bulged and widened in fear in the water below him, and he looked away with distaste, knowing from experience that her face would soon darken into a revolting shade of blue. Xavier kept his cold eyes averted as Portia convulsed beneath him, refusing to give in to his rising panic.

Everything is going to be all right. I'll find another way out and no one will ever know I was here. I'll be long gone before she's even discovered.

Finally, after what seemed to Xavier like hours, her body went limp and sank heavily to the bottom. One last feeble gush of water spilled over the side as the struggle ended.

Xavier's heavy breathing was the only sound in the room as he gazed down at Portia's lifeless body with grim satisfaction. The job was almost done.

A high-pitched ring filled the silence of the room, and Xavier jumped in alarm as Portia's cell phone vibrated against the marble countertop. He looked over at the phone with narrowed eyes.

Crossing to silence the call, he recognized the face that flashed on the screen. It was Jane Bishop, Portia's literary agent. He pushed the button to send the call to voicemail, and the display went dark again. But Jane Bishop's meddlesome face had heightened his anxiety.

It'll only be a matter of time before the old bat sends out the calvary.

Xavier knew he'd better hurry. He'd gotten through the hardest part of the plan already. It was time to move on to the next stage. He turned to survey the room. Puddles of water surrounded the tub, and the cotton robe rested in a sodden heap several feet away. Splotches of blood made a trail from the tub to where he stood by the sink.

He looked down to see two bloody scratches on his forearm.

"Shit!"

Grabbing a plush hand towel, he wrapped it around his arm and tried to think. He'd screwed up, but he still had a chance. He'd always managed to find a way out before. This time would be no different. He just needed to keep his head straight and act fast. Pulling more towels off the rack, he fell to his knees and began wiping up the water.

* * *

Xavier gave one last look around the room and sighed. He'd done what he could to correct his mistakes. The floor was relatively clean, his wine glass had been rinsed and dried, the empty pill bottle was on the counter, and Portia's body was motionless in the cooling water.

Now he needed to focus on his escape. The whole ordeal had taken much longer than he'd planned, and the hotel was bound to be quiet and deserted by now. Small towns like Willow Bay never had much of a nightlife, even if it was a Friday. His plan of mingling in with the crowd that was leaving the event would no longer be feasible.

By now the only one hanging around will be a bored security guard.

No, he'd have to move on to plan B, and he'd need to do it fast. The longer he hung around, the more likely he'd encounter a witness. Or make another mistake.

Zipping his jacket, Xavier felt the right pocket to reassure himself that the thick roll of cash and Cartier watch were still safely inside. He pulled his hood up to cover his head and opened the door.

The suite was located at the end of the hall just as he'd recommended to Portia, telling her it would protect her privacy and shield their relationship from the prying eyes of the public and press.

If she'd suspected he had wanted to avoid the cameras positioned on each floor by the elevator, she had never mentioned it. She'd trusted him after all.

Head down, Xavier stepped into the corridor and hurried toward the stairs at the end. A red EXIT sign glowed overhead as he slowly pushed the metal door open.

Half expecting to hear the wailing of an alarm, he relaxed his shoulders and stepped into the hot, dimly lit stairwell. A faint click, click, click made him look down.

Drops of water fell from his still-soggy jeans and splashed onto the concrete floor. But was that what he'd heard? Shaking away a feeling of unease, he began to hurry down the stairs. Fourteen flights of stairs and he'd be outside and home free.

But the clicking started again, and this time Xavier

recognized the sound of high heels descending the stairs a few flights below him. Startled, he leaned over the rail and looked down into the upturned face of an equally startled young woman with long, bright pink hair. Her eyes, rimmed with heavy black liner, widened at the rage etched on his face, then dropped to take in the hoody and wet jeans.

Knowing he had only seconds to act, Xavier hurled himself forward, banging down the stairs toward the only person that had seen his face. The only person that would be able to place him at the hotel. He had to stop her before she got away. He had to make sure she didn't have a chance to tell anyone what he'd done.

Continue reading *Her Last Summer: A Veronica Lee Thriller, Book One* by Melinda Woodhall

And don't forget to sign up for the Melinda Woodhall Newsletter to receive bonus scenes and insider details at www.melindawoodhall.com/newsletter

Melinda Woodhall

ACKNOWLEDGEMENTS

SEPTEMBER IS A SPECIAL MONTH AROUND my house. It marks a few special birthdays, the official end of a long, hot Florida summer, and the start of a new (and hopefully exciting) school year. So, when I decided to release the fourth book in my Bridget Bishop series in September, I knew it would be a challenge to get it done on time. Luckily, with the support of my much-loved family, I somehow managed to make it work.

As always, I'm grateful for the consistent support and love of my amazing husband, Giles, and my five one-of-a-kind children, Michael, Joey, Linda, Owen, and Juliet.

I also know how lucky I am to have the encouragement of my extended family, including Melissa Romero, Leopoldo Romero, Melanie Arvin Kutz, David Woodhall, and Tessa Woodhall.

The positive feedback from readers continues to provide me with motivation whenever I start to falter, as does the constant and enduring presence of my mother in my memory and my heart.

ABOUT THE AUTHOR

Melinda Woodhall is the author of heart-pounding, emotional thrillers with a twist, including the *Mercy Harbor Thriller Series*, the *Veronica Lee Thriller Series*, the *Detective Nessa Ainsley Novella Series*, and the new *Bridget Bishop FBI Mystery Thriller Series*.

When she's not writing, Melinda can be found reading, gardening, and playing in the back garden with her tortoise. Melinda is a native Floridian and the proud mother of five children. She lives with her family in Orlando.

Visit Melinda's website at www.melindawoodhall.com

Other Books by Melinda Woodhall

Her Last Summer	*Catch the Girl*
Her Final Fall	*Girls Who Lie*
Her Winter of Darkness	*Steal Her Breath*
Her Silent Spring	*Take Her Life*
Her Day to Die	*Make Her Pay*
Her Darkest Night	*Break Her Heart*
Her Fatal Hour	*Lessons in Evil*
Her Bitter End	*Taken By Evil*
The River Girls	*Where Evil Hides*
Girl Eight	

Made in the USA
Monee, IL
05 February 2023

27153103R00194